THE TITLE MARKET

MORE WILDSIDE CLASSICS

THE TITLE MARKET

EMILY POST

WILDSIDE PRESS

THE TITLE MARKET

This edition published in 2006 by Wildside Press, LLC.
www.wildsidepress.com

CHAPTER I

PRINCE SANSEVERO DIMINISHES
THE FORTUNES OF HIS HOUSE

Her excellency the Princess Sansevero sat up in bed. Reaching quickly across the great width of mattress, she pulled the bell-rope twice, then, shivering, slid back under the warmth of the covers. She drew them close up over her shoulders, so far that only a heavy mass of golden hair remained visible above the old crimson brocade of which the counterpane was made. The room was still darkened so that the objects in it were barely discernible, but presently one of the high, carved doors opened and a maid entered, carrying a breakfast tray. Setting the tray down, she crossed quickly to the windows and drew back the curtains.

Sunlight flooded the black and white marble of the floor, and brought out in sharp detail the splendor of the apartment. The rich colors of the frescoed walls, the mellow crimson damask upholstering, might have suggested warmth and comfort, had not a little cloud of white vapor floating before the maid's lips proclaimed the temperature.

She was a stocky peasant woman, this maid, with good red color in her cheeks, but she wore a dress of heavy woolen material and a cardigan jacket over that. Her thick felt slippers pattered briskly over the stone floor as she went to a clothes-press, carved and beautifully inlaid, took out a drab-colored woolen wrapper trimmed with common red fox fur, and, picking up the tray again, mounted the dais of the huge carved bed.

"If Excellency will make haste, the coffee is good and very hot."

The covers were pushed down just a little, and the princess peered out.

"What sort of a day have we, Marie? Isn't it very cold?"

"Oh, no! It is a beautiful day. But Excellency will say that the coffee is cold unless it is soon taken."

So again the Princess Sansevero sat up in bed. Her maid placed the coffee tray before her, and wrapped her quickly in the dressing-gown. The plain woolen wrapper had looked ugly enough in the maid's hands, but its drab color and fox fur so toned in with the red-gold hair and creamy skin of its wearer that an artist, could he have beheld the picture, would have been filled with delight. It would not in the least have mattered to him that there was a chip in the cup into which she poured her coffee, nor that the linen napkin was darned in three places. The silver breakfast service belonged to a time when such things were chiseled only for great personages and by master craftsmen. That it was battered through several centuries of constant handling rather enhanced than diminished its value. Of the same antiquity was the bed—seven feet wide, its four posts elaborately carved with fruits and flowers, and with cupids grouped in the corners of the framework supporting a dome of crimson damask that matched the hangings. What difference could it make to the artist that the springless mattress was as hard as a rock, and lumpy as a ploughed field? With painted walls and vaulted ceilings that were the apotheosis of luxury, what did it matter that the raw chill from their stone surface penetrated to the very marrow of her Exalted Excellency's bones? Unfortunately, however, it was she who had to occupy the apartment and to her it did matter very much, for her American blood never had grown used to the chill of unheated rooms.

"I think I can heat the bathroom sufficiently for Excellency's bath," ventured the maid.

The princess shivered at the mere suggestion. She knew only too well the feeling of the water in a room that was like an unheated cellar in the rainy season of late autumn. "No, no!" she exclaimed, "fill me the little tub, in my sitting-room."

As she spoke, a door opened opposite the one through which the maid had entered, and the prince came in. A fresh color glowed under his olive skin, his hair was brushed until it was as polished as his nails; also he was shaved, but here his toilet for the day ended. The open "V" of his dressing-gown (his was made of a costly material, quite in contrast to the one his wife wore) showed his throat; bare ankles were visible above his slippers. With the raillery of a boy he cried:

"Can it really be possible that you are cold! No wonder they call yours the nation of ice water! I know that is what you have in your veins!" With a spring he threw himself full length across the bed.

"Sandro, be careful! See what you are doing! You have spilled the coffee."

"Oh, that's nothing!" he said gaily; "it will wash out."

"On the contrary, it is a great deal. It makes unnecessary laundry and uses up the linen—we can't get any more, you know."

At once his gay humor changed to sulkiness. "*Va bene, va bene!* let us drop that subject."

Immediately the princess softened, as though she had unthinkingly hurt him, "I did not mean it as a complaint; but you know, dear, we do have to be careful."

But the prince stared moodily at his finger-nails.

She began a new topic cheerfully. "I hope to get a letter from Nina today; there has been time for an answer."

Sansevero had been quite interested in the idea of a possible visit from Nina Randolph, his wife's niece, a much exploited American heiress. But now he paid no attention. He still stared at his nails. The princess scrutinized his face as though in the habit of reading its expression, and at last she said gently:

"What have you in mind, dear? Tell me—come, out with it, I see quite well there is something."

For answer he sat up, took a cigarette from his pocket, put it between his lips, searched in both pockets for a match, and, failing to find one, sat with the unlighted cigarette between his lips, sulkier than ever.

He felt her looking at him, and swayed his shoulders exactly as though some one were trying to hold him. "Really, Leonora," he burst out, "this question of money all the time is far from pleasant!"

A helpless, frightened look came into her face. It grew suddenly pinched; instinctively she put her hand over her heart.

"I have not mentioned money." She made an effort to speak lightly, but there was a vibration in the tone. Then, as though gathering her strength together, she made a direct demand:

"Alessandro, tell me at once, what have you done?"

For a moment he looked defiant, then shrugged his shoulders. "Well, since you will know—" he sprang from the bed, pulled a letter out of his pocket, and, quite as a small boy hands over the note that his teacher has caught him passing in school, he tossed her the envelope, and left the room.

Her fingers trembled a little in unfolding the paper; and she breathed quickly as she read. For some time she sat staring at the few lines of writing before her. Then suddenly thrusting her feet into fur slippers, she ran into the next room. "Sandro," she said, "come into my sitting-room; I must speak with you."

He followed her through her bedroom into an apartment much smaller and, unlike the other two rooms, quite warm. Just now, all the articles of a woman's toilet were spread out on a table upon which a dressing-mirror had been placed; and close beside a brazier of glowing coals was a portable English tub; the water for the bath was heating in the kitchen.

Seeing that there was no means of avoiding the inevitable, he said doggedly: "I thought to make, of course, or I would not have gone into the scheme." Then something in her face held him, and at the same time his impulsive boyishness—a little dramatic, perhaps, but only so much as is consistent with his race—carried him into a new mood.

"Leonora, I suppose I am in the wrong—indeed I am sure I am utterly at fault; but help me. Don't you see, *carissima*, this time I did not *wager*—it was a business venture!"

In the midst of her distress she could not help but smile at the absurdity.

"Scorpa is doing it all," he continued—"not I. You know what a clever business man *he* is! He assured me that it was a rare chance—the opportunity of a lifetime. It was because I wanted so to restore to you what my gambling had cost, that I agreed. I did not think it possible to lose. But help me this once; believe me, I do know, and with shame, that were it not for my accursed ill luck we should be living in luxury now. But just this once—you will help me, won't you?"

His wife seated herself in a big armchair, and looked at him wearily, running her fingers through the heavy waves of her hair. She had beautiful hands—beautiful because they seemed part of her expression; capable hands with nothing helpless in her use of them; the kind that a sick person dreams of as belonging to an ideal nurse; gentle and smooth, but quick and firm.

"It is not a question of willingness, Sandro." Her voice was as smooth and strong, as flexible, as her hands. "You know everything we have just as well as I. I never kept anything from you, and what we have is ours jointly—as much yours as mine. I have, as you know, only two jewels of value left, and they would not bring half the amount of this debt."

"Leonora, no! you have sold too many already; I cannot ask such a thing again."

His wife's smile was more sad than tears; it was not that she was making up her mind for some one necessary sacrifice—it was a smile of absolute helplessness. "If only I might believe you! We now have nothing but what is held in trust for me. I am not reproaching you—what is gone is gone. But Sandro! where will it end?"

The maid knocked and entered with two pails of hot water, which she poured into the tub. She spread a bath towel over a chair, moved another chair near, put out various articles of clothing, and left the room again.

The princess threw off her slippers, and tried the temperature of the water with her toes.

"I think, Sandro, we had better give up Rome," she said. "The money saved for that will pay the greater part of the debt. It is the only way I can see. But go now; I want to take my bath. We can talk more by and by." She smiled quite brightly, and the prince, emboldened by her cheerfulness, would have taken her in his arms. But she turned away, her hand involuntarily put up as a barrier between herself and the kiss that at the moment she shrank from. He took the hand instead and pressed it to his lips.

When he had gone, she bathed quickly, partially dressed herself, and called her maid to do her hair. Sitting before the improvised dressing-table, she glanced in the mirror, and her reflection caught and held her attention a long moment. A curious, half-wistful, half-pathetic expression crept into her eyes as the realization came to her sharply that she was fading. There were lines and shadows and pallor that ought not to be in the face of a woman of thirty-five. She smoothed the vertical lines in her forehead, and then let her hands remain over her face, while behind their cool smoothness her mind resumed its troublesome thoughts.

It was not like meeting some new difficulty for which the strength is fresh; it was struggling again with emotions that have repeatedly exhausted one's endurance. Just as she had every hope that her husband was cured of the gambler's fever, here he was down again with an even more dangerous form of it. The man who knowingly risks is bad enough; but the man who cannot see that he risks, and cannot understand how he has lost is the hardest victim to cure. All of her capital was gone except a small property which her brother-in-law, J. B. Randolph, held for her in trust and on the income of which they now lived. Ten years before she had had considerable money, enough for them to live not only in comfort but in luxury. A large amount had been sunk in a Sicilian sulphur mine, and to this investment she had given her consent, not yet realizing her husband's lack of judgment. But aside from this, cards and horse races and trips to Monaco had limited their living in luxury to a periodic pleasure of three or four months. Now in order to open the palace in Rome, they had to practise the most rigid economics the other eight or nine months in their villa in the country.

Yet in spite of all, her compassion went out to Sandro. He was so gay, so boy-like, that he acquired ascendancy over her sympathies in spite of her judgment. And by the time her maid had coiled her great golden waves of hair and helped her into a short, heavy skirt, a pair of stout boots, a plain shirt-waist, and a rough, short coat and cap, her feeling of resentment against him had passed. She drew on a pair of dogskin gloves, and went out.

In the stables she found the prince helping to harness a pony.

"Are you going to drive to the village?" she asked as cheerfully as though there had been no topic of distress.

"Yes; will you come with me?" he returned eagerly. She nodded her assent and as they started down the road they talked easily of various things. It was the prince who finally came back to the topic that was uppermost in their minds. He looked at her tenderly as he said:

"You do believe, my darling, don't you, that to have brought this additional trouble to you breaks my heart? I have taken everything from you—given you nothing in return. Yet—I do love you."

"Oh, *va bene, va bene, caro mio*; we will talk no more about it. Do you really agree to stay in the country all winter and give up Rome?"

"Of course," he said, with the best grace in the world. "It is all far too easy for me—but for you!—Ah, Leonora, no admiration, no new interest! no amusement! a year of your beauty wasted on only me."

"Be still; you know very well that I care nothing for all that. It is always this horrible fear of your leaping before you look. Sandro, Sandro! can you really see that one more plunge—and we are done? Now we can give up our savings, and the jewels; another time—don't let there ever be another time!"

He looked up the road and down; there was not even a peasant in sight. He put his arm about her and drew her to him. "Look at me, Leonora! On the name of my family and on that which I hold most sacred in the world I swear it: you will never again have to suffer from such a cause."

She inclined toward his kiss, and love dominated the sadness in her eyes. Who could be angry with him—impulsive, affectionate, warm-hearted child of the Sun, or Italy—since both are the same.

A turn in the road, around a high wall topped with orange trees, brought them into the little town and the village life. A couple of ragged urchins sitting before the door of one of the cavelike structures that are called dwellings, grinned as the princess looked at them. An older girl bobbed a courtesy and pulled one of the children to her feet, bidding her do the same. The men uncovered their heads, as the noble padrones passed.

Before one house the little trap stopped. Immediately the door opened and a woman came out. She was young and handsome though the shadow of maternity was blue-stenciled under her eyes. She courtesied, then looked anxiously at the prince.

"Excellency would speak with me?" she asked, "has Excellency decided?"

"Yes," the prince answered, "Pedro will wed thee at the house of the good father—tonight at eight." At his first words she clasped her hands in thanksgiving, but when he continued that she was to wear no veil or wreath, her joy gave way to a wail.

"Excellency would shame me," she sobbed, "I am a good girl and Pedro my husband by promise."

Sansevero looked helpless for a moment and then seemed wavering. The woman caught at the opportunity and repeated her cry, this time to the princess, but there was no indecision in the latter's manner as she spoke now in her husband's stead.

"Thou knowest, Marcella, that the veil and the wreath are only for such as are maidens! Say no more, I speak not of goodness, Pedro comes to the house of the padre—at eight. Be a faithful wife and mother, and so shalt thou have honor—better than by the wearing of a wreath."

She put her hand on the girl's head, with a kindness that took away all sting from her words. And Marcella made no further protest, although as the pony-cart drove on, she remained weeping before the door.

Sansevero himself looked dejected. "Don't you think, dear one," he protested, "that you were rather severe! What difference can it make after all, whether the poor girl wears a few leaves in her hair or a bit of tulle?"

But the princess was inflexible. "It would not be just to the others," she answered, "since we made this rule there has been a great difference in the village. It is almost rare now that the family arrives before the wedding. The question of irregularity never used trouble the girls at all. The only disgrace they seem able to feel is that they may not dress as brides; and that being the case, I think we have to be strict."

"All right, wise one," said the prince as he drew up at the post-office, "I am sure you know best." He looked at her with such obvious satisfaction that two urchins standing by the road-side grinned. The post-master hurried out with the mail, and the princess looked through the letters. One with an American stamp held her attention. As she read, her cheeks flushed with pleasure, her eyes grew bright, a sweet and tender expression came into her face.

"Nina is coming!" she cried. Gladness rang in her voice. "Coming for the whole winter—let me see, the letter is dated the fifteenth—she will sail this week. Oh, Sandro, I am so happy!"

For a moment it would have been hard to say which looked more pleased, the prince or the princess. But then, as though by thought transference, in blank consternation each stared at the other, and exclaimed in the same breath, "But how about Rome?"

In silence the prince turned the pony about and slowly they drove back up the hills.

CHAPTER II

THE PRINCESS PLANS TO RECEIVE
THE AMERICAN HEIRESS

When the pony-cart arrived at the castle the princess alighted, too preoccupied with her own thoughts to notice that her husband drove off in the opposite direction from the stables. Her forehead was wrinkled and her head bent as she walked between the high hedges of ilex toward the south wing of the building. Her worry over their inability to pay the debt was increased by the fact that their creditor was the Duke Scorpa.

There had been a feud between the Sanseveros and the Scorpas for over a century, and while the present generation tried to ignore it, the princess felt instinctively that like the people of Alsace Lorraine, who never really forgave the government that changed their nationality, the Scorpas never forgave the Sanseveros for lands which they claimed were unjustly lost in 1803, when a daughter of the house married a Sansevero and took a portion of the Scorpa property as her dowry. That these same lands were distant from either county seat, and of comparatively small value, in no way mitigated the Scorpa resentment, and every time they looked at the map and saw the triangular piece painted over from the Scorpa red to the Sansevero blue, there was bad feeling.

When the old Prince Sansevero was alive, he and the present Duke, who was then a violent tempered youth, had several unfriendly encounters about the boundary line of this same property. All this had seemed very trivial to Alessandro, the present Prince, who looked upon the Duke as one of his best friends—but Alessandro had no perspicacity. He believed others to be as free from guile as himself.

Reaching a small postern gate at the end of the path, the princess opened it by pressing a hidden spring. This led directly into the apartments at the end of the south wing next to the kitchen offices—the only ones at present in use. She went directly to her own sitting-room, from which the evidences of her toilet had meantime been removed.

This room better than anything else proclaimed the manner of woman who occupied it. It had been arranged by one to whom comfort was of paramount importance, and, in spite of a certain incongruity, the whole effect was pleasing and harmonious. The frescoes on the walls were almost obliterated by age, and were partially covered by dull red stuff. Against this latter hung three pictures from the famous Sansevero collection: a Holy Family by Leonardo da Vinci, a triptych by Perugino, and a Madonna by Correggio. Hardly less celebrated, but sharply at odds with the ecclesiastical subjects of the paintings, was the mantle, carved in a bacchanalian procession of satyrs and nymphs—a model said to have been made by Niccola Pisano.

The floor, of the inevitable black and white marble, was strewn with rugs; and in front of desk and sofa bear skins had been added as a double protection against the cold. The furniture was modern upholstery, with gay chintz slip-covers. Frilled muslin curtains were crossed over and draped high under outer ones of chintz. And everywhere there were flowers—roses, orange blossoms, and camellias; in tall jars and short, on every available piece of furniture. Scarcely less in evidence were photographs, propped against walls, ornaments, and flower jars; long, narrow, highly glazed European photographs with white backgrounds, uniformed officers, sentimentally posed engaged couples, young mothers in full evening dress reading to barefooted babies out of gingerly held picture books. There were photographs of all varieties; big ones and little ones, framed and unframed—the king and the queen with crown-surmounted settings and boldly written first names, and "*A la cara Eleanor*" inscribed above that of her majesty. In the other photographs the signatures grew in complication and length as their aristocratic importance diminished. Books and magazines littered the tables; French, Italian, and English in indiscriminate association. A workbasket of plain sewing lay open among the pillows on the sofa. An American magazine, with a paper-knife inserted between its leaves, was tossed beside a tooled morocco edition of Tacitus. A crucifix hung beneath the Correggio; a plaster model of the Discobolus stood between the windows.

And in the midst of old and new, religious and pagan, priceless and insignificant, sat her Excellency, the ex-American beauty and present chatelaine of the great family of the princes of the Sansevero, in a golf skirt and walking boots, a plain starched shirtwaist and stock tie, adding to the wrinkles in her forehead and in the corners of her eyes by trying to figure out how, with forty thousand lire, she was going to pay a debt of sixty thousand lire and have enough left over to open the great palace in Rome, and realize a dream that had always been in her heart—to take Nina out in Roman society, to give herself the delight of showing Rome to Nina, and the greater delight of showing Nina to Rome.

She glanced up at two photographs, the only ones on her desk. The first was of her husband, taken in the fancy costume of a troubadour, with the signature "Sandro" across the lower half, in characters symbolical of the song he might have sung, so gay and ascending was the handwriting. The other picture was of a young woman in evening dress. The face was bright and winning rather than pretty; the personality really chic, and this in spite of the fact that the girl's clothes were over-elaborate. Her dress was a mass of embroidery, and around her throat she wore a diamond collar. Diamond hairpins held the loops of waving fair hair—very like the princess's own—and two handsome rings were on the fingers of one hand. It in no way suggested the Italian idea of a young girl; yet there was a youthful freshness in the expression of the face, a girlish slimness of the figure that could not have been produced by touching up the negative. Under the picture was written in a clear and modernly square handwriting, "To my own Auntie Princess with love from Nina."

The name "Auntie Princess" carried as much of Nina's personality to the mind of her aunt as the picture itself. It was the one her childish lips had spoken when she was told that her aunt was to marry a prince. Most distinct of all Eleanor Sansevero's memories of home was one of Nina being held up high above the crowd at the end of the pier to blow good-by kisses to the bride of a foreign nobleman, being carried out into the river whose widening water was making actual the separation between herself and all that till then had been her life.

It was only for a little while, she had thought at the time. She would go back once a year or so, surely; and Nina should come over often. But in the intervening fifteen years, though the Randolphs had been in Europe many times, they had always chosen midsummer for their trip, and the princess had joined her sister at some northern city or watering-place. This visit, therefore, was to be Nina's first glimpse of her aunt's home, and the princess was determined that she should not spend the time desolately in the country! She might come here for a little while—for reasons that the princess would have found hard to explain to herself, she did not want Nina to get a false impression. Yet for nothing would she have exposed her husband's failing—even to her own family. With the weakness of a true wife, she never dreamed that all her world suspected, if it did not actually know, of the great inroads on her fortune that his gambling had made.

The princess went back to her accounts, but no amount of auditing made the sum they had saved any larger. A large pearl pendant that had been the Randolphs' wedding present to her, and a ruby that had been her mother's, were her only remaining possessions that could bring anything like the sum needed; with them and perhaps notes on her next year's income, they might make up the full amount. But how to sell the jewels was the problem. There is little demand for really fine stones in Italy, and besides, they might be recognized. Long before, she had sold her emerald earrings and had false ones put in their places. She had hated wearing the imitations, but she had worn the real ones constantly, she feared their sudden absence might be noticed.

Indeed, as it was, one day out in the garden, when Scorpa was sitting near her, she thought she saw a knowing gleam in his eyes. Afterwards she tried to assure herself that it was a trick of her own consciousness; but she had not worn the earrings again in the daytime—nor ever if she knew that Scorpa was to be present.

She threw down her pencil. The first thing at all events was to find out how much she could realize on her stones, and to do that she would have to go to Paris. Taking a railroad gazette out of a drawer, she looked up trains. Eight-thirty mornings, arriving at—

The door burst open. The prince, exuberant, his face wreathed in smiles, skipped, rather than walked, into the room. In pure joyousness he pinched her cheek.

"What do you think, my dear one? It is all arranged. We can have *la bella* Nina; we shall go to Rome as usual. And you, you more than generous, shall not sell any jewels!"

His wife did not at once echo his gladness; in fact she seemed frightened.

"What has happened? You have not made a wager and won?"

He looked reproachful, almost sulky. "Leonora, unjust you are. Have I not promised? But I will tell you. I have arranged it all with Scorpa. I have let him have the Raphael—as security, practically—that is, I have sold it to him for a hundred thousand lire—a loan merely—and he has given me the privilege of buying it back at any time, with added interest, of course. There will be no need of paying for years. He is enchanted, as he has always wanted the picture, and says he only hopes I may never wish to take it back."

"No, don't let us do that," the princess broke in, then hesitated, "I can't tell you how I feel about it, but—I don't trust Scorpa. It is a hard thing to say, but I have always believed he persuaded you into buying the 'Little Devil' mine, knowing it could not be worked. Of course, dear, that heavy loss may not have been his fault, but I'd so much rather never have any dealings with him. Besides, the very thing I wish to avoid is letting people know we must get money."

"But, *cara mia*, listen: It is all so well thought out, no one will know. You see, we go to Rome; this picture hangs in an empty house, which through the winter is very damp, and bad, therefore, for the painting. Scorpa keeps his house open and heated; he takes care of it on that account. Is that not a wonderful reason?"

"Whose reason was that?"

"Scorpa's own!" He danced a few steps in his excess of delight.

His wife arose and put her hand on his arm. "To please me, do not send the picture. I can sell the jewels and have false stones put in their places. We need not have any one know. But I don't want to remain in the duke's debt!"

"The picture is already in his possession."

"In his possession? But how?"

"He drove over here just now, followed me in his motor-car, and took it back with him."

The princess was evidently frightened. "What are his reasons?" she said to herself, yet audibly.

Her husband looked at her, his head a little on one side, then he said banteringly: "My dear, you Americans are too analytical. You always look for a motive. Life is not of motive over here. Have you not learned that in all these years? We act from impulse, as the mood takes us—we have not the hidden thought that you are always looking for."

"You speak for yourself, Sandro *mio*, but all are not like you. However, since the picture is gone—and since you have made that arrangement—let it be. I may do Scorpa injustice; he has always professed friendship for you—as indeed who has not?" She looked at him with the softened glance that one sees in a mother's face.

Sansevero seated himself at the desk and took up the photograph of Nina. "When will she arrive?" he asked buoyantly; then with sudden inspiration, "Write to Giovanni and ask him to hurry home. If Nina should fancy him, what a prize!"

The princess frowned. "On account of her money, you mean?"

"Ah, but one must think of that! We have no children; all this goes to Giovanni—with Nina's immense fortune it would be very well. We could all live as it used to be; there are the apartments on the second floor in Rome, and the west wing here. I can think of nothing more fitting or delightful. Has she grown pretty?"

"I don't know that you would call her pretty," mused the princess.

"Besides *you*, my dearest, a beauty might seem plain!" His wife tried to look indifferent, but she was pleased, nevertheless.

"Tell me, Sandro, you flatterer, but tell me honestly, am I still pretty? No, really? Will Nina think me the same, or will her thought be 'How my Aunt has gone off'?"

Melodramatically he seized her wrists and drew her to the window; placing her in the full light of the sun, he peered with mock tragedy into her face. "Let me see. Your hair—no, not a gray one! The gold of your hair at least I have not squandered—yet."

"Don't, dear." She would have moved away, but he held her.

"Your face is thinner, but that only shows better its beautiful bones. Ah, now your smile is just as delicious—but don't wrinkle your forehead like that; it is full of lines. So—that is better. You make the eyes sad sometimes; eyes should be the windows that let light into the soul; they should be glad and admit only sunshine." Then with one of his lightning transitions of mood, he added, not without a ring of emotion, "*Mia povera bella.*"

But Eleanor reached up and took his face between her hands. "As for you," she said, "you are always just a boy. Sometimes it is impossible to believe you are older than I—I think I should have been your mother."

CHAPTER III

NINA

A ponderous, glossy, red Limousine turned in under the wrought bronze portico of one of the palatial houses of upper Fifth Avenue. As the car stopped, the face of a woman of about forty appeared at its window. Her expression was one of fretful annoyance, as though the footman who had sprung off the box and hurried up the steps to ring the front doorbell had, in his haste, stumbled purposely. The look she gave him, as he held the door open for her to alight, rebuked plainly his awkward stupidity.

Yet, in spite of Mrs. Randolph's petulant expression, it was evident that she had distinct claims to prettiness, though of the carefully prolonged variety. The art of the masseuse was visible in that curious swollen smoothness of the skin which gives an effect of spilled candle-wax—its lack of wrinkles never to be mistaken for the freshness of youth. Much also might be said of the skill with which the "original color" of her hair had been preserved. She was very well "done," indeed; every detail proclaimed expenditure of time—other people's—and money—her own. She trotted, rather than walked, as though bored beyond the measure of endurance and yet in a hurry. Following her was a slim, fair-haired young girl, who, leaving the footman to gather up a number of parcels, turned to the chauffeur. Even in giving an order, there was a winning grace in her lack of self-consciousness, and her voice was fresh in its timbre, enthusiastic in its inflection.

"Henri," she said, "you had better be here at three. The steamer sails at four, and an hour will not give me any too much time. Have William come for Celeste and the steamer things at two. The Panhard will be best, as there is plenty of room in the tonneau." Then she ran lightly up the steps and into the house.

The first impression of a visitor upon entering the hall might have been of emptiness. In contrast to the over-elaborateness characteristic of all too many American homes and hotels, obtruding their highly colored, gold-laden ornament, the Randolph house rather inclined toward an austerity of decoration. But after the first general impression, more careful observation revealed the extreme luxury of appointments and details. The one flaw—if one might call it such—was that every article in the entire house was spotlessly, perfectly brand-new. The Persian rugs, pinkish red in coloring and made expressly to tone in with the gray white marble of the hall, were direct from the looms. The banister, of beautiful simplicity, was as newly wrought as the stainless velvet with which the hand-rail was covered. From the hall opened faultlessly executed rooms, each correctly adhering to the "period" that had been selected. The library was possibly more furnished than the rest of the house; but even here the touch of a magician's wand might have produced the bookcases of Circassian walnut ready filled with evenly matched, leather bound, finely tooled volumes. It would have been a relief to see a few shabby, old-calf folios, a few more common and every-day, in cloth or buckram!

On the mind of a carping critic the universal newness might have forced the question, "Where did the family live before they came here? Did all their accumulation of personal belongings burn with an old homestead? Or did they start fresh with their new house, coming from nowhere?" One could imagine their having superintended the moving-in of crates and boxes innumerable, but the idea of vans piled with heterogeneous personal effects that had accumulated through years—Impossible!

As Mrs. Randolph and her daughter entered, a servant opened the doors leading into the dining-room, and Mrs. Randolph turned at once in that direction.

"You don't want to go upstairs before luncheon, do you, Nina?"

"Yes, for a moment, Mamma. I want to speak to Celeste about the things for my steamer trunk." Her mother suggested sending a servant, but Nina had already gone. She entered an elevator that in contrast to the severity of the hall looked like a gilt bird cage with mirrors set between the bars, pushed a button, and mounted two flights.

On emerging, she went into her own bedroom, which, from the Aubusson carpet to the Dresden and ormolu appliques, might have arrived in a bonbon box direct from the avenue de l'Opéra in Paris. At the present moment two steamer trunks stood gaping in the middle of the floor, tissue paper was scattered about on various chairs, the dressing-table was bare of silver, and a traveling bag displayed a row of gold bottle and brush tops. Nina threw her packages on a couch already littered with empty boxes, wrapping-paper, new books and various other articles.

"Have the other trunks gone, Celeste?"

"Yes, Mademoiselle."

"Any messages for me?"

"Mr. Derby telephoned that he would be here soon after

lunch. Miss Lee also telephoned. And Mr. Travers."

Nina listened, half absently, except possibly for a flickering interest at the mention of Mr. Derby. She went into an adjoining room that had a deep plunge bath of white marble, and a white bear rug on the floor. A sliding panel in the wall disclosed a safe, from which she gathered together several velvet boxes, and carried them to her maid.

"Are these all that Mademoiselle will take?"

"Yes, that is enough—I don't know, though, the emerald pendant looks well on gray dresses." She got another velvet box and threw it on the floor. "I ordered the Panhard to be here for you at two o'clock. They can put the trunks in the tonneau. My stateroom is 'B,' yours is 107."

Quickly as she had entered, she was gone again, into the elevator and down to join her mother.

"Really, Nina," Mrs. Randolph said as soon as her daughter was seated, "I can't see what you want to go to Rome for. I am sure it's more comfortable here. I hate visiting, myself." As she spoke she set straight a piece of silver that to her critical eye seemed an eighth of an inch out of line.

"But, Mamma, you know how keen I have always been to see Aunt Eleanor's home. Being with her can hardly seem visiting; and Uncle Sandro—"

"What your aunt ever saw in Sandro Sansevero," interrupted her mother, "I'm sure I can't imagine. He's always bobbing and bowing and gesticulating, and he talks broken English. He makes me nervous! I'd infinitely rather be without a title than have it at that price."

"You have always told me that theirs was a love match, that Aunt Eleanor did not marry him for his title."

"That is just the senseless part of it!" Mrs. Randolph retorted with a fine disregard for consistency. "If she had married him for his name—which, after all, is a good one, although princes are as common in Italy as 'misters' are here—that would have been one thing. But she was actually in love with him! She is yet, so far as I can see!"

Nina burst out laughing, and, as though catching the infection, Mrs. Randolph laughed too. They were interrupted by the butler's announcing "Mr. Derby!"

John Derby was a young man of twenty-five, broad shouldered and well over six feet. His features were a little too rugged to be strictly handsome, but his spare frame was as muscular as that of a young gladiator. So much at least our colleges do for the sons we send to them. John Derby had made both the 'Varsity eight and the eleven; he had been a young god at the end of June when, captain of the victorious boat, his classmates had borne him on their shoulders to their club-house. That night there had been toasting and speeches and what not—he was a very "big man" of a very big university; and perhaps nothing that life might ever give him in the future could overshadow this experience.

All hail to the victor—and glorious be his remembrances. Exit our Greek god at the end of June, to be replaced by a young American citizen about the first of July—one small atom who thinks to make the same sized mark on the great plain of life that he made on the college campus. All the same, there were good clean ideals back of John Derby's blue eyes, and fresh, healthy young blood surged through his veins. What is the world for, if not for such as he to conquer?

Thousands had called "Derby! Derby! Go it, Derby!" when he made his famous sixty-yard run down the gridiron. Yet it is well to remember that the victory came at the end of ten years' training at school and college, after many bruises, some dislocations, and not a few breaks. With such discipline, there was after all no reason to wonder that he donned overalls and went to a desolate settlement of brick chimneys, smelters, and shack dwellings, set on the sides of hills, which, because of sulphurous fumes, were bleak as sandhills in Sahara.

He had taken up his work at Copper Rock exactly as he had taken up his practice under the athletic coaches. He gave all the best of him, from the earliest to the latest possible hours; and night saw him stretched on a bunk which would have made his mother wince, but upon which he slept the sleep of healthy, tired youth.

Three years he had spent in this place. Twice in that time furnace explosions had sent him home to be nursed. But he suppressed the horrors and related only enthusiastic tales of metallurgical possibilities. In the main, however, he was strong enough to stand it. It did him a vast amount of good; and the end of three years saw him saying good-by with something akin to regret to the bleak shacks on the bleaker hills, and to the men he had grown to know and appreciate.

An improved form of blast furnace that he had patented, eased his first strenuous need of money. And the present moment found him vice-president of a mining and smelting company, temporarily back among his old friends, and somewhat in his old life again. He was too busy and too interested in his work to spend any effort outside of it; but there were one or two houses where he went, and one of them was the Randolphs'. The Randolph and Derby country places adjoined, and since early boyhood he had been as much at home in one house as in the other.

Mrs. Randolph had taken his college achievements complacently as a tribute to her discernments in having nurtured an eagle in her own swan's nest. But his work at Copper Rock seemed to her a fanatical whim. She no more appreciated the benefit of the experience than she understood the persevering grit that was the real reason for her liking him. Nina, having adored him as a Greek god, continued her allegiance to the workman at Copper Rock. She had written him letters regularly; she had even sent him provision baskets. To herself she questioned whether the end he was striving for might not be reached by smoother roads; but if any one else suggested that he was doing an irrational thing, she flew up in arms. And now as he came into the dining-room his "Hello, Nina!" was much as a brother's might have been, and he kissed Mrs. Randolph's cheek.

"Will you have lunch, John?" she smiled up at him. "It is all cold by now, I dare say!"

"No, thanks, I lunched downtown; but I'll sit here if I may." He picked up a knife from the table and cut the string of a package he held in his hand. "I brought you these, Nina. Have you read all of them?"

Nina finished a mouthful of nectarine and picked up the books one by one.

No, she had not read any of them. So he went on to explain: he knew the cowboy story was a corker, and another, of Arizona, described an Indian fight in the Bad Lands that was capital. He did not know much about the others, but the man at the shop had told him two were very funny; he had bought the rest on account of their illustrations.

Nina laughed deliciously with real joy—she loved his selection, because it seemed to express him.

"It was awfully sweet of you, Jack. And I shall adore them! I am so glad you did not bring the regular selection of 'Walks in Rome.'"

"What I ought to have brought you," he answered, "was a big thick journal—one of those padlocked ones—to write up Italian court life as it really is. You mustn't miss such a chance! It could be published after everybody mentioned in it, is dead, including yourself. Wouldn't it be great!"

"You need not make fun of me. I don't think you half appreciate how wonderful it is going to be," Nina returned enthusiastically. "Think of it, I am going to live in a palace!"

Derby threw back his head and laughed.

"What do you call this house? It is a great deal more of a palace than the tumble-down, musty ones of Italy."

Mrs. Randolph seemed enchanted with this rejoinder, for she laughed rather exultantly as she exclaimed, "Nina will be ready enough to come home at the end of a week!"

Instead of answering Nina jumped up from the table, calling "There you are at last, Father darling!"

Her father, a man of distinguished presence, had come into the room looking at his watch from force of habit. And though his eyes rested upon his daughter with very evident pride and affection, the custom of quickly terminated interviews and the economy of precious time gave a sharp, decisive curtness to his manner. Every one who came in contact with him felt the impelling necessity of coming to the point as clearly and tersely as possible. Just now, with a "Hello, John, my boy," he held out his hand to Derby and shook his head negatively in answer to his wife's inquiry if he wanted luncheon.

"Well, are you ready to start?" he asked his daughter, smiling. And then to Derby he added, "Excuse Nina for a few moments, John; I want to speak with her. You are going down to the steamer with her, of course?" As Derby answered affirmatively, Nina picked up her books and followed her father.

In his own study he drew her to a sofa beside him, and from a number of papers in his pocket he handed her an envelope.

"Here is your letter of credit. I doubt if you will need the whole amount of it. If, on the contrary, you find you want more for anything special, write or cable to the office."

Out of another pocket he drew a white muslin bag, such as bankers use. It held a quantity of Italian gold and a roll of Italian bank notes. This was "change" to have with her when she should arrive. He talked with her for some time on various topics; on the beauty of Italy, the charm of the people; of his admiration for Eleanor Sansevero. "But dearest," he ended, "one word on the subject of European men: you will probably have a good deal of attention. I don't want to spoil your enjoyment, but you must remember the hard, cold fact that it will be chiefly because you are Miss Millionaire."

"I am sure they couldn't be any more after 'Miss Millionaire' over there than here." She began calmly enough, but grew vehement as she continued: "How many of the proposals that I have had from my own countrymen during the past two years have been for me, the girl, and not merely for your daughter?"

Her father, having stirred up her resentment, now tried to soothe it down again.

"You must not get cynical, little girl. Every advantage in this world must have its corresponding disadvantage. I merely want you to follow your extremely sensible and well-balanced head. Only, remember," he added with bantering good-humor, "I am not over keen about foreigners, so don't bring a little what-is-it back with you, and expect because it has a long string of titles dangling to it, that it will be welcomed with any enthusiasm by your doting father! So, away with you!" He again looked at his watch. "Better get your things together; you haven't any too much time."

As soon as Nina left him, instead of rejoining his wife and Derby he sat at his desk and was immediately absorbed in making figures with the stub of a pencil on the back of an envelope. He was still there when Nina, in coat and furs, came downstairs again to the library, where her mother and Derby were now waiting.

"Well, are you ready at last? Where is your father? What is he doing now?" her mother demanded with a pout, as if his absence were quite Nina's fault, and as if whatever his occupation might be it especially annoyed her. She fluttered to the doorway of his study and looked in.

"James, I really think you might give some thought to your family. Nina is going now." She spoke in a babyish, aggrieved tone. He did not look up, and Mrs. Randolph did not repeat her remark; she turned instead to her daughter. "Go in and tell your father that I think he might pay you some attention."

Nina went over behind his chair, and gently put her cheek down to his. She did not interrupt him, but let him finish the calculation he was doing; and he turned to her after about a minute.

"All right, sweetheart, come along."

Having put his envelope in his pocket, he dismissed whatever it meant completely from his mind, and Nina held his undivided attention as he went down the steps with her to the motor, into which Derby had already put Mrs. Randolph. As soon as they were all in and the machine started, Nina leaned forward and called to the butler, "Good-by, Dawson!" And for once the man's face lost its imperturbability, as he answered fervently, "Good-by, miss, and a safe return—home!"

"Safe return—home." For a moment the question entered her head—was there any doubt of her returning? With the apprehension came also a slight sense of excitement—but soon she had forgotten. While they sped toward the dock, Mrs. Randolph, possibly a little piqued that her daughter could want to spend the winter away from her, showed her authority by endless directions and counsels. As she completely monopolized the conversation as far as Nina was concerned, the two men talked together, and Nina's responses gradually drifted into a series of "Yes, Mamma's," to admonitions that were but half heard, until her wandering attention was brought up with a sharp turn by her mother's impatient exclamation:

"For goodness sake, Nina, try to be less monotonous!"

Nina roused herself quickly. "I am sorry, Mamma dear! I did not think there was anything for me to say. Please don't be put out with me, just now when I am going away!"

They had by this time arrived at the steamer, and went for a moment to see Nina's cabin, where they found Celeste trying to reduce to some semblance of order the innumerable baskets of fruit and boxes of flowers with which it was crowded.

Derby looked perhaps a trifle chagrined at the profusion, as Nina gave a cursory glance at the cards that Celeste had affixed to each opened box. But with a curious little smile—one that had real sweetness in it—Nina picked up a particular bunch of violets, and looked at Derby over their clustered fragrance as she lifted them to her face. She let the look thank him—and then she pinned the flowers on.

Mrs. Randolph did not see the wordless scene, as she was busy reading cards and making characteristic comments. Mr. Randolph had stopped to make sure that the luggage was attended to. He now appeared, and with him Mrs. Gray, with whom Nina was to make the crossing. Mrs. Gray shook hands with every one, called Nina a "precious child," told her where the steamer chairs had been placed, and disappeared. On the promenade deck Nina found a throng of young girls and men waiting for her. They all chattered together in a group and plied her with questions: Was she going to be presented at court? Was she going to live in an old castle? What was her uncle the prince like? How wonderful to spend a season in Rome? They wished they were going, too—and so they went on.

But at a moment when the others were all talking loudly, John Derby managed to draw Nina aside. He looked down at her with an expression half-quizzical, half-serious. "This is about the time we come to the 'great divide,'" he said. "Your trail lies to the palaces of the Old World; mine to dig holes in remote corners of the New. You'll write me, won't you? My letters will be pretty dull, I am afraid—same old story: a laborer's day, and occasionally a

Sunday's ride to get the mail at the nearest ranch."

"Then I'll make mine doubly thick—so they will seem like packets. I may even write that famous journal and send it in instalments to you!" Then suddenly the banter died of her eyes and voice and she said half-sentimentally: "Dear old Jack! Most of every one I shall miss you. I hope things will go famously for you. You have my address?"

"Yes; and mine is Breakstone, Arizona, care of Burk Mining Company. Well," he smiled, "good hunting to both of us!"

There was still plenty of time before the ship sailed, but Mr. Randolph was leaving. He had been talking with another financier who was seeing his own family off, and now came up between his daughter and Derby.

"If you will go with me now," he said to the latter, "we can talk over the Louisiana sulphur proposition on the way to my office." Then he turned to Nina: "It is barely possible you may see John in Italy before the winter is over."

Nina raised her eyebrows as she looked at Derby. "You said you were going to Arizona!" she said accusingly.

But Derby's expression showed that he was as much in the dark as she. Mr. Randolph wagged his head as though altogether pleased with the situation. "Of course, he is going to Arizona, and very likely he'll stay there—on the other hand, maybe he won't. Now that's something for you to think about besides speculating on the length of name of each stranger you meet." He kissed her affectionately on both cheeks and, giving Derby barely a chance to shake hands with her, hurried him away.

People were beginning their final good-byes, and from where Nina and her friends stood by the deck rail, there was a clear view of the gang plank and the ship's departing visitors. It was from this vantage that several pairs of envious young masculine eyes, looking downward, saw the right hand of the great and only James B. Randolph affectionately laid on the broad shoulder of an ex-oarsman and football player. And for as long as the two were in sight it was the ex-oarsman who talked, and the great financier who listened.

CHAPTER IV

THE DUKE SCORPA MAKES A DEAL

In the branch office of Shayne & Co., in the Via Condotti, Rome, Mr. Shayne arose from his desk, rearranged his diamond scarf-pin in his gray satin Ascot tie, flicked two imaginary particles of dust from his tight-fitting cutaway coat, whisked his silk handkerchief out of his breast pocket and in again, so that the lavender border was visible, cleared his throat, and stood in an attitude of agreeable expectancy.

Directly the door of his private room was discreetly opened, admitting a square-jawed, beetle-browed man, heavy and ugly—a coarse type, yet not without distinction. The two men did not shake hands. Mr. Christopher Shayne bowed blandly, deferentially, yet not servilely, and again he cleared his throat. The visitor nodded as though there upon an affair of business that he was anxious to have terminated as speedily as possible.

"Will you be seated?—I think you will find this chair comfortable." Mr. Shayne indicated a chair with a wave of his hand. "The letter which I have from your Excellency is a trifle indefinite. But I take it that you have something of more than ordinary importance to communicate." He finished his sentence by giving his mustache a thoughtful twirl upward, first on one side and then on the other.

The Duke Scorpa let his rat-like eyes rest a moment upon the alert face of Mr. Shayne before he answered: "You said once in my presence that you had long wanted to acquire a Raphael. I am in a position at present to offer you one."

"A Raphael!" Shayne showed genuine surprise. "I do not remember one in your collection."

"It is not in my own collection. Before giving you further details, however, I must be assured that you are still anxious to purchase, and also that you will observe strict secrecy with regard to it."

"In answer to the first, such an opportunity is beyond question of interest to me; in answer to the second, my reputation should be a guarantee of my discretion. I hope the picture you have in view is not the Asanai one—for there is much doubt as to its being genuine."

"No, the one I speak of is the Sansevero Madonna."

In spite of himself Mr. Shayne blew a long whistle. "The Sansevero Madonna with the doves!" he reiterated. "That *is* a prize! I am astonished, though—" It was on his tongue to say that he had thought the Prince Sansevero beyond the suspicion of illegal sale of treasures; but, checking himself in time, he finished his sentence—"that he should be willing to part with it. Besides, it is a dangerous thing for him to sell, on account of its celebrity."

"So I told him." The Duke Scorpa lied perfectly. "But it is better, after all, to sell one thing that will bring in a good price than to sell a number of things that bring in little, and yet incur the same amount of risk in getting them out of the country." Here the duke's manner became almost confidential. "As I told you, I am of course acting merely in the interest of my friend the Prince Sansevero. Selling against the law of my country would be abhorrent to me personally. But my friend, poor fellow, is hard pressed for money. And, as he argues, the picture is his, and has been in his family since long before our government ever made such laws. He considers he has a right—or should have—to dispose of property that is his own. The government would pay not more than half what you will give me, I am sure."

"Of course, of course. I have long coveted that Raphael. On the other hand, as I said, the picture is so very well known and so excellent that it could hardly be palmed off as a copy. Also the canvas is large, which will make it very difficult to conceal. It is still at Torre Sansevero, I suppose?"

"No, it is here in Rome. It is removed from the frame and is at present in my palace. I suppose the offer that you once told me you would make still holds good?"

The American looked shrewd. "Did I name a sum? I do not remember. Ah, yes. But that was for a very rich man who has since bought a Velasquez. I doubt if he will buy any more."

Scorpa rose as though to leave. "My friend wants five hundred thousand lire."

Mr. Shayne laughed scornfully. "Preposterous!" he said, and from that they argued for nearly half an hour; but in the end it was settled that the picture should change hands, and the price agreed upon was two hundred and fifty thousand lire.

In the matter of payment the duke was punctilious about protecting his friend the Prince Sansevero from the consequences of his transgression of the law. Shayne agreed to make his payments in cash, so that Sansevero's name should not appear on the checks.

But Christopher Shayne was more than skeptical about the duke's disinterestedness. "There is a rake-off for this one somewhere," he thought. He also thought that for once he had been mistaken in his judgment of character. Sansevero had been, in his opinion, a man who would sooner starve than defraud the government. So strongly did he believe this that although he had, as the duke knew, long coveted the Raphael, he would never have dared to approach Sansevero.

After the duke had gone Shayne went out and personally sent a code cable announcing his purchase.

"Well," he said to himself, "it's no business of mine. But duke or no duke, he is a slick one. I don't like him. I can tell, though, whether it is the Sansevero picture as soon as I lay my eyes on it—but what gets me is that the prince chose such a go-between. Why didn't he come to me direct?" He didn't puzzle over that long, however; planning to get the picture out of Italy occupied his attention. An excellent idea presented itself: some furniture ordered by his firm should carry it in a sofa, and his partner should be advised by cipher letter to remove the picture. J. B. Randolph would buy it, without doubt—no need to tell him how it came into Shayne & Co.'s hands. They could swear they bought it in London. Plausible stories of masterpieces discovered in out of the way corners were easily enough manufactured. So these thoughts all being to his utmost satisfaction, he went whistling down the street.

The Duke Scorpa at the same time was being driven cheerfully homeward. That had been a stroke, that idea of pretending he was merely the intermediary. He had got the picture for a loan of one hundred thousand, and had one hundred and fifty thousand clear profit. There was nothing to show his transaction with Sansevero. No money had passed between them, not even a scrap of paper. He had torn up the prince's I. O. U., and that was all the evidence there had been. Christopher Shayne, besides, was a shrewd man and reliable, and one who never had been caught in a questionable transaction. To be sure, Scorpa had given Sansevero his word (but again there was no proof), that he would let him retrieve the picture at an advanced price that should be merely the accrued compound interest on the money lent. In case of his being able to reclaim it, Scorpa would pretend that the picture was burnt or stolen—time enough to cross bridges when he came to them. But that chance was beyond all probability. There was no way for Sansevero ever to secure enough money to get back the picture—unless, indeed, his younger brother Giovanni should marry the great American heiress who was on her way to Italy for the winter.

"I hardly think that likely," said the Duke Scorpa to himself, as he stroked his heavy chin with his fat hand, "for I intend to annex that little fortune myself."

CHAPTER V

DON GIOVANNI ARRIVES

It was a few days after Nina's arrival in Italy; one of the glorious mornings when the famous Sansevero gardens were full of golden light, bringing into high relief the creamy marble of statues that in other centuries had been white. Against the deep waxy green of shrubs and hedges, the fountains seemed to be tossing liquid diamonds; and beyond the marble balustrades of the descending terraces, the hills rolled away in soft gray billows of young olive leaves and powdered slopes of blossoming orange branches. In contrast with this background of green and marble and roses and flowers and fountains stood Nina reaching up to pick a pink camellia. In front of her, the princess was looking vaguely into the finder of a camera.

"Now what shall I do? Just press the bulb and let go?"

"W-w-ait a moment until my teeth stop chattering!"

Nina had taken off her coat and was wearing a dress as summery in appearance as the garden. "All right, Auntie. This ought to be lovely—I hope gooseflesh and a blue nose won't show."

The picture taken, she lost no time in getting back into her long fur coat again and wrapping it tightly around her, still shivering.

"I do hope the pictures will be good—I am going to write under them 'In a rose garden at Christmas Time.' I shall not tell that I never was so cold in my life as at this minute. What I can't understand is how the flowers are hypnotized into believing it warm weather. It is every bit as cold as New York, yet if we were to ask these same shrubs to live in our gardens, they would hang their heads and die at the mere suggestion." Nina wanted to take snap shots of the princess, but the latter refused to remove her coat, and the incongruity of furs dispelled the midsummer illusion. Slipping her hand through her aunt's arm she drew her into a brisk walk. The temperature of Italy is low only by comparison with its summery appearance, and by the time they reached the terrace end she was in a glow.

She looked up at the irregular stone pile of the old castle, against which semi-tropical vines climbed so high as partially to cover even the great square tower; and involuntarily she exclaimed, "It is so beautiful, so beautiful—it almost hurts; even the color of the sunshine—the brilliancy, yet the softness—and then to be with you!" Enthusiastically she pressed her aunt's arm.

"But tell me," she went on, "what rooms are these along here? Do I know them? Let me see—mine is far around on that side over there, isn't it?"

"That is your room in the corner, the one by the fountain of the dolphins."

Just then there was the sound of tramping on the gravel walk. Nina turned, and the next instant her curiosity was aroused. "Who in the world were all these people?" As her aunt paid no attention, she repeated her question, and the princess casually glanced in their direction. It was probably a party of Cook's tourists. Yes, she recognized the conductor.

Nina watched the party with increasing interest. "Look how funny that little woman is. When the guide tells her anything, she follows his directions as though he had a string tied to her nose." Nina began to laugh, and the princess turned to see two of the tourists, who, like rodents, seemed to be judging a statue of Hermes entirely by the sense of smell. The party came nearer, and the princess turned away. But Nina, alert, exclaimed, "The guide is pointing you out to them."

"Very likely; one gets used to that. Come, let us go on; they will be all over here in a few minutes." The crowd craned after her as she went down the terrace, followed by Nina.

"Do you mean to say you give up your own home like this to strangers?" the girl asked. "It must be a perfect nuisance!"

"It is all a matter of custom," the princess answered. "Besides, the people don't annoy us. They go usually on the lower terraces; at most they come up to the old courtyard galleries, perhaps mount the tower to see the view, or go into the catacombs."

At the bare mention of catacombs Nina was greatly excited, and looked eagerly toward the tourists who were going under the archway where the drawbridge once had been, but the Princess showed very little interest. They were merely underground passageways that were probably used by slaves, although there was one that undoubtedly was built as a means of escape. It ran many kilometers and ended in a cave in the forest. "Oh, come! Please come!" Nina fairly dragged her aunt after the party to the steep dark entrance leading from an old stone dungeon that was falling in ruins. The tourists were descending in an awed silence in which nothing could be heard but the groping shuffle of cautious feet, broken by the hollow echo of the guide's voice reciting his sing-song jargon of what he supposed to be English. He held a lantern that revealed a long alleyway of crumbling, mud-colored stone.

Nina tried to make out something of his glib discourse, but soon gave it up.

"What is he talking about?" she whispered.

The princess disentangled the tradition from the overburdening names and dates: those scratches he was pointing out on the walls were supposed to be a cryptic message from some refugees in need of provisions. It was not a very authentic story, though.

As the princess spoke in English, two tourists detached themselves from the huddled group around the guide and sidled up to her.

"Can you tell me," asked one, a wizened small person who, in the flickering light of the lantern, was strongly suggestive of a mouse, "are there many buried here? The guide has been explaining, and I am stupid, I know, but for the life of me I can't understand a word he says." Her voice was a little dejected, and altogether apologetic.

"We do not think there are any," the princess answered.

The little tourist blinked, hesitated, and then asked, confidentially, "Did the guide say you were the princess of this castle? We couldn't make out."

By this time two others, inquisitive and gaping, joined the spokeswoman, who, as the princess assented, exclaimed, "My!"

That ended the conversation for the time being; and the party trooped on in silence. But after a little the small mousy one's curiosity overcame her diffidence. "Land, it'd be queer to live in a place like this! Do you come down here much, Your Highness?"

Nina nearly giggled, but the princess replied, "I have been down only once or twice. There is no use to which we can put these passageways nowadays. There was a deep pit that descended from one of the upper rooms of the castle through a trap in the floor. The bottom of it was far below here, but it is all done away with and cemented over now."

"You know, Your Highness," returned the little tourist, now glibly at ease, "I think it'd be a good place for growing mushrooms."

The guide interrupted by mounting a pair of stairs and holding up his lantern with the order to "come this way." They all stumbled up the crumbling steps after him and suddenly found themselves behind the altar of a chapel that stood at the far end of the garden.

"For pity's sake!" cried the little tourist, her eyes again blinking—this time at the light. "I never was in such a wonderful place in all my life. My! It won't seem like anything at all to go down cellar at home after I get back! Is this the way you go to meeting? Oh, no—you said you hadn't been down often. Maybe this is the way to go when it rains! It don't rain much here, does it? My, but that's an idea—to go underground to church. I wonder how ever you get used to it." And then irrelevantly she added, "All these beautiful churches over here in Yurrup, not a pew in one of 'em."

"They bring out these kneeling chairs for service," the princess said, pointing to a number against one wall of the chapel.

Again all the tourist could say was her ever ready "My!"

"Would you like to see some of the castle?" the princess asked. "There is a picture gallery not usually opened to visitors, also some apartments with frescoes that are worth seeing." Then to the guide, "You may take them into the west wing." The tourists looked variously, according to their several dispositions; the little one beamed.

"Oh, that's real kind of Your Highness," she exclaimed, her small gray person fluttering, more than ever like a mouse. "I must say that's real kind. I just dote on pictures. Do you like crayons? Well, I like oils best myself, but there are some who have a taste for crayons. The photographer's son—out where I live—he is real talented. He did some beautiful portraits. Folks thought he ought to come over here right away and study art. But others thought there was just as good art right at home. Now, what'd you say?"

Her good intention quite won the princess, and her accent warmed her heart in a way that Nina would have been at a loss to understand.

They had reached the west door, and the Princess sent a gardener around to the main entrance for the porter to bring his keys. The old man came quickly enough, fumbling in the pocket of his greatcoat, but he did not look at all edified at the whim of Her Excellency which allowed a lot of strangers to track mud through the best rooms of the Castle. He preceded the party, however, with all signs of deference, unlocking doors as they went.

The little New Englander was meekly trailing after the guide, leaving Nina and her aunt for the moment alone.

"Oh, but these are beautiful rooms, Aunt Eleanor! Why don't you use them?"

"We do in summer sometimes, but one needs a staff of servants to keep them up. Besides in winter it is impossible to get them warm."

"Then why," Nina spoke as though she had discovered an

obviously simple solution, "don't you have the proper heating put in? You won't mind if I ask you something, will you?"

"Ask what you like, dearest."

"Why don't you make yourself more comfortable? For instance, why don't you have modern plumbing put in? And don't you prefer electric light?"

The Princess smiled as though she had never felt the need of any of these things. "You have left the land of modern improvements and come over to the land of romance!" For a moment she kept the illusion, but the next she seemed to change her mind, for she said practically and with no veiling of the facts: "Quite apart from the difficulty of putting pipes and wires through these thick stone walls, even if every modern improvement were already installed, the cost would make it prohibitive to attempt either heating or lighting."

Nina gasped, "I don't understand! You don't have to think of such a thing as the expense of keeping warm, do you?"

"Indeed we do. Fuel is a very serious item."

"But, you have plenty of money, surely. I thought living abroad—especially in Italy—was cheap."

"I did have a bigger income than now—one does not get as good a rate of interest as one used." She colored a little at the false inference and dwelt with more emphasis on the next sentence.

"When we go to Rome we spend much more money; we have all the rooms open there, and we have a great number of servants—in short we live like princes." She smiled brightly. "But you see in order to do that we have to live quietly and save during the rest of the year."

Nina looked perplexed. "That sounds very queer," she said. "I should think you would even things up and be more comfortable all the time."

"Then we would have nothing. It would be additional expenditure on things that don't matter, and no money left for things that do. Opening these rooms, for instance, would not greatly add to our pleasure. After all, we can only sit in one room at a time. To have many guests and motors and horses for hunting, and to have big shooting parties—all that is an expense not to be thought of. It amuses us more to go to Rome, so we prefer to save for nine months in order to live well the other three."

Nina was trying to do a sum in mental arithmetic; she could not quite make the diminished interest account for her aunt's evident lack of income, but did not like to ask for more details. However, something else happened that diverted her attention. They went through innumerable rooms, always to the distant droning sing-song of the guide's explanations.

Finally they came to the picture gallery. It was not a notable collection, with one or two exceptions; and one of these exceptions was strikingly absent. The guide left the group and approached the princess, exclaiming, "Excellency! The Raphael!"

"It has been sent to be repaired." Her hesitation was scarcely perceptible. "The background was sinking a little."

The man quite forgot himself and in his excitement dared a retort—"It was one of the best preserved Raphaels extant." But the expression in the princess' straight-gazing eyes held his further speech in check, and though she said no word the man cringed.

"Pardon, Excellency," he said, and went back to explain to the waiting group that the great painting of the Sansevero collection at that moment was being carefully examined, by experts, as to its preservation. Nevertheless, there was a look in his face that caused Nina to turn to her aunt with an apprehension, that gave rise to a vague suspicion that the princess, who was walking slowly, her head very high and her beautiful shoulders well back, was struggling to hide some strong emotion. She thought later that she might have been mistaken, for a moment later her aunt asked with her usual composure, "Have you a watch on? What time is it?"

Nina consulted the diamond and enamel trinket hanging on a chain around her neck. "It is ten minutes to one. Is it lunch time?"

"Nearly. Are you hungry? We are not having lunch today until half after. I have a surprise for you."

"For me? What is it to be?"

"My young brother-in-law, Giovanni, comes home today. I expect him on the twelve-thirty train. Your uncle has gone to the station to fetch him—they ought to arrive at any moment."

Nina's face looked brightly expectant. "Tell me something about him! Is he half as good-looking as his pictures?"

"Ah? So she has been examining his photographs!"

"Of course!" Nina laughed. "Oh, please tell me something about him! Does he speak English? French? Or shall I have to struggle in broken Italian? Is like Uncle Sandro?"

"Wait until you see him."

"At least tell me does he speak English?"

"He speaks beautiful French."

"Which means, I suppose, that he speaks monkey English!"

But the princess vouchsafed no reply.

"Well, but really, I *do* think you might tell me something! Is he attractive?"

The Princess assumed a tantalizing air—"That also I am going to leave you to find out when you see him. At all events he is young—that is compared to your uncle and me. It has been dull for you, darling, with no one your own age."

Nina interrupted her reproachfully. "Don't you dare! To hear you, one might suppose you were a hundred. I don't care a bit whether Don Giovanni is a Calaban or an Antinous—All the same," she laughed, "had I better tidy my hair—or does it not matter?"

The tourists were all filing out of the castle now, and as the porter locked the doors, the princess shook hands with the little American.

"Thank you, Your Highness," she said, "you have been real kind. We—I didn't think, when I left home that I was going to be talking this way to princesses. I never dreamed they were like you; and you talk beautiful English, too."

With a warm impulse the princess laid her left hand over the cotton-gloved one in her right.

"Ah, but I was an American myself," she said, "and it does me good to see a country-woman."

They parted. Again the guide made a deep reverence to "Her Excellency," but to Nina the look in his eyes seemed both sly and suspicious.

In the meantime, the pony-cart carrying the prince and his brother was jogging slowly up the hills from the station.

Don Giovanni Sansevero—by his own title the Marchese di Valdo—was still on the hither side of thirty, but if a reputation for being "irresistible to women" goes for anything, he must by this time have had some experience in their ways. At all events, his appearance so tallied with hearsay that, whether founded upon fact or not, the reputation remained.

He was supple and beautifully built, his bones were small and finely jointed, his features chiseled with classic regularity—later on his lips might grow coarse, but as yet they were merely full. The chief characteristic of his expression was its mobility, but it was the mobility of an actor who knows every emotion that the muscles of a face can command. Sansevero's face, also changeable as an April day, was the spontaneous expression of unconscious mood. Giovanni was of a type to smile sweetly when most angry, or to assume an air of sulkiness when at heart he might be well content. Just now, with an assumption of extreme indifference, he turned to his brother.

"What is she like, this heiress of yours whom you are so anxious to have me marry?" he asked. "Plain, stupid, a nonentity?—So much the better—those make the easy wives to manage. Give me a woman with little real success—I mean, one who has seen only the imitation fire that is lighted when man pursues with reason and not with feeling. The American men make it easy for the rest of us—they are what you call curtain raisers in the play of love. They keep the gallery busy until the entrance of the hero. I hope she is not a beauty."

"*Per Bacco*, how you do talk!" interrupted the prince. "I have no chance to answer. Miss Randolph is not a beauty; but she is *simpatica*; she has an air, a *chic*."

"So much the better, so long as the *chic* is one of appearance and not of personality. I don't want my wife to be a siren." Suddenly he laughed and hit his brother's knee. "But what nonsense! Imagine a cold American miss having the power to make a man's pulses leap! Oh, don't make a face like that—I am not speaking of my honored sister-in-law; she is indeed of the true type of our mother." Mechanically both men indicated the sign of the cross at the word "mother."

"But," continued Giovanni, "I am not exactly worthy of a saint—it would not suit my disposition. It is bad enough associating always with good Brother Antonio as it is. By the way, where is he?"

He gave a shrill whistle and looked back down the road for the gray figure of his inseparable friend and companion: not a monk as the name indicated, but a Great Dane. A distant cloud of dust proclaimed that the whistle had been heard. "Poor Sant Antonio!" he called as soon as the dog had caught up, "Where have you been? I suppose you were meditating along life's highway. No," he continued, "it were best I did not pretend to be better than I am; my good monk would not absolve me else. Still, do you know, sometimes I seriously doubt even Brother Antonio's morals!" He shrugged his shoulders and laughed in great delight. Sansevero seemed undecided whether to be shocked or amused; ordinarily he would have laughed easily enough, but Giovanni in some way had seemed to involve Eleanor in his levity.

"Well," continued Giovanni, "I suppose at least Miss America, not being a Catholic, will make no objections to Sant Antonio's short-comings!"

At this Sansevero bristled, "Giovanni, I will ask you not to air your irreligious remarks about that dog with an unseemly name, in connection with the family of my wife."

For answer Giovanni blew a whistle into the air.

Sansevero grew sulky. "I warn you! Don't let Leonore hear you make remarks that she might think slighting about her darling! She is like her own child to her!"

For a few moments both men were silent. Giovanni's face was no longer mocking; he was watching the beautiful lope of his huge dog. Sansevero looked straight ahead, quite pensively for him. "Poor Leonore," he said at last. "It is often such as she who have no children!" Unconsciously he sighed.

Giovanni smiled, "I don't see what she wants of another child than you!"

"And you will inherit—"

"Please! I am not quite so bad as that. Believe me, I should rejoice for you if you had children. Leonore would have made a wonderful mother. Even I might be respectable if a woman such as she loved me as she loves you. But," he grew flippant again, "to marry one of those nose-in-the-air, soulless, school-teacher prudes—Never! And in any event, my dear, I am not so sure I want to marry your heiress. I am very well as I am!" He shrugged his shoulders. A moment later, though, he put a question. "What is her first name?—I have forgotten."

"Nina."

"Nina! Really a charming name, that! One that can be said without breaking consonants against the teeth. There was a girl once, very pretty, but she was called—I can never pronounce it—E-d-i-t-h—those are the letters. But Ni-na! It has a delicious sound." He let it slip over his tongue. Then he put his head on one side and asked quizzically, "How much has she?"

Sansevero looked up quickly; he hesitated a moment, then answered stiffly: "She has a great fortune, but she is also my niece."

Giovanni raised his eyebrows, and then burst into shouts of laughter.

"What has come over you? It was you who suggested the match! You know as well as I that my debts don't disturb me in the least. It is quite easy always to—borrow, if one must pay."

CHAPTER VI

LOVE, AND A GARDEN

Don Giovanni arrived on Tuesday, and Saturday found him out on the terrace leaning over the balustrade beside Nina. His expression was unusually animated, for he was making the most of his first chance to talk to her without the presence of a third person. Not that they were alone—the Princess Sansevero was too much of an Italian to leave a young girl for a moment unchaperoned. But she was walking about with the head gardener, discussing the possibilities of saving a grove of cypress trees that showed signs of dying; and though she kept the young people well in sight, she could not overhear their conversation. Giovanni's big dog, St. Anthony, was lying outstretched in the sunshine.

In the full light, Nina had ample opportunity for observing that her companion was quite as good-looking in detail as in general effect; and the rhythmic inflection of his voice—he spoke in French—she thought truly attuned to his surroundings. He was one of those who, like Italy itself, give to strangers only the suggestion of their meaning, and he interested Nina chiefly as a new unsolved problem.

Gradually the habitual sleepy expression had returned to his eyes, and his voice grew dreamy. "We of Italy," he was saying, "live, endure, die, if need be—always for the same reason—woman and love! Your men in America"—his teeth glittered as he smiled—"tell me, Mademoiselle, do you believe they know what it is to love? Do they hide it, perhaps, from us Europeans?"

"I should think," answered Nina sagely, "that love means more to our men than to you." (A remark that John Derby had made came into her mind as she spoke: "You will find your own countrymen go in for the real thing, where the foreigner spends all his time talking about it.")

Don Giovanni was too thoroughly a European to become argumentative. "You see, I speak only from hearsay," he continued, with that air of agreeing with her which only the Latin possesses. "I have always been led to suppose that love plays a very small part in the lives of your countrymen." He held the thread of the conversation, but his manner said plainly that he only waited humbly to be enlightened. "I should have said," he went on, "an illustration of love in my country as contrasted with yours is shown in the gardens—just as our gardens bloom all the year, so love blooms always in our hearts; flowers and love, they go together; nowhere in the world are they so perfect as in Italy."

"So cultivated?" asked Nina.

He took no notice of the quip. "If to cultivate is to think of and to nurture, to strive always for greater perfection, then, yes, let us say cultivated."

There was a challenge; there was also a look of pity that annoyed her. It was this that she resented. She felt that she was being enmeshed in an invisible web, and she sought for a means of escape. Seeing none she might be sure of, she dropped the figurative speech and took refuge in platitudes.

"In America we admire a man for what he does—over here you do nothing. Each day for you is the same. You spend your time as a woman might, unless you go into the army, the church, or diplomacy. For instance, you, yourself, what is your ambition? Is there anything you are trying to do?"

Indolently he shrugged his shoulders, and with a half-lazy arrogance he answered, "Why should I try to create a personal and trivial future, when I can, without striving, merely survive from a far more glorious past? Listen, Mademoiselle, do you think as much can be accomplished by one short generation as by many? For instance, could a garden such as this be produced in the lifetime of one man?" He waved his arm in a circular motion. "It is not alone its plan and its fountains, and its green shrubbery that make it what it is, but the history of human lives that is planted in its every turn and corner. The gardens of America are but newly born from the minds of your landscape architects; in most of them the trees are but newly planted. This garden was already stately with ilex and cypress when the first white men of North America were sowing a little corn. How can you feel romance in a garden where there is no tradition save of the hours a few laborers have spent in digging?"

Suddenly a look of real ardor came into his face, an animation into his expression that gave a new charm to his words. "On this terrace where we now stand, leaning upon the marble of this very railing, countless men who were heroes, poets, philosophers, and fair women who were their sweethearts, have looked, as we do, over the hills laden with blossoming trees. Up that path yonder to the monastery have gone pilgrims, sinners, martyrs, and many lovers to have their vows blessed, or to find a haven for broken hearts. In the *allée* of cypress trees have walked many of the great lovers of Italy's romance. From this terrace end Beatrice herself is said to have thrown a rose of that very bush's parent stem to her

immortal lover. Every corner of the garden holds its story of meet-
ings that made of it a paradise, of partings that made of it an
inferno. What is paradise, but love? Inferno, but the sorrow of
love? Down before us, and even up here on this terrace, scenes
have been enacted in feud and in peace, horrible scenes of blood-
shed and cruelty, and again scenes of splendor—gatherings of
church, ceremonials of state, but chiefly scenes of love—some
beautiful and happy, others no less beautiful because they were
tragic. Shall I tell you some of the stories?"

Nina nodded an eager assent; Giovanni's manner held her
completely.

"Almost where you are standing, Cecilia Sansevero was
stabbed by Guido Corlone before he killed himself, so that they
might be together in the next world. Out of that window, the third
from the end, another daughter of our house descended by a silk
ladder. They—she and her lover—took the path directly below
here; the guards saw them. This happened just beside the statue
yonder. He drew his sword and stood before her, but the guards
were too many, and he was killed. She had poison in a locket that
she wore, and almost before they could drag her arms from about
her lover's neck, she also was dead."

"Horrible!" cried Nina. Her face, mobile as Giovanni's own,
had unconsciously reflected, in changing expressions, the progress of his narrative. "To think that in such a place as this such
things really happened." She shuddered, then added, "But, Don
Giovanni, are there no pleasant stories? Please think of some."

"Oh, any number. Once there was a small house in the
valley—a lodge it would be called now. A very pretty girl lived
there. This time it was the son of our house, a young, hot-headed
fellow like all of us." Giovanni let just enough fire gleam in his eyes
to give Nina a glimpse of another phase of him. "Well, this son—
whose name was the same as mine, Giovanni, a Prince Sansevero—he was mad about this girl. He would marry her or he would
take his life. She was the star of his destiny, the crown of his life,
and all the rest of it. They were going to send her away—she was to
go into a cloister; he was locked up in the castle. But the old custo-
dian, who adored the boy, let him escape by the underground passage. He came out in the church. She had gone there to pray,
knowing nothing of the underground way—it was kept a pro-
found secret in those days. As the girl knelt, Giovanni appeared
suddenly beside the altar. Her duenna thought him an apparition,
and the two fled up to the monastery—that one you see from
here."

"And then—?" said Nina breathlessly.

"The Father Abbot relented and married them."

Nina tried to discern the path to the monastery; in her imagination she saw them hurrying along on the night of their escape.

"And then? In the end what became of them?"

"She bore him fifteen children; thirteen of them were girls."

Giovanni's manner was so casual as he said this that Nina laughed long and deliciously. He swung himself lightly over the balustrade and gathered her a long-stemmed rose from the bush whose early branches were supposed to have known the touch of Beatrice. Perhaps the legend was untrue, but his action, like the afternoon, held much that was alluring. Something of this allure lay in Giovanni's having the same name as the people he told about. Something, too, in the carelessness, and yet the pride, of his telling, made his tales enchanting, and seemed in some way to include his own personality in the chain of romance as its final link. The garden was spread before her. The underground passage she knew, and it wound directly beneath her feet. The chapel, the statue, the ruins of the little temple, the monastery encircling like a low crown the summit of the distant mountain, all were before her; and beside her was a son of the same race, of the same blood. She wondered vaguely why it was so much more apparent in Don Giovanni than in her uncle the prince. Prince Sansevero seemed quite modern; the Marchese di Valdo, though more modern actually than his brother, still seemed to keep his touch on the age that was past.

"Do these old legends please you, Mademoiselle? Or are you too restless? Too progressive? Americans, like the horse Pegasus, leap into the air without any need of foundation to stand on. We, over here, build, like the coral reefs, slowly perhaps, but always from the foundation up."

"I think," said Nina slowly; "it is the mystery of the past that makes it so wonderful. We never can know quite enough about it. All legends are like pictures seen through a fog; it lifts and shows a glimpse, then as quickly closes in again. I always want to know what happened next."

As she said this, she realized that she was more or less making an allegorical description of Giovanni himself. He was like his country and its traditions, revealing himself only in glimpses. He attracted her immensely through his subtle impersonality underlying all that was seemingly personal. She could not fathom his depth, nor determine his shallowness—she did not even guess which it might be. She was irresistibly drawn to him; yet she was on her guard, as one who, looking down from a great height, in fear of vertigo clings to the parapet over which he leans. The parapet she clung to was her own good American common sense. Yet she feared she did not know what. A little gleam in Giovanni's dark eyes, a curious, deliberate, intentionally produced expression of his smiling lips, swept over her sensibilities with a feeling that was as terrifying as it was delicious—and both perhaps because it was strange.

A little look—like triumph—flickered in his face; he laughed joyously. "Mademoiselle, you are—adorable!" he said.

CHAPTER VII

ROME

Christmas and New Year's passed, and the Sansevero household moved to Rome. The princess was impatient to have Nina meet people, but from the first glimpse of the domed City its immortal charm claimed the American girl, and for a little while she had neither time nor inclination for anything but sight-seeing. She fairly hungered for history and tradition, and she soon made the discovery that if Don Giovanni *did* nothing, he at least *knew* a great deal.

She marveled at his memory. He seemed to have every name and date in the history of Rome and Italian art at the tip of his tongue. One afternoon they were going through the apartments of the Borgias; the princess, tired out with sight-seeing, was sitting at the edge of the room, and Giovanni was following Nina and pointing out the story illustrated in the frescoes.

"I have found at least one thing you could do!" she laughed. "You'd make a wonderful guide for Cook's."

But he was not at all amused by this sally; in fact, he let her see that he was annoyed. This same sort of unexpected response had baffled her several times before. Any American youth would have fallen into the manner of a guide at once. She remembered that John Derby on one occasion, at a County fair, had insisted upon climbing on the stand of a barker and was the success of the show. On the other hand, this Italian prince appreciated things which John Derby would have brushed aside. He was a delightful companion, the most delightful she had ever known, but every now and then he became suddenly and inexplicably offended—and always over some stupid trifle, like this suggestion of hers about Cook's.

"I only meant," she ventured appeasingly, "that you hold all of Rome's history in the palm of your hand. Is there anything that you don't know?"

His gesture was expressive. He raised his eyebrows and opened both hands palms upward. "I am Roman—since a thousand years."

Nina changed the subject. "I wish," she said, "that they had wheeling chairs with head rests. I have a crick in my neck and my eyes are going crossed from looking so much at ceilings."

Giovanni's ill temper had been for a moment only. He smiled

now and whimsically suggested that they write to the director of the Vatican asking that litters be provided. Why not? He grew quite enthusiastic over his description of how charming she would look between tall negro bearers, with a little black boy trotting beside her, carrying a long fan—no, in place of the fan he should carry a little stove.

"My idea was not half so picturesque," she laughed in answer. "I think I had a dentist's chair in mind—a red fuzzy plush one on wheels."

"And with me to push it?" He said it eagerly enough. Here was a contradiction of his late irritation! She did not dare, as a matter of fact, to answer; his melodies and his discords were too easily transposed.

She turned her attention to the fresco before her; it was one with the portrait of the kneeling Borgia.

"He looks like a burglar!" she exclaimed with a shudder. Then she hesitated, but Giovanni's mood being too uncertain to take into consideration she finished her sentence, "Do you know who he looks like—? The Duke Scorpa."

Again he was angry. "Please, Miss Randolph, do not say anything of that sort."

"But why shouldn't I?" She colored under his reproof, but held to her point.

"Because you are of the household of the Sansevero. A little remark—even so little as a tenth of that, might be imprudent. Rome is today almost what it was. There still is a very frail bridge uniting the Scorpas and the Sanseveros; the ravine is always there; a torrent from the glacier may descend at any time."

"Then I shall say it in a whisper! He looks like a burglar, and like a cut-throat and—like Scorpa!"

Giovanni scowled. "I warn you, Mademoiselle, be prudent!" A note of tension in his voice brought Nina to a sudden halt.

"There is no one here but Aunt Eleanor—I doubt if even she can hear."

"In Rome it would not be the first time if walls had ears."

"I am sorry," she said so simply, so candidly, that Giovanni was charmed. He became light and amusing. He elaborated the legends of the frescoes with the lives of the painters' until she felt as though they were yet living. Finally they reached the side of the room where the princess was waiting. There was no impatience in her voice, but she looked tired, and Nina cried penitently:

"Ah, Aunt Eleanor! Why did you not call me sooner? I get so carried away by all the things I see, and the tales Don Giovanni tells me, that I have no sense of time."

They descended the stairs to the inner court of the Vatican, where they found their carriage, an old-fashioned C-spring landeau, all very dignified and perfectly appointed, and in striking contrast to the pony-cart in which the princess was trundled about at Torre Sansevero.

By the time they crossed the Ponte S. Angelo the color had come back a little into the princess's face. Nina, with no sign of fatigue, sat brightly alert, while Giovanni opposite, prattled ceaselessly, except for the interruption necessitated by his constantly taking off his hat as his sister-in-law bowed to passing acquaintances.

They had not far to go along the Corso Vittorio Emanuele before they came to the dingy pile of yellow stone that for centuries had borne the name of Palazzo Sansevero. The landeau turned under one of its three broad archways, and entered the courtyard. A plain stone stairway, worn and dingy like the rest of the façade, led into a vestibule of unpromising darkness. The *portiere*, however, was very gorgeous and imposing in his knee breeches, white silk stockings, gold-trimmed coat, and his three-cornered hat with the prince's cockade at the side. He moved majestically down the steps, carrying a silver-headed mace, like a drum-major's, and saluted as the "nobilities" entered the palace. They ascended to a vast stone hall with a grand stairway at its further end, that quickly effaced the impression of the entrance. From an antechamber, they passed through five or six rooms hung with tapestries and paintings, and adorned with sculptures, until they arrived at the one where the princess really lived. This last was a huge, dignified, mellow, and splendid apartment, in every way worthy of the palace in which it stood, and of the great lady who occupied it now, no less than of all the great ladies who had occupied it in the past. In its present furnishings there were deep sofas with light and table arrangement, so that one might lounge and read and at the same time be near the great open fire. Many bibelots of silver and porcelain made a contrast to the other rooms, that were more like museum galleries; and everywhere— here as in the country—were flowers and the army of autographed photographs marching across tables and banked high against the walls.

As soon as the family had entered, the tea-tray was brought in and placed near the fire. Following the Roman custom, according to which the daughter of the house pours the tea, the princess motioned Nina to fill the office, and she herself sat at her desk and began rapidly writing on a pad of paper. Giovanni carried tea and muffins to her, while Nina poured out her own cup and helped herself to a third cake.

"Are these really so good?" she asked half wistfully. "Or are even these little cakes seemingly delicious only because they are in Rome? I am sure the cook at home made plenty that were every bit as good!" She said this last as though to convince herself.

"They are wonderful little cakes—they are very celebrated!" Giovanni said it with an aggrieved air that made Nina laugh. As though wilfully misunderstanding her, he turned to his sister-in-law.

"Such curious ideas Miss Randolph has about Rome! One would suppose, to hear her, that it was a land of witchcraft—even our food is to be taken with suspicion."

"Not at all," retorted Nina, with a turn of manner that would have done credit to an Italian, "a land of enchantment, which makes ordinary cakes—very ordinary little cakes, I tell you!—seem small squares and rounds of ambrosia. And, furthermore—I can assure you it is much more comfortable here than in the country."

If Giovanni thought she was going to stay sentimental very long, he did not know the American temperament. For she now went into a long dissertation upon the discomfort of Torre Sansevero, where she nearly froze to death. Candle light she had not minded, though she much preferred electricity.

"Have you entirely obliterated the gardens from your memory, Mademoiselle?" Giovanni asked in an undertone, and with a romantic inflection. But Nina's mood was not, at that moment, attuned to gardens.

"Ah, I love Rome—just Rome itself! There is no other such place in all the world! I thought I loved Paris. Paris is gay and beautiful. But Rome is glorious—splendid!"

Giovanni's chagrin at her apparent indifference to the gardens was changed to enthusiasm at her appreciation of his beloved city, for to have her love Rome was like having her love the greater portion of himself—who was but part of Rome.

"The only detriment is," continued Nina, "that at night I dream of marble statues parading against backgrounds of cobalt blue under groined arches of gold—like the ceilings in the rooms of the Borgias and—this one! Why this is exactly like them! There is the same face as the St. Catherine—" then suddenly she sat up, leaning eagerly forward—"Auntie Princess, I don't want to have a party at all! I don't want to meet people! I like to think of Rome as inhabited with those of long ago." Then with one of her sudden checks upon a tendency to become over sentimental, she added gaily, "The little cakes of today, are good at all events! Give me another, please!"

Giovanni slid out of the corner of the sofa like smooth steel springs unfolding; neither hastily, nor with effort. She watched him; fascinated by his grace and litheness. Suddenly, though, she felt uncomfortably certain that he knew what was passing in her mind, and this conviction immediately put her out of humor. For the space of a few minutes she disliked him. He seemed to know that too, for his next sentence was:

"Are all young girls in America so unreasonably capricious, so whimsically balanced mentally as—a young girl I once met?"

"How was she?" Nina's curiosity was aroused in spite of her.

"Very inexperienced, and therefore uncertain. Like the person who in dancing counts one, two, three—one, two, three, for fear of losing time—or like the inexperienced swimmer who measures constantly the distance to shore."

"Children, you are chattering nonsense," the princess interfered. "Here, you lazy ones, help me to write the invitations!"

Nina arose and went to look over her aunt's shoulder. "Oh, but it is for day after tomorrow!" she exclaimed. "Do you mean to say that any one will come at such short notice?" That the invitations were merely visiting cards with "Informal Dance" written in the corner, and a date not forty-eight hours ahead, astonished her. She asked about the details. How could they arrange for the decorations, favors, supper? But the princess smiled complacently. Candles were all the decoration necessary! the favors would be trifles that could be bought in half an hour; and as for supper—what could young people want more than lemonade or tea, sandwiches, and cakes? The only question was where they should dance.

The princess turned to Giovanni. "I think it is best in the picture gallery, don't you?"

"The floor is not so smooth as in the Room of the Aenead, but come, let us go and decide." He led the way, and they followed. The Room of the Aenead was next that in which they were sitting. The portrait gallery, filled with treasures from the days of Italy's grandeur, was still beyond. It was this apartment of all others that most appealed to Nina. For a moment she forgot why they had come into the gallery, and her attention remained fixed upon the canvases. With the ever-vigilant Giovanni at her side, she seemed to be walking in a day that was past, to be enveloped in a fairy mantle! She put her hand on a group said to be the work of

Michelangelo, running her fingers over the face of one of the figures with awe in her touch.

"To think," she said very softly, the wonder breaking through the low tone of her voice, "to think that Michelangelo's own living hand has been where mine is now—still more, he has been in this very room! Not alone he, but Raphael, Correggio, and Pinturicchio! And all this is called home by my own aunt. *Mine!*" A little quiver had come into her throat. "It is too wonderful! Yet it gives me the strangest sensation—I can't exactly explain it, but it is as though I were not born at all. Do you know," she had turned to Giovanni wistfully, "I think I can understand just a little of the way you feel—it is as though you were securely planted like a tree. In the beginning, long ago, you were put into the earth with the first things sown. I am merely a leaf, blown from what branch I do not even know—belonging nowhere, coming from nothing. I think I see for the first time what you mean, over here, but just *being* and not caring to do more than survive from the gloriousness of all this." She spread her arms out as though bewildered.

"Now you see," Giovanni answered her, as though there were a new and strong bond of sympathy between them, "why decorations are unnecessary. Can you imagine these walls, which for centuries have looked down upon every great personage of Rome, being decked up like a Christmas tree because a number of people whose achievements are in no way illustrious are coming for an hour or two?"

"I think," said Nina, "that I shall dance like a wraith. It seems almost a sacrilege to bob around and prattle in such surroundings. How silly their sainted ghosts might think us!"

"I never thought of the old masters as saints exactly. But come, Mademoiselle—let us pretend—in each of those chandeliers are burning a hundred wax candles. It is the night of the ball—we open it so—will you dance?"

Again there appeared a Giovanni that she had never seen before, his lazy arrogance vanished, as, whisking a handkerchief out of his pocket to wave in his hand, he became a sprite—a dancing faun, a reincarnation of the spirit of Donatello.

Twice he traversed the length of the gallery, and then, with a vigor added to his grace, he caught Nina and swung her with him into his whirling dance. It had been perfectly done; even in his *abandon* there was no lack of ceremony. There was none of the "come along" spirit of youth in America. He was in this, just as he was in everything else, a remnant of a past age; he had merely been transformed into a Bacchant! He was in no way a mere young man who had grabbed a young girl around the waist and made her dance.

But as the princess watched them, her feelings were strongly at variance. Admiration played the greater part. Even a much less biased mind than hers could not have failed to appreciate the wonderful grace of the man and the girl, for Nina was as graceful as he. Yet the princess looked vaguely troubled, too, at the thought that Giovanni was perhaps overstepping his privilege.

"Giovanni! Nina!" she called, but she might as well have appealed to the wind that blew through the courtyard below, and instead of their heeding she felt her own waist encircled as Sansevero, who had entered by the door behind her, swept her into the dance with him. "But, Sandro!" she exclaimed, resisting, "it is . . . not seemly! What if . . . the servants . . . should . . . see us?" But, joining Giovanni in the tune he was whistling, Sansevero seemed to have caught some of his brother's humor. If Giovanni had become the spirit of grace, Alessandro had become the spirit of recklessness, and Eleanor was whirled, breathless, not as one dances usually, but madly, so that her feet barely touched the floor. To add to the revelry of the scene, the Great Dane, who was never far from Giovanni's side, now joined the general whirl and leaped round and round as though he had but newly come from a bath, his deep bark punctuating the valse the two men were whistling. The princess felt an apprehensive dread of a servant's intrusion, and again a breathless "Sandro, stop!" escaped her lips just as—

The portière was lifted and the footman announced, "*Suo Eccellenza il Duca di Scorpa!*"

"Ah, I hope I do not intrude upon the family gaiety!" The duke's face was insinuatingly bland and his manner smooth as an eel.

The dancers stopped instantly. The princess flushed, but otherwise only one who knew her intimately might have guessed that she was conscious of having been put in the position of a careless and undignified chaperon. But she winced inwardly, and felt no reassurance in the knowledge that the duke's tongue was known to be more skillful in the art of embroidering than the fingers of the most expert needlewoman. Sansevero followed his wife's cue, but without feeling her dismay, for he, it must be remembered, liked Scorpa. He had the naïve manner of a child caught doing something foolish, but that was all. Giovanni welcomed the duke suavely, yet, as the princess led Scorpa into the living rooms, Nina had an exhibition of a real side of Giovanni that she was destined to remember ever after.

She never in her life had imagined that such fury could be depicted in the human countenance. His nostrils dilated, and his jaw was squared.

"I'll kill that viper yet!" he muttered between his teeth, and, reaching out for the first thing to hand, his long smooth fingers locked around the neck of the Great Dane—so tight that the dog, half strangled and snarling, lunged at his tormenter. Nina cried out in horror, but instantly Giovanni's temper vanished as it had come. He relaxed his fingers with a caress; and the animal fawned on him.

"Forgive me, Mademoiselle." He said it as lightly as though there had been only some trivial inattention to overlook.

The whole scene had taken place in a moment—so quickly, in fact, that as Nina and he followed the princess through the adjoining rooms, she half wondered if her senses had deceived her. What manner of man was this indolent, graceful descendant of a feudal race? As he approached the duke, Nina unconsciously held her breath. Half expecting to see them draw daggers then and there, she glanced fearfully from one to the other; but Giovanni, smiling his sleepy-eyed smile, talked as though he thought the duke the most charming man in the world.

CHAPTER VIII

OPENING DAY AT THE TITLE MARKET

On the evening of the dance the Princess Malio, stiff, thin, and sour, and the old Duchess Scorpa, stolid, ugly, and squat, sat together in a corner of the ballroom—that is to say, the picture gallery—of the Palazzo Sansevero.

"So that is the new American heiress!" said the duchess. "Very presentable, I call her. My Todo might do worse than marry her—but of course"—her face drew itself into the grimace that did duty for a smile—"my Todo would have little chance for her favor in competition with your nephew."

The princess bowed in acknowledgment and strongly protested against the idea of any one's being able to compete with a Duke Scorpa.

The conversation between these two old women was always forced into just such channels of conscious politeness. It was rarely that they disclosed the antagonism that formed the chief spice of their lives. But the princess could not control an impulse to destroy, if possible, the satisfaction of her rival.

"My dear Duchess," she insinuated dulcetly, "do you really credit her fabulous fortune?" Her manner expressed her pity for the other's credulity. "Such a sum as five hundred thousand *lire* a year too much oversteps the mark of probability."

But the complacency of the duchess was not so easily disturbed. "Oh, no, that is not right!" she broke in. "I have been assured that she has five hundred thousand *dollars* a year. Dollars! And there are five *lire* in every dollar, remember."

"Dollars!" echoed the princess—and her voice rose several notes above normal pitch; in fact, she nearly screamed. "I am very certain you are misinformed." But her skepticism barely covered her real chagrin because her nephew was a cadaverous nonentity, with little to recommend him to a title hunter. As she looked at the girl in question, however, there was a decided relish in her next remark:

"I think Giovanni Sansevero will carry off that prize! See the way she is smiling up at him. Ah! and now they are dancing together. Certainly they make a suitable looking couple."

The duchess straightened her dumpy figure to its greatest possible height. For once she forgot herself. "Would any one marry a Sansevero when there is a Scorpa to choose!"

"It has happened," chuckled the princess.

The threatening break in their habitual politeness was averted by the arrival of a third old lady, the Marchesa Valdeste. As her husband was the receiver of the "*Gran Collare de l'Anunziata*," a distinction that gave him the rank of cousin to the king, the duchess and the princess both rose for a moment in deference. The "collaress" seated herself with them. In contrast to theirs, her face was sweet and fresh, with an expression almost like that of a young girl. Her whole personality was gentle, and she punctuated what she said by a curious little swaying motion, a bending of the body from the waist, very suggestive of the way a flower bends on its stalk to the breeze.

The marchesa was also much interested in the new heiress, and although a certain finish of demeanor now modified their remarks, none of them attempted to conceal her ambition to secure Nina's money for her own family.

The Princess Malio was more eager than skeptical as she asked the marchesa, "Have you heard the story of her half a million dollar income? Do you believe it possible!"

The marchesa turned her little hands over, palms up. "She has something incredible, but I cannot say how much. Maria Potensi asked the American ambassador if the celebrated James Randolph was as rich as reputed, and he said—"

The duchess became almost apoplectic in her eagerness. "He said—"

The marchesa looked for all the world like a young girl telling a fairy tale. "He said"—she breathed it in wonder—"that Mr. Randolph's wealth was so fabulous that it was beyond computing! And *this* is his *only child!*"

An awed stillness fell upon the group, each old lady looking and longing according to her own nature. It was the marchesa who at last broke the silence. "I cannot deny that I should like my Cesare to be so fortunate as to win her, but I must confess she and Giovanni Sansevero make a charming couple!"

"Dancing, yes," snapped the duchess, "but for my taste they dance too fast!"

"She is doubtless thinking of her tub of a son, who moves with about the grace of an elephant," whispered the Princess Malio behind her fan.

"I can imagine nothing more graceful than the picture they make at this moment," the marchesa answered, wistfully regarding the two slim figures whirling down the length of the room, dancing, dancing on! as though it were the first, and not the tenth, time they had traversed the great gallery; the elastic poise of each the same, the gold-colored gauze of Nina's dress exactly matching the rippling waves of glorious hair only a shade below the sleek black head of her partner.

Yet the marchesa was perhaps no more anxious than either of the others to have Giovanni bear off the American prize. "My Cesare does not return from England for another month," she added only half audibly, and then she sighed.

Suddenly the old princess pounced like a lean cat upon a new thought. "Ah, ha! There is some trouble brewing! Maria Potensi has found your picture of dancing grace a bit too charming. Di Valdo is biting his mustache, and she is giving herself away! I always thought the wind sat in that quarter. Now—she is losing her temper—and with it her discretion!"

"Maria Potensi is above suspicion," interrupted the marchesa. "I do not believe there is a word of truth in what you imply."

"But how do you account for her jewels? I am interested to hear. There were none in the Potensi family, nor in her own!"

"She says quite frankly that they were given her by an old Russian who is her god-father."

"Every one knows," rejoined the princess, "that di Valdo has made heavy debts, yet he is not a gambler like his brother Sansevero, and he has no personal extravagances that account for the sums borrowed."

The "collaress" answered nothing, and the fat duchess, who had so far been only a listener, drew her head in like a snapping turtle as she made the satisfactory observation that her "Todo" was now the partner of the heiress.

The Duke Scorpa and Nina, standing for the commencement of a quadrille, suggested rather a brigand and a princess than a duke and a titleless daughter of the democracy. Nina was holding her head very high, yet easily and unconsciously, because it was her natural way of standing. The dancing had brought color to her cheeks, and her eyes were sparkling; but it was at the evening in general, not at the man who at that moment was trying to please her. She could not bear the duke's sharp little black eyes, his brutal square jaw, his unctuous manners; and as he took her hand to lead her down a figure of the quadrille, its thickness felt to her imagination like a paw.

Dancing vis-à-vis were Giovanni and the Contessa Potensi. Nina did not know her name or anything about her, but she felt at first sight a subtle antagonism, and, following an instinct that she would have found difficult to account for, she turned her attention away toward a second personality, which fascinated her in as great a degree as that of the Potensi had repelled.

"Who is that over there?" she asked of the duke. "I mean the slender girl in black."

"The Contessa Olisco. She was a Russian princess. Her name was Zoya Kromitskoff. I thought the name of Zoya pretty once—that is, until I heard the name of N-i-n-a!"

As he said her name they were just turning around the last figure, and she might not, without attracting attention, snatch her hand from his; but his familiarity in using her Christian name made her cheeks burn. In the final courtesy she barely inclined her head, and at the close of the dance went in quest of her aunt without noticing his proffered arm. At this unheard-of behavior, the duke hurried after her, biting his mustache.

"Ah, ha!" ejaculated the old princess in the ear of the Marchesa Valdeste, "that cuttlefish of a Scorpa has thrown his tentacles out too far, and the goldfish is scurrying away in alarm." She fanned herself in agitated satisfaction at her triumph over the duchess—who was pretending that she had noticed no coolness in the American's treatment of her son.

The next moment the Princess Sansevero brought Nina to present her to the marchesa. Nina had been dancing at the time of the arrival of the "collaress" and must therefore be presented at the first opportunity. The marchesa, with a few kindly remarks about her dancing, would have let her return to her partners, but the duchess moved ponderously aside on the sofa, making a place for Nina. Without prelude she began, "Is it true that you have five hundred thousand dollars a year? Or is rumor mistaken—is it only five hundred thousand *lire?*"

The baldness of the question left Nina for the moment speechless; then presently, "I have what father gives me," she answered evasively.

"But you are the only child of the American multimillionaire, 'Jemmes Ronadolf,' yes?"

Nina nodded in affirmative.

"The Duke Scorpa, with whom you danced just now, is my son!" Her manner clearly demanded that the American girl recognize the great favor that she had received. "He is my only son," she reiterated, "and the head of the family of the Scorpa. You must come to tea tomorrow. I especially invite you, though we are regularly at home."

The condescension of her demeanor can hardly be described. Nina turned helplessly toward the Princess Malio, but found in her a new inquisitor: "American fathers are proverbially generous"—her ingratiating smile so ill suited her features that it seemed almost not to belong to her—"of course your dot will be colossal?"

Again Nina gasped, but before she was obliged to answer the Marchesa Valdeste laid her hand upon her arm. "Come, my dear," she said, with her soft Sicilian accent, "it is a pity to miss so much dancing. It is not right for a young girl to sit with old ladies at a ball," and, holding Nina's hand in hers, she led her away. They had taken only half a dozen steps when she tapped a young officer lightly with her fan.

He wheeled quickly. "Ah, Marchesa!" He bowed ceremoniously.

"Count Tornik," said the marchesa, "will you take Miss Randolph to the Princess Sansevero, or where her numerous partners may find her?"

Count Tornik bowed again, this time to Nina. "Will you dance? I don't dance as well as di Valdo." Nina looked up at him, suspicious and displeased, but there was no conscious deprecation in his manner, which indeed proclaimed that whether he danced well or badly was a matter unlike unimportant to him.

"Yes, let us dance," she said.

As he put his arm around her it seemed to her that "an animated tin soldier" expressed him perfectly. He held her stiffly, and so closely that her nose was crushed against the gold braiding of his uniform. He was so tall, and his shoulders were so square, that she could not see over them, and to add to her discomfort, he danced, not as did the Italians, but round and round like a whirling dervish. Before they had gone ten yards she was so dizzy and uncomfortable that she stopped.

Again Tornik bowed, offered his arm, and without addressing a further remark to her, led her to the Princess Sansevero. As he took leave of her his expression showed a glimpse of understanding, a momentary illumination. She felt for an instant a possibility of his attractiveness, but just as she became curious he was gone.

The men she met after this were a mere succession of dancing figures, and at the end of the evening, when her aunt came into her room to kiss her good night, she could sleepily distinguish only one or two people out of the kaleidoscope of confused impressions. And even these few melted off into shadows as she danced on and on through dreamland with Giovanni, amid gardens and marble statues, to the magic rhythm of wonder-world music.

But while Nina slept with a happy little smile still lying in the corners of her mouth, the princess in her own room was having an animated conversation with her husband.

"Leonora, my treasure!" he exclaimed joyously, "things go well for Giovanni with *la bella* Nina? *Hein?* With her fortune! And to have such an air and grace, too—it is really Giovanni that is a lucky one!" Before his wife could interrupt he went on, "Five hundred thousand dollars income—that is to be her dot, isn't it? Why, we can have all the rooms at Torre Sansevero opened, and you, my beautiful one, shall have again the comfort that your wretch of a husband has deprived you of!"

His excited appropriation of Nina's fortune for the general family coffers jarred; and the princess at once checked his rapidly soaring imaginings.

"Not so fast! Not so fast! Remember the American girl is used to arranging her own marriage, and besides . . . for nothing in the world would I try to influence her. Should it turn out unhappily I could never forgive myself . . . never!"

Sansevero looked at his wife in open-eyed amazement. "What has come over you, my dear! I am not proposing to sell your Miss Millions to a rag gatherer. She has no amount of beauty—yes (as he followed Eleanor's expression), she has a charming countenance—*molto simpatica*—also a distinction that is really rarer in your country of beautiful women. Giovanni, on his side, certainly has all that one could ask in the way of good looks and intelligence. He is young, and he is the sole heir to my titles and estates—She would be getting a very good exchange for her dollars, I am thinking. There is no use to make a face like that; I am not trying to sell her to an ogre. Why, he does not even gamble—"

"No—but do you think Giovanni can be true to a woman?"

Sansevero laughed. "What would you have? Are you becoming a Puritan miss, Leonora *mia?*" He shrugged his shoulders. "He is young and he has heart! Would you have for a nephew-in-law a St. Anthony?"

As the princess still looked worried, he seemed afraid that he had hurt his project. "Giovanni is of a type that women like," he said reassuringly, "and probably he has had his successes—that is all I meant. Don't be so suspicious! I want merely to further the interests of two young people who are in every way suited to each other. Giovanni may be an anchorite, for all I know."

Eleanor stood turning her wedding ring round and round on her finger. Then she looked anxiously into her husband's face.

He was puffing at a cigarette that he had lighted, and his eyes looked back into hers with the perfectly innocent expression of a child's.

CHAPTER IX

A DOOR IS OPENED THAT
GIOVANNI PREFERS TO KEEP CLOSED

The eyes of La Favorita boded good to no one! As a hostess her deportment left much to be desired, but since her visitors were limited to her very intimate friends it mattered, perhaps, little. At all events, as guest after guest arrived in her over-decorated salon, she looked up expectantly, and then resumed her expression of ugly indifference.

"*Per Bacco!*" she muttered quite audibly enough for one to overhear, "this crowd seems to think I have asked all Rome to supper!"

She attacked two young men of fashion as they entered. Fortunately, her manner somewhat modified the rudeness of her words—and the ill humor of her tone carried no conviction. "You cannot come in. I did not invite you! I have no room!"

Instead of being angry, one, the Count Rosso, answered her in a voice that was half jesting, half conciliatory, in the familiar second person singular: "But thou art quite mad, my dear! We were all asked at Zizi's supper. I, for one, call it very ungracious of you to try to dispense with our agreeable society."

La Favorita lapsed once more into indifference. "Oh well, I don't care"—she shrugged her shoulders—"I don't care whether you all go or stay!"

A moment later a group that had formed at the end of the room made a great noise, and the hostess, suddenly rousing again, swept toward them with the floating motion of the professional dancer. "I wish you to understand," she said in a fury, "that you are to comport yourselves in my house as you would in the palaces of the nobility!"

The group fell into a half-sympathetic hush as she moved back again to the door of the entrance. A little woman—a *café* singer—broke into a snatch of song:

> "*The moon has two sides, a black and a white*
> *When the heart is dark there can be no light.*"

Laughing, she snapped her fingers. "Fava has been in a bad temper ever since that American heiress came to Rome. She fears that Miss America will cut the leading strings of Giovanni."

"Why pout at that? Giovanni will then be rich—a rich lover is better than a poor one any day!" laughed another soubrette.

"What is the matter with Fava, anyway?" put in a third. "She was quite delighted with the American's arrival at first. Now she might draw a stiletto at any time."

"The matter is that she has heard the millionairess is pretty, and she fears she will take Giovanni's heart as well as his name!"

"Fava jealous! A delicious thought that! Yet I am not sure that I should care to be in Giovanni's shoes if he wants to get away from her," observed Rigolo, the actor.

Favorita again swept toward the group, her voice strident: "*Per Dio!* Do you suppose I can't imagine what you are all talking about, with your long ears together like so many donkeys chewing in a cabbage patch? You need not imagine to yourselves that I am jealous. No novice could hold Giovanni long. It is I who can tell you that, for I know such men and their ways fairly well—I have had experience! Me!"

The others took it up in chorus: "Favorita has had some experience, *hein!* A race between the countries! Italy and America at the barrier. Holla, zip! they are off! La Favorita in the lead—America second, coming strong." And so it went on. Favorita had returned to her position by the door. She was more quiet, and in repose it might be seen that her face looked drawn—her eyes, if one observed closely, beneath the black penciling showed traces of recent weeping. "Tell me something," she said to Count Rosso. "What is she like, this Miss Randolph? Is it true"—her breath came short—"that Giovanni is trailing after her?"

"Say after her millions, rather! I hope he gets them for your sake, Fava. Then you can have the house in the country that you have always wanted."

"I'd rather he got his money some other way. It does not please me that he should marry!"

"Aren't you unreasonable? Can't you give him up for a few weeks?"

"If you call marriage a few weeks."

Rosso, laughing, threw his hand up. "How long does a honeymoon last? A few weeks and he will be back."

But the dancer's eyes filled, and she set her sharp little teeth together. "I cannot bear it! *Ah Dio!* I cannot! She is young—and surely she loves him."

"Every woman thinks the man she prefers is alike beloved by every other woman he meets! I have not heard that she loves him!"

"Be quiet about what you have heard—what I want to know is, does he return it? I am told she is attractive; if she is—I shall—"

Count Rosso chanced upon the right remark in answering, "Could a man, do you, think, who has had your favor, be satisfied with a cold American girl? Do not be stupid!"

Favorita was slightly pacified. "Is she at all like me? Paint me her portrait!"

"Her eyes are—m—m—rather nice; her skin—yes, good; her features—imperfect; she holds herself haughtily—chin out, and her back very straight, and"—as a last assurance, he added, "she speaks broken Italian."

La Favorita's coal-black eyes lit with a new light, and her whole body seemed to flutter. Her carmine lips parted as, with an expression of quick joy, she clapped her hands together and exclaimed, "American accent! *Per Dio!* She has an American accent!"

In her delight she threw her arms about the count's neck and kissed him on the lips. With perfect impartiality she turned to two other men standing near and kissed them also, repeating to herself the while, "An American accent!"

The next arrivals she received as though they were both expected and welcome; greeting them with the unintelligible exclamation, "Imagine speaking the only language in the world worth speaking with an American accent!"

"But why do we not go into the dining-room?" asked her stage manager, a heavy puff of a man. "I have a void within."

"May the void always stay, great beef!" she laughed. Then, with a shrug and a wave of her arms, as though to sweep every one out of the room, she cried petulantly, "Go! and eat, all of you. I am glad, if only you go!"

The company, for the most part, laughed and went into the dining-room, whence the sound of revelry gradually grew louder. The Count Rosso alone remained with the hostess. "Come, Fava, don't be so headstrong—you're spoiling the party."

"Spoiling the party! Do you hear the noise they are making? Is that the way to conduct one's self in a lady's house—I said a lady's house! Why do you look at me like that? Am I not a lady just as much as that daughter of an Indian squaw from over the Atlantic? Those in there"—she pointed with her thumb toward the dining-room—"they would not behave so in the Palazzo Sansevero!" Then, without another word, she followed where she had pointed, so fast that her thin draperies fluttered behind the lithe lines of her figure like butterfly wings. On the threshold of the dining-room she paused, like the bad fairy at the christening.

"Why should you think you can behave in my house as you would not behave in the house of a princess?"

The count, who had followed her, seemed relieved that she mentioned no specific name. Her remark seemed to touch a chord of sympathy in the company, for the women, especially, became very quiet. Favorita sat down at the end of the table between the manager and an empty place.

"Eat something, my girl!" he said to her. "It will be the best thing you can do!"

"My need is not the same as yours—I have emptiness of heart."

Her alert hearing caught a footfall, and she was looking eagerly at the door when Giovanni Sansevero entered. At once her face became transfigured. "Ah, there thou art, my mouse!" she said, pulling out the chair beside her for him.

He smiled and nodded familiarly to all at the table.

"At least it is good for the rest of us that you come, Prince!" said the manager. "Fava is in a frightful mood." But there was that in Giovanni's expression that made the manager's speech turn quickly from any too personal allusion, and a qualifying clause was trailed at the end of his sentence, "She may show you more politeness."

Giovanni looked annoyed. The dancer, to appease him, said gently: "You know I am nervous from overwork. The rehearsals have been doubled lately. If you don't come when I expect you, I imagine horrors!" The manager was about to put his fork into a grilled quail, when she whisked it away and put it on Giovanni's plate. The former was obliged to vent his indignation against her obstinately turned back and deaf ears. She was conscious of nothing and of no one but Giovanni, whom she was feeding with her own fork. His appetite, however, paying small compliment to her attention, she arose, and he followed her into the other room. Whereupon her guests, less constrained without her, drank and were merry.

In the salon Giovanni's musical, caressing voice was saying, "You look bewitching tonight, Fava *mia!*" He covered her with his glance, so that she preened herself. He laughed lightly at her vanity, and, leaning over, kissed her lovely shoulder. Quickly, with both hands she held him close, her cheek against his.

"*Carissimo,*" she said tensely, "if you ever love any other woman—"

"I love you," he said, against her lips; "let there be no doubt of that." And there was a long silence between them.

Giovanni was not one of those who can withstand a woman of beauty. He loved La Favorita passionately; she perhaps more than any one else could hold him—a Griselda one day, a fury the next, but always alive and always beautiful.

Yet he might have indulged his curiosity as to what she would do if seriously aroused to jealousy, had it not been for his innate hatred of all exhibitions of feeling, which seemed to him *bourgeois*. He knew that if the dancer had an idea that he might be falling in love with Nina, she would be capable of any scandal. On the other hand, he could not imagine Favorita's being jealous of the American girl. He had often congratulated himself that she was not jealous of her only real rival, the Contessa Potensi, his devotion to whom, however, he had managed to keep so quiet that very few persons in Rome had a suspicion of it.

The contessa, on the other hand, looked upon Giovanni's attention to the dancer as an artifice practised solely on her account, so that the world would the less suspect his attachment to herself. Neither woman had until now felt any jealousy of Nina. To their Italian temperament she had seemed too cold a type, too antipathetic, to be a danger. The contessa was quite willing to have Giovanni marry the heiress, for she never doubted that the end of the honeymoon would find him tied more securely than ever to her own footstool.

Giovanni, at present, with his arms about the dancer, was raining a succession of kisses upon her lips, her eyes, her hair. He could feel that she was all on edge about something, but, man-like, he preferred to keep things on the surface and not stir depths that might be turbulent. His efforts, however, were of small avail.

"Swear to me by the Madonna, and by your ancestors, that you will not marry!"

With sudden coldness Giovanni drew away from her. He let both arms hang limp at his sides. "Why let this thought come always between us!" Then, exasperated into taking up the discussion, he crossed his arms and faced her: "We might as well have this out. I am not engaged—I swear that; but whether I ever shall be or not, you have no cause for jealousy. Marriage in my world, you know very well, is not a matter of inclination, but of advantageous arrangement. There is every reason why I ought to marry, and if that is the case why not one as well as another? My brother has no children; I am the last of my name."

With a cry she flung her arms around his neck and broke into a storm of weeping. "You shan't marry her! You shan't. She shall not have your children for you!"

But Giovanni grew impatient. He unclasped her hands and pushed her away. "If you make these scenes all the time, I won't come near you! Please, once for all, let us have this ended. If there is one thing I can't endure, it is a woman who cries. Here, take my handkerchief. Come now—that is right, be reasonable." His tone modified, and he lightly and more affectionately laid his hand upon her shoulder. "Come here a minute, I want to show you a picture." He led her, as he spoke, before a long mirror.

"Now, *cara mia*, tell me, do you think that a man who possessed the love of such a woman as that would be apt to run seeking elsewhere?"

La Favorita looked at her own reflection, at the slender yet full perfection of southern beauty, and she saw also the returning ardor in the face of her lover as he, too, looked at her image. Her black eyes grew soft, her lips parted slightly—with a sudden exuberance he caught her to him, and this time he held her so tensely that, although her plaint was the same, her tone was altogether different. "But I don't want you to marry—even without love, I don't want you to," she pouted softly.

"You are an idiot, Fava!" But the words were whispered caressingly. "It would be much better for you if I did."

CHAPTER X

MR. RANDOLPH SENDS FOR JOHN DERBY

Meanwhile, one morning in New York, the express elevator of the American Trust Building shot skyward without stop to the twentieth story, at which John Derby alighted. He emerged upon a broad space of marble corridor, leading to the offices of J. B. Randolph & Co. Derby, being known—and, moreover, on the list of those expected—escaped the catechism to which visitors usually were subjected, and was shown into the waiting room without question. When, some minutes later, he was admitted to Mr. Randolph's private office, he caught the sign of battle in the ruffled effect of the great financier's hair, for he had a habit, when excited, of running his fingers up over his right temple until his iron gray locks bristled. But, whatever the cause of his annoyance, it was put aside as he held out his hand in unmistakable welcome to Derby. "Hello, John, good work! You have got here nearly a day ahead of the time I expected you. What is the latest news? Did you have any trouble in the swamp district?"

"None at all. We find the quick sands average only about thirty feet, and the tubes go easily below. Everything is going along splendidly. Better than I had ever dared to hope."

Mr. Randolph nodded his satisfaction. "And now," he said, "I'll tell you why I wired for you. The Volcano Sulphur Company is buying every available mine, and it is time for us to look into the Sicilian possibility. How soon can you leave for Italy?"

"As soon as you say, sir."

"Have you secured your assistant engineers?"

"Jenkins came on with me, for one, and I am pretty sure I can get a man named Tiggs—a good mechanic, who was with me at Copper Rock."

"And how soon can you get your machinery? You'll have to take everything in that line with you. Otherwise, you might get off by—tomorrow? The *Lusitania* sails in the afternoon." He added this last with impatient regret.

Derby pondered a moment, and then answered briskly: "I can make it. Jenkins can follow with the machinery on a Mediterranean boat. There will be no delay over there, as I'll have time to make my arrangements."

"Good!" Mr. Randolph seemed pleased, then asked abruptly, "How well do you speak Italian?"

"Fluently, very; grammatically, not at all."

Mr. Randolph smiled. "Fluently will be good enough. Especially if you pick up an assortment of expletives in the Sicilian vernacular. Go to Rome first. Look about and get information on the Sicilian mines, especially those that are unproductive by the present mining system. Lease one and try your process. If it works—we have the biggest thing in the way of a sulphur control imaginable. You'd better get an option on every sulphur mine you can, to lease on a royalty basis. Our Italian correspondent will be notified to honor your drafts. You will have to use your own discretion as to necessary expenses—of course, you are to send a weekly statement to the office. The royalty to you on your inventions will be ten per cent. on the net, not the gross, earnings. Still, if it all turns out well, you ought to make a nice thing out of it."

A swift gleam of eagerness leaped into the young man's face. Mr. Randolph looked at him sharply. "I did not know that you were so mercenary, John."

"In my place any man would want millions, or else that—" He broke off abruptly, leaving his meaning unexpressed. But his eyes had something wistful in their direct appeal, which perhaps the older man understood, for his expression was unusually kind as he asked with apparent irrelevancy, "Have you heard from Nina?"

Derby flushed even under his tan, but he answered frankly: "Yes, I have had letters regularly—bully ones—full of Italy and the high nobility. Isn't it just like her to remember her friends at home!" Then he added ardently, "There was never any one like Nina—never! Of course, every man in Italy is in love with her by now."

"Humph!" was Mr. Randolph's answer, as his hand went up through his hair until it stood straight on end. "Had she the disposition of Xantippe and the ugliness of Medusa she would be called a goddess divine by the titled sellers. But what can I do? I can't keep her locked up at home—for the matter of that, she is run after about as badly over here—" and he added gently in an altered tone, "My poor little girl! Sometimes I think how much better off she would have been as the daughter of a man without money. At present, of course, she is beset with every possible danger. I don't think Nina will lose her heart easily, mind you, but there is an underlying excitement in her letters that gives me some uneasiness as to the state of her emotions. I do not relish the possibility of her marrying one of those ingratiating, cold-hearted, and seemingly ardent noblemen." Then, as though to qualify his general statement, he continued, "My sister-in-law married a decent sort of a man, and I imagine they are happy—but she'd have done much better if she had married your uncle. He never cared for any one else, and I hoped it would be a match. But Alessandro Sansevero came along and swept her off her feet. She was a great beauty, and I believe he married her for love—which is more than I can hope in Nina's case."

Into Derby's face there came a look like that of the small boy who gazes hungrily into a bakery shop window as he protested. "No one could know Nina well and not love her. She is the squarest, the truest, just as she is the most beautiful, girl in the world."

"No,"—Mr. Randolph spoke quite slowly, for him—"Nina is not beautiful—sweet, and unspoiled, and lovable, yes; but she is not a beauty."

Derby's face kindled with indignation, and he retorted unguardedly, "I grant you she hasn't one of those pleased-with-itself, don't-disturb-the-placidity-of-my-peerless-perfection sort of faces; the valentine sort that strikes a man at first sight, but that at the end of a week he would do anything for the sake of varying its monotony. But Nina—the more you look at her the more lovely she becomes, *unless* she gets the notion that some man wants to marry her money—and then it is time for me to take to the prairies! Her eyes get hard, her mouth goes up on one side and her features seem to set and freeze. She has only one hard side, but that is adamant! Poor girl, I can hardly blame her. As she says herself, there are proposals on her breakfast tray every morning—with all the other advertisements."

Mr. Randolph looked directly into the blue eyes before him, as though to probe their depths. "I want my girl to marry a man whom she can look up to because he is trying to accomplish something himself," he said emphatically, "and not one who will lay his hat down in the front hall of my house instead of at his own office. And," he added grimly, "a coronet in place of the hat is still less to my liking."

A curiously restrained, almost diffident, expression, which in no way suited his personality, came into Derby's face, and he abruptly rose to take leave.

Mr. Randolph rose also, but, instead of terminating the interview, crossed the room, saying, "Before you go, John, I want to show you a prize I have found." He turned a canvas that stood face to the wall, and lifted it to a sofa for a better view.

It was a marvelous picture: a Madonna and child; and on the shoulder of the Madonna was a dove.

"It is supposed to be a Raphael," said Randolph, "and I am convinced that it is. The story is rather interesting. Raphael painted two pictures that were almost identical. One is in the Sansevero family. Their collection in Rome I have seen, but this picture has always hung at Torre Sansevero, their country estate, and I have never been there. However, as I said, Raphael painted two. The second belonged to the Belluno family and was sold long ago into France. There it became the property of a Duc du Richeur, and during the Revolution it was supposedly destroyed. Some time ago Christopher Shayne, the dealer, bought among other things at an auction a nearly black canvas. On having it cleaned, this was the result—without doubt the lost Raphael!"

"Jove, that's interesting!" exclaimed Derby. "I'd like to see the other. Perhaps I'll have the chance, although Nina wrote that they were leaving for Rome, and that was several weeks ago. But now good-by, sir. Tiggs and Jenkins are to meet me at the Engineers' Club at noon. I am sure I can get off tomorrow."

Mr. Randolph held the younger man's hand in a long clasp as he said, "Good-by, my boy, and—luck to you!"

As Derby left the office, the sudden prospect of seeing Nina so soon set his thoughts in a turmoil unusual to the condition in which he managed pretty steadily to keep them. Of all the things that this young man had accomplished, none had been more difficult than preserving the attitude toward Nina that he had after careful deliberation determined upon. To his chagrin the task became more, instead of less, difficult, as time went on. In the long ago, it had been she who adored and he who accepted the adoration—in the way common with the big boy and the little girl. He had taught her to swim, and to ride, and to shoot. And—though he did not realize it—from his own precepts she had acquired a directness of outlook and a sense of truth that embodied justice as well as candor, and that was in quality much more like that of a boy than a girl.

Then came the time when he was no longer a boy. He went out West, and work made him serious, and absence made him realize that he loved her as that rare type of man loves who loves but one woman in his life. But she, never dreaming of any change in his feelings, went on thinking of him always as of a brother. Often, when he returned from a long absence, and she ran to meet him with both hands outstretched, he looked for some sign from her—some fleeting gleam such as he had caught in other women's eyes. But always Nina's glance had met his own affectionately, but squarely and tranquilly. His coming, or his going, brought smiles or gravity to her lips, but her eyes showed no sudden veiling of feeling, no new consciousness of meaning unexpressed. When she laughed, they danced as though the sunlight were caught under their hazel surface. When she was serious, they were velvety soft. To John hers was the sweetest, brightest, and assuredly the most expressive face in the world. But he knew the distrust and coldness that would undoubtedly be his portion should he ever forget the rôle that up to the present he had played to perfection—that of her brotherly, affectionate friend. Her very expression, "Dear old John"—generally she said "Jack"—her entire lack of reserve or self-consciousness in his presence, put him where he belonged.

And the other women—undoubtedly there were lots of the every-day kind, waiting all along the stream, just as there always are when a man is young and fairly good to look upon. And there were the different, and far more dangerous, "other women," who wait at the whirlpools for a man who has that elusive but distinctly felt magnetism which some personalities exert, seemingly with indifference, and quite apart from any effort or intent. But John Derby lashed his heart to the mast of hard work and resolutely turned his eyes and ears from the sirens. And so he saw the years stretching on, always crammed with tasks that he was to accomplish, but without hope of ever winning the girl he loved, because of the barrier of her money.

Only a short time before, when a letter from her had come to Breakstone—a long letter full of the beauty and charm of Italy and the Italians—Derby had gone to the edge of the forest and—for no reason that any one could see, save the apparent joy of swinging an axe—chopped a tree into fire-wood.

"D—n it all," he muttered as the chips flew, "I could support a wife—if she wasn't so all-fired rich." Later he carried a load of his wood across the clearing to the camp and slammed it down. "Oh, hell, I hate money!" he exclaimed vehemently to Jenkins.

Jenkins, a Southerner, took the statement placidly. "Looks like you're workin' powerful hard to get what you don't care for. Some of that kindlin' 'd go good under this soup pot."

Derby laughed and fed the fire. But "Shut up, Jenkins, you ass!" was all the latter got for a retort courteous.

CHAPTER XI

ROME GOES TO THE OPERA

On the evening of the first court ball, the Sanseveros gave a small dinner, after which they went to the opera. The guests were the Count and Countess Olisco, Count Tornik, Don Cesare Carpazzi, and Prince Minotti. Don Cesare Carpazzi, a thin swarthy youth, sat just across the corner of the table from Nina. Although his appearance was one of great neatness, it was all too evident, if one observed with good eyes, that the edges of his shirt had been trimmed with the scissors until the hem narrowed close to the line of stitching; and his evening clothes in a strong light would have revealed not only the fatal gloss of long use, but also careful darning. The old saying that "Clothes make the man" was refuted in his case, however, as his arrogance was proclaimed in every gesture.

Sitting next to him was the Countess Olisco, the Russian whom Nina had noted and admired at her aunt's ball. As there were but nine at dinner, and the conversation was general, Nina had time to observe closely her appearance. She had the broad Russian brow, the Egyptian eyes and unbroken bridge of the nose. She was the most slender woman imaginable, and her slenderness was exaggerated by the fashion of wearing her hair piled up so high and so far forward that at a distance it might be taken for a small black fur toque tipped over her nose. She rarely wore colors, but tonight, because of the etiquette against wearing black at court, her long-trained dress was of sapphire blue velvet, as severe and as clinging as possible.

Nina divined better than she knew, when she put the little Russian and Carpazzi in the same category. Fundamentally they were much the same, but whereas he was always bursting into flame, the contessa suggested a well banked fire that burned continually, but within destroyed itself rather than others. Thin, white, and self-consuming, she was like the small Russian cigarettes that were never out of her lips. Fragile as she looked, she had a will that brooked no obstacle, an energy that knew no fatigue.

Aside from her appearance, the story that Giovanni had related of the contessa's marriage was in itself enough to arouse the interest of any girl alive to romance. According to him, she was the daughter of a Russian nobleman of great family and wealth. The Count Olisco (a mild-eyed Italian boy, he looked) had been attached to the legation at St. Petersburg. Zoya was only sixteen years old when she announced her intention of marrying him. Her father, furious that the Italian had dared approach his daughter, demanded his recall, whereupon she told him the astonishing news that Olisco had never, to her knowledge, even seen her. But she declared that if her father did not marry her to him, she would kill herself.

She did take poison but, being saved by the doctors, who discovered it through her maid, she sent the same maid to tell the Count Olisco the whole story. The romance of her act, coupled with her beauty and her birth, naturally so flattered the young Italian that he offered himself as a suitor, and, her father relenting, they were married.

Nina was left for some time to her own thoughts, as her Italian (not particularly fluent at best) was altogether lacking in idiom, and she missed the point of most that was said. In the first lull, the Count Olisco asked her the usual question put to every stranger, "How do you like Rome?"

The Countess Olisco, like an echo, caught and repeated her husband's inquiry, "Ah, and do you like Rome?"

And then Carpazzi hoped she liked Rome—and this very harmless subject was tossed gently back and forth, until Prince Minotti gave it an unexpectedly violent fling by remarking, "I suppose Signorina, that you have been impressed"—he held the pause with evident satisfaction—"with the great history of the Carpazzi, without which there would be no Rome!"

All at once the young man in the threadbare coat became like a live wire! His hair, which already was *en brosse*, seemed to rise still higher on his head, his thin lips quivered, and his hands worked in a complete language of their own. He put up an immediate barrier with his palms held rigidly outward. All the table stopped to look, and to listen.

"Does a Principe Minotti"—he pronounced the word *"Principe"* with a sneering curl of the lips—"dare to criticize a Carpazzi?" He threw back his head with a jerk.

"What is he?" whispered Nina to Tornik, who was sitting next her. "Is he a duke?"

"A Don, that is all, I believe."

Softly as the question was put and answered, Carpazzi heard. Showing none of the fury of a moment before he spoke suavely, though still with arrogance.

"Signorina is a stranger in Rome; the Count Tornik also is a foreigner, which excuses an ignorance that would be unpardonable in an Italian."

Tornik at that moment pulled his mustache, looking at it down the length of his nose. It was impossible to tell whether the movement hid annoyance or amusement. Nina was keen with curiosity.

"Of course," Nina said sweetly, eager to soothe his over-sensitive pride, "I have heard of the Carpazzi, but I do not know what is the title of your house. I asked Count Tornik whether you were a duke."

"I am Cesare di Carpazzi!" He said it as though he had announced that he was the Emperor of China.

"The Carpazzi are of the oldest nobility," Giovanni interposed. "Such a name is in itself higher than a title."

Don Cesare bowed to Don Giovanni as though to say, "You see! thus it is!"

The subject would have simmered down, had not Tornik at this point set it boiling, by saying in an undertone to Nina, "Why all this fuss? It is stupid, don't you think?"

He spoke in French, carelessly articulated, but the sharp ears of Carpazzi overheard.

"Why all this fuss!" he repeated. "It is insupportable that an upstart of 'nobility' styled p-r-ince"—he snarled the word—"a title that was *bought* with a tumbledown estate, *dares* to speak lightly the great name of the Carpazzi, a name that is higher than that of the reigning family."

His flexible fingers flashed and grew stiff by turns. Nina had seen a good deal of gesticulating since she had come to Rome; she had even been told that the different expressions of the hand had meanings quite as distinct as smiles or frowns or spoken words, and Carpazzi's fingers certainly looked insulting, as with each snap he also snapped his lips.

"You know whereof I speak, Alessandro and Giovanni—not even the Sansevero have the lineage of the Carpazzi!"

"Certainly, certainly, my friend," answered Giovanni. "No one is disputing the fact with you."

"But I should think," ventured Nina, her velvety eyes looking wonderingly into his flashing black ones, "that you would accept a title, it would make it so much simpler—especially among strangers who do not know the family history. A duke is a duke and a prince for instance—"

Up went his hand, rigid, palm outward, and at right angles to his wrist, "There you are wrong. A duke or a prince may be a parvenu. For me to accept a title—Non! It would mean that the name of *Carpazzi*,"—he lingered on the pronunciation—"could be improved! The name of Minotti, for instance, what does it say? Nothing! It is the name of a peasant. It may be dressed up to masquerade as noble, if it has 'Principe' pushed along before it. But it could not deceive a Roman. It is not the 'Principe' before Sansevero that gives it renown. Don Giovanni Sansevero is a greater title than the Marchese Di Valdo, by which Giovanni is generally known. Yet Di Valdo is a good name, too, let me tell you."

The Princess Sansevero kept Minotti's attention as much as possible, so that it might appear that Carpazzi's arraignment had not been heard. All that Carpazzi said was perfectly true. There was little therefore that Minotti could have answered. He was a man of plebeian origin. His father, a rich speculator, had bought a piece of property and assumed the title that went with it. To a Roman the name Carpazzi was a great deal higher than that of any number of dukes and princes.

The question of "Good Taste," however, was another matter and the princess changed the subject by asking:

"Does any one know what the opera is tonight?"

The Contessa Olisco announced: "La Traviata." "They are to have a special scene in the third act," she said, "to introduce a new dance of Favorita's." She did not look at Giovanni, and yet she seemed to be aiming her remarks at him. To Nina it all meant nothing. Once or twice she had heard the name of the celebrated dancer, but it merely brushed through her perceptions like other fleeting suggestions; nothing ever had brought it to a full stop.

The talk turned on other topics, and as the meal was very short, only five courses, the princess, the contessa, and Nina soon withdrew to another room. The conversation there, as it happened, came back to the subject of Carpazzi.

Zoya Olisco lit her cigarette and spoke with it pasted on her lower lip. She smoked like this continually, and never touched the cigarette except to light it and put a new one in its place.

"Though I see what he means," she said, "I should, were I in his place, claim a title! They need not take a new one. My husband told me that the Carpazzi were of the genuine optimates of the Roman Duchy."

"I think Cesare regrets in his heart," said the Princess Sansevero, "that his ancestors did not accept one, but I agree with him now."

She stirred her coffee slowly and then added, "I am fond of the boy, but I do not think I shall have him to dinner soon again. He is too uncontrolled."

The contessa agreed. And then, with her eyes half shut to avoid the smoke of her cigarette, she stared with fixed curiosity at Nina.

"Do you find people here like those in America?" she asked.

"Yes, some are quite like Americans," Nina answered, and added frankly, "but you at least are altogether different from any one I have ever seen!"

"Really, am I?" The contessa raised her eyebrows and laughed. "I know of what you are thinking!" She said it with a deliciously impulsive candor. "You are thinking of my marriage. Yes, it is true! The instant my father said 'no,' I took poison. It was the only way. Had fate willed it, I would have died. But fate willed that I should be—just married." She laughed again.

Nina glanced at her aunt, whose answering smile said clearly, "I told you she was like this."

The contessa lit another cigarette—everything she said and did seemed incongruous with her appearance, she was so fragile and so young. Nina became more and more fascinated as she watched her.

"But supposing that, after meeting him, you had not liked him?" she asked.

"That is impossible. I know always if I like people. I like people at sight—or I detest them! For instance, I detest Donna Francesca Dobini. She is a beauty, I know. She has charming manners; so has a cat. She is all soft sweetness. Ugh! I hate her!—But I like you."

Nina was delighted, but she could not help being amused. "You don't know me in the least," she laughed. "I may be a perfectly horrid person."

The contessa shrugged her shoulders. "That is nothing to me. No doubt I adore some very horrid persons!" Then impetuously she ran her arm through Nina's as they walked through the long row of rooms to the one where their wraps were. "I *like* you!" she repeated; "that is all there is to it!"

In the hall they were joined by the men, and started for the opera.

Here, Nina had an unusual opportunity to see Roman Society, as the house that night was brilliant with the people who were going afterwards to the Court Ball. Donna Francesca Dobini, a celebrated beauty, was rather affectedly draped in a tulle arrangement around her shoulders. The Contessa Olisco, who for the time being was forced to do without her cigarette, said to Nina:

"Look at her, there she is! She is 'going off,' so that she has to wrap tulle about her old neck to hide the wrinkles."

She moved the column of her young throat with conscious triumph as she spoke. A moment later, as though Nina would understand, she whispered: "There is the Potensi! No! In the box opposite. She has on a dress of purple velvet. Sitting very straight, and quantities of diamonds."

Nina put up her opera glass and encountered an insolent stare, as though the Contessa Potensi were purposely disdainful of the American girl.

"She is the same one with whom Don Giovanni danced opposite in the quadrille! Heavens! but she is a disagreeable person!"

"She has reason for looking disagreeable," announced the Contessa Zoya with a meaning laugh; but more she would not say.

Giovanni leaned over Nina's chair. "Do you find the Romans attractive? How does our opera compare with that of New York?"

"The house seems made of cardboard," Nina answered. "I never thought our opera houses especially wonderful—"

"No?" Giovanni rallied her. "Is it possible that you have anything in America that is not the most wonderful in the world! I am sure you will say your opera house is bigger! And richer! and more comfortable! Yes? Of course it is!" He laughed. "My apple is bigger than your apple. My doll is bigger than your doll! What children you are, you Americans!"

"If we are children," retorted Nina, piqued by his laughter, "we must be granted the advantages of youth!"

With a sudden gravity, but none the less mockingly, Giovanni besought her for enlightenment.

"We gain in enthusiasm, energy, and honesty," she announced sententiously. "A country and a people never attain perfection of finish until they have begun to grow decadent. I'd rather have my doll and my big apple than sit, like an old cynic, in the corner, watching the children play!"

She was immensely pleased with this speech,—mentally she quite preened herself. Giovanni looked amused, but the Contessa Potensi caught his glance from across the house, and his smile faded as he bowed. Nina, who had good eyes, saw a complete change in her face as she returned his salutation.

"Do you like that woman?"

"She is one of the beauties of Rome," he said evasively.

"No, but do you like her?" Nina could not herself have told why she was so insistent.

"She is an old friend of mine," he said lightly; then changed the subject. "Do you follow the hounds, Miss Randolph?"

"At home, yes." But she came back to the former topic. "Does she ride very well, the Contessa Potensi?"

"Wonderfully." This time he answered her easily. "But I am sure you ride well, too. Any one who dances as you do, must also be a horsewoman."

There was something in Giovanni's manner that excited suspicion, but she did not know of what. She half wondered if there had been a love affair between him and the Contessa. Maybe he had wanted to marry her and she had accepted Potensi instead. She wondered if Giovanni still cared; and for a while her sympathy was quite aroused.

The curtain went up and every one stopped talking. At the beginning of the *entr'acte* Giovanni left the box, and Count Tornik took his chair. He was a strange man, but Nina was beginning to like him. Notwithstanding his brusque indifference, he had a charm that he could exert when he chose. Giovanni's speeches were no more flattering than Tornik's lapses from boredom.

As a matter of fact, in spite of his assumed bad manners, the social instinct was so strong in him that, just as a vulgar person shows his origin in every unguarded moment or unexpected situation, Tornik's good breeding was constantly revealed. And in appearance, he was an attractive contrast to the Italians, tall, broad-shouldered, very blond, and high cheekboned; he might have been taken for an Englishman.

Presently her Majesty, the Dowager Queen, appeared in the royal box, and every one in the audience arose.

"Shall we see both queens tonight at the ball?" Nina asked the Princess Sansevero.

"No; only Queen Elena. The Queen Mother has never been present at a ball since King Umberto's tragic death."

"I wish this evening were over," said Nina, with a half-frightened sigh.

The Contessa Olisco, who had caught the remark and the sigh, asked sympathetically, "But why?"

"I was nervous enough over going alone to the presentation the other afternoon, but to go to a ball is much worse."

"But you won't be alone. We shall be there! You may have your endurance put to the test, though. Are you very strong?"

Nina laughed. "You mean, have I the strength to stand indefinitely without dropping to the floor?"

"Ah! you know, then, how it is. Still—if it is hard for us, think what it must be for their Majesties. Tonight, for instance, the King does not once sit down!"

Nina opened her eyes wide. "I thought the King and Queen sat on their throne. But then—I had an idea the presentation would be like that, too—and that I should have to courtesy all across a room, and back out again."

The Contessa Zoya seemed to be occupied with a reminiscence that amused her. "If you have a special audience, you do, or if you go to take tea. We had a private audience yesterday with Queen Margherita and—I had on a long train—and clinging. Of course, entering the room is not hard—I made my three reverences very nicely, very gracefully, I thought,—one at the door, one half-way across the room, and one directly before the Queen, as I kissed her hand. But when the audience was over, the distance between where her Majesty sat and the door of exit—my dear, it seemed leagues! One must back all the way and make three deep courtesies! The first was simple, the second, half-way across the room, was difficult. I was already standing on nearly a meter of train, and when I got to the door—well, I just walked all the way up the back of my dress, lost my balance and *fell out!*"

Nina laughed at the picture, but was glad the presentation had not been like that.

"When you go to take tea with the Queen it is difficult, too," Zoya, having begun to explain, went on with all the details that came to mind. "Since two years Queen Elena has given 'tea parties' of about thirty or forty people. Her Majesty talks to every one separately, or in very small groups, while tea and cake and chocolate and iced drinks are served by the ladies in waiting—there are never any servants present. It is of course charming, and the Queen puts every one at ease, but there is always a feeling that you may do something dreadful—such as drop a spoon or have your mouth full just at the moment when her Majesty addresses a remark to you. At the Queen Mother's Court things are more formal—more ceremonious. I always feel timid before I go. And yet no sovereign could be more gracious, and her memory is extraordinary. She forgets nothing. Yesterday she asked me how the baby was. She knew his age, even his name and all about him. She asked me if he had recovered from the bronchitis he was subject to. Think of it!"

Nina looked long at the royal box, and could well believe the contessa's account. Her Majesty was talking to the Marchesa Valdeste.

Of all the older ladies to whom she had been presented, Nina liked the marchesa best. Her face had the sweet expression that can come only from genuine kindness and innate dignity. At a short distance from the royal box Don Cesare Carpazzi was talking to a young girl. Don Cesare's expression was for the moment transfigured; instead of arrogance, it suggested rather humility; both he and the young girl seemed deeply engrossed.

Tornik told Nina that she was Donna Cecilia Potensi, the little sister-in-law of the contessa in the box opposite. He also added that Carpazzi was supposed to be in love with her, and she with him, but they had not a lira to marry on. There were no poorer families in Italy than the Carpazzis and the Potensis.

Certainly there was nothing in the appearance of the young girl to indicate wealth, but her plain white dress with a bunch of flowers at her belt, and her hair as simply arranged as possible, only increased her Madonna-like beauty.

Nina was enchanted with her, and instinctively compared her appearance with that of the sister-in-law, glittering with diamonds. "The Contessa Potensi was a rich girl in her own right, I suppose," Nina remarked aloud.

With a suspicion of awkwardness Tornik glanced at Giovanni, who had returned to the box. The latter began to screw up his mustache as he replied in Tornik's stead. "The Contessa Potensi inherited some very good jewels from her mother's family, I am told."

"Her mother was an Austrian, a cousin of mine," Tornik drawled. "I never heard of that branch of the family's having anything but stubble lands and debts. However, it is evident she has got the jewels! I felicitate her on her valuable possessions. *Elle a de la chance!*" He shrugged his shoulders. Tornik's detached and impersonal manner gave no effect of insult, and Giovanni, beyond looking annoyed, made no further remark. But the Princess Sansevero interposed:

"Maria Potensi has a passion for jewels, as a child might have for toys, and she accepts them in the same way. She tells every one about it quite frankly; in that lies the proof of her innocence."

But the Contessa Zoya showed neither sympathy nor credulity, and there was no misinterpreting her meaning as she said:

"It is true, Princess, you know the Potensi well, and I only slightly—but if my husband offered a diamond ornament—"

"He would never give her another! Is that it?" put in Tornik.

"No—nor any one!" The intensity of her tone alarmed Nina, who was beginning to feel confused by the succession of violent impressions. Scorpa, Giovanni, Carpazzi, Zoya Olisco, all struck such strident notes that their vibrations jangled.

Another act and *entr'acte* passed. Nina saw Giovanni enter

the box of the Contessa Potensi. In contrast to her greeting across the house, she seemed now scarcely to speak to him. He talked to her companion, the Princess Malio, who bobbed her head and prattled at a great rate; but as he left the box Nina saw him lean toward the Contessa Potensi as though saying something in an undertone. She answered rapidly, behind her fan. Giovanni inclined his head and left.

This small incident made a greater impression on Nina than its importance warranted. And the Contessa Potensi occupied her thoughts far more than the various men who had come into the box, and who seemed little more than so many varieties of faces and shirt-fronts. She noticed that many of the older men wore Father Abraham beards and clothes several sizes too big. On account of the Court Ball those who had orders wore them, frequently so carelessly pinned to their coats that the decorations seemed likely to fall off. The Marchese Valdeste—a really imposing man—had two huge ones dangling from the flapping lapel of his coat, and a sash with a bow on the hip that would put any man's dignity to a supreme test.

"The ballet is very important tonight," Nina heard the marchese saying to the Princess Sansevero. "La Favorita is to appear in the Birth of Venus. She does another dance first—a Spanish one, I think."

As he spoke, the ballet music had already begun, and the Spanish *coryphées* were twisting and bowing, and straightening their spines as they danced to the beat of their castanettes. Then they moved aside for the *ballerina*.

It may have been intended as a Spanish dance, or Eastern, or gypsy—but it was more likely a dance of La Favorita's own imagination. She appeared clad in a thin slip of transparent and jetted gauze. Upon her feet were socks and ballet slippers of black satin. A black mask covered the upper part of her face, and her black hair was drawn high and held with a diamond bracelet; she wore a diamond collar, long diamond earrings, and the gauze of her upper garment—which could hardly be called a bodice—was held on one shoulder with a band of diamonds. For the space of a second she faced the audience, standing still and rigid; then, with a quiver, the rigidity was shattered! A serpent's coiling was not more swift than the movement of her dazzling, glittering form, which twirled and turned and bent, while the twinkling rapidity of her steps was faster than the eye could follow. A twirl, another twirl, a flash—and she was gone.

The *coryphées*, who had seemingly danced well before, were

now so awkward by comparison that Nina and Tornik laughed aloud.

"They look like cows," commented Tornik.

"Or nailed to the ground," Nina rejoined. She leaned forward, eager for Favorita's reappearance.

To make a background for the second dance, the stage hands had moved in folding wings or screens of sea green. The calciums had gradually been turning to the blue of moonlight, and now, at the back of the stage, Venus arose, veiled in a mist of foam.

Seeming scarcely to touch her feet to the ground, the dancer was a puff of the foam itself, a living fragment of green and white spray. She caught her arms full of the sea-colored gauze, like a great billow above her head, and then with a swirl she bent her body and drew the diaphanous film out sideways, like a wave that had run up on the sands. Drawing it together again, she seemed to produce another breaker.

So perfectly was the fabric handled that it seemed exactly like the spray of the sea, which, in its freshness, clung to her, and at the last, by a wonderful illusion, she gave the appearance of having gone under the waves.

For several seconds the house remained absolutely hushed, and in that moment Nina found herself vaguely groping through a confusion of ecstatic, yet slightly shocked, sensations. She wondered whether La Favorita had really nothing on except a number of yards of tulle which she held in her hands.

But the verdict of the audience was voiced by a torrent of bravos and handclappings that thundered until La Favorita, having thrown a long mantle about her, came out into the glare of the footlights.

She bowed and kissed her hands, her smiles of acknowledgment sweeping the house from left to right, but at the box of the Sanseveros her smile faded, and she threw back her head with a movement of triumph.

Nina was startled into fancying that she looked long, directly, and particularly at her.

CHAPTER XII

A BALL AT COURT

The Sansevero party left the opera shortly after ten o'clock, and a little while later drove into the courtyard of the Quirinal. Entering a side door, they ascended a long staircase, upon each step of which was stationed a royal cuirassier, all resplendent in embroidered coats, polished high boots, and veritable Greek helmets, which seemed to add still further to their unusual height. Between their immovable ranks the guests thronged up the stairway to the Cuirassiers' Hall. Here, at the long benches provided for the purpose, they left their wraps in charge of innumerable flunkies in the royal livery—which consists of a red coat, embroidered either in gold or in silver, powdered hair, blue plush breeches, and pink stockings.

Nina followed her aunt and uncle through an antechamber into the throne room and beyond again into the vast yellow *sala di ballo*. Here also the cuirassiers, who were stationed everywhere, added a martial dignity to the splendor of the scene. The people were all massed against the sides of the room; and although certain important personages had seats upon the long red silk benches placed in set rows, the great majority of those present stood, and stood, and stood. In contrast to her weary waiting at the afternoon reception when, a few days before, she had been presented at court, Nina found so much to interest her tonight that she did not remark the time. One side of the room was quite empty save for the big gilt chair reserved for the Queen, and the stools grouped around it for ladies in waiting. Three especial stools were placed at the left of the queen for the three "collaresses"—those whose husbands held the highest order in Italy, the Grand Collar of the Annunciation.

It was the most brilliant gathering that Nina had ever seen, chiefly made so by the gold-embroidered uniforms and court orders of the men. The dresses and jewels of the women differed very little from those seen at social functions elsewhere. With a rare exception, such as the Duchessa Astarte and the Princess Vessano, whose toilettes were the most *chic* imaginable, the great ladies of Italy followed fashions very little. Not that Nina found them dowdy—far from it: they had a distinction of their own, which, like that of their ancient palaces, seemed to remain superior to modern decrees of fashion. Nearly all of them had lovely figures, which they did not strive to force into newly prescribed outlines.

A remark that a foreigner in New York had made to Nina came back to her, and she now realized its truth. It was that the one great difference between the women of Europe and those of America was that in Europe one noticed the women, while in America too often one noticed merely the clothes. The Roman ladies wore plain princesse dresses, the majority of velvet or brocade, and with little or no trimming save enormous jewels often clumsily set, but barbarically magnificent.

Here and there, to Nina's intense interest, she found, strangely mingled with the others, people of the provinces, who, because of distinguished names, had the right to appear at court, yet who looked as though they were wearing evening dress for the first time in their lives. Near by, for instance, was a lady whose rotund person was buttoned into a tight-fitting red velvet basque of ancient cut, above a skirt of pink satin. A court train, evidently constructed out of curtain material, was suspended from her shoulders. Broad gold bracelets clasped her plump wrists at the point where her gloves terminated, and a high comb of Etruscan gold ornamented the hard knob into which her hair was screwed.

Princess Vessano represented the other extreme—that of fashion. She was in an Empire "creation" of green liberty satin with an over-tunic of silver-embroidered gauze. Her hair was arranged in a fillet of diamonds, which joined a small banded coronet, also of diamonds, set with three enormous emeralds. Around her throat she had a narrow band of green velvet bordered with diamonds and with a pendant emerald in the center that matched pear-shaped earrings nearly an inch long. Yet in a crowd of three thousand persons neither the grotesque lady nor the princess was remarkable.

The crush of people became greater and greater until it seemed impossible to admit another person without filling the center of the ballroom and the royal space. As there was no music, the chatter of voices made an insistent humming din. At last! the Prefetto di Palazzo sounded three loud strokes, with the ferule of his mace, upon the floor, the sound of voices ceased, the doors into the royal apartments were thrown open, the band struck up the royal march, and their Majesties entered, followed by the members of their suite. Every one made a deep reverence, and the Queen seated herself upon the gold chair. The King stood at her left. As soon as the Queen had taken her place, the dancing commenced, led by the Prefetto di Palazzo and the French ambassadress. But as a wide space before the Queen's chair was reserved out of deference to their Majesties, the rest of the ballroom was so crowded that dancing was next to impossible. Presently the King made a tour of the room—followed always by two gentlemen of his suite, with whom he stopped continually to ask who this person or that might be, sometimes speaking to special guests.

The Queen likewise singled out certain strangers of distinction. In this way she sent for a United States senator, who was making a short visit in Rome, and kept him talking with her for a considerable time. Her Majesty sat through the first waltz and quadrille. Then she and the King promenaded slowly through the assemblage, speaking to many people as they passed. Some careless foot went through Nina's dress, tearing a great rent, just as she made her reverence to their Majesties, who were approaching. The Queen smiled sympathetically and held out her hand for Nina to kiss, at the same time exclaiming her sympathy, then, quite at length, her admiration for the lovely dress. Nina flushed with pleasure, feeling that the damage to her prettiest frock had been more than repaid.

Giovanni was standing with Nina at the time, and after their Majesties had passed, he looked quizzically at the torn hem that Nina held in her hand. "Is it altogether spoiled?"

Nina laughed. "If I were sentimental, I should keep it always in tatters in memory of the Queen!"

"But as you are not sentimental—I hope it can be mended. May I tell you that her Majesty's admiration was well deserved? It is a most charming costume and not too elaborate. The touch of silver in the dress is just enough to go with the silver fillet over your hair. White is seldom becoming to blondes, but it suits you admirably."

She looked up, frankly pleased. "It is nice, really? I am so glad!" She was perfectly happy, and her smile showed it. The whole evening had been delightful. The disagreeable impressions made by the Contessa Potensi and Favorita were forgotten as she danced with Giovanni, who performed a feat of rare ability in finding a passage through the crush.

Presently he said to her, "When their Majesties have gone into an adjoining room, then the rest of us can go to supper."

As he spoke, Nina saw them disappear through the doorway. "Are they not coming back?" she asked.

"No. They have gone."

"But do they never dance?"

"Never! Queen Margherita and King Humbert always opened

the ball by the *quadrille d'honneur*, with the ambassadors and important court ladies and gentlemen. But the present King abolished all that."

At the end of the waltz Tornik managed to find Nina and announced supper. In the stampede for food there was such a crush that people stepped on her slippers and literally swept up the floor with her train. Tornik, being a giant, and able to reach over any number of smaller persons, finally secured a *pâté* and an ice. Standing near her, two young men were stuffing cakes and sandwiches into their pockets. Amazed, she drew Tornik's attention. He shrugged his shoulders. "Who are they?" she whispered. "Princes, for all I know," was his rejoinder. "Poor devils, many of them never get such a feast as this."

CHAPTER XIII

CORONETS FOR SALE

According to Italian etiquette, strangers must leave cards within twenty-four hours upon every person to whom they have been introduced. Therefore the afternoon of the day following the ball was necessarily spent by Nina in three hours of steady driving from house to house. Finally, as she and the princess were alighting at the Palazzo Sansevero, Count Tornik drove into the courtyard, and together they mounted to the apartments used by the family.

Nina settled herself in the corner of a sofa, pulling off her gloves. Tornik dropped into a loose-jointed heap in a big chair opposite. Suddenly he sat up straight, his eyebrows lifted.

"I did not know!" he said. "May I felicitate you, mademoiselle?"

"On what?" she asked, puzzled.

"Since you wear a ring, it is evident that your engagement is to be announced. Will you tell me who is the fortunate man?"

She saw that he was gazing at the emerald she wore on her little finger. "Is there reason to think I am engaged—because of *this?*"

"Certainly, what else? A young girl's wearing a ring can mean but one thing."

"On my little finger? How ridiculous! My father gave it to me. Sometimes, at home, I wear several rings. Does that mean I am engaged to several men?"

"Then you are still free?"

He hesitated as though under an impulse to say something sentimental, then apparently changed his mind, and relapsed into his habitually detached indifference of manner.

"They have curious customs in your country," he said casually. "A friend of mine was in America last year. He told me many things!"

"Did he? What, for instance?"

"He said that the women sat in chairs that balanced back and forth—"

"Chairs that—" she interrupted. "Oh, you mean rocking-chairs! That's true, you don't have them over here, do you? I did not mean to interrupt. You said we rock—"

"Not you, it's the older women who balance all day on verandas, and let their daughters do whatever they please! In an American family, I am told, the young girl is supreme ruler. Is that true?"

Nina, laughing, shrugged her shoulders. "I don't know—I never thought about it! But over here I suppose a girl does not count at all? Tell me, according to your ideas, what her place should be."

"Oh, I do not say *should*. I merely state the fact: over here, a young girl plays a very small rôle. But then, for the matter of that, most people belong naturally in the background, and very few, whether they are women or men, have their names on the program."

"And you? What part do you play?"

For a moment his eyes gleamed. "That depends upon whether fate shall cast me to support a *diva* or to occupy an empty stage."

"And if fate allowed you to choose, I could easily imagine that you would prefer a part with very little action and as few lines as possible."

"You are quite wrong. I do not object to saying all that a part calls for, and, above all, I like action."

"That's true; I had forgotten! You are a soldier! I wonder why you went into the army?"

"It is the only career open to me."

Nina was thinking of Giovanni and his point of view as she asked, "Why are you not content to be merely Count Tornik?"

"You mean that I, like Carpazzi, should live on the illustriousness of my name? If I were very poor, perhaps I should."

"How curious!" Nina exclaimed. "Does not a career mean making money?"

"On the contrary, it means spending it! One must have a great deal of money to go to any height in diplomacy."

"Then you are rich?" Nina already had acquired a brutal frankness of direct interrogation through her Italian sojourn.

"Not exactly." He looked bored again. "But I have a little—though perhaps not enough for my ambition. If only there were a serious war, I'd have a good chance." Then he added simply, "I am a good soldier!"

The princess, who had been summoned to the telephone, now returned and seated herself beside Nina on the sofa. "I have just been talking with the Marchesa Valdeste, and she told me that the Queen said most gracious things of you, dear; called you the 'charming little American.'" The prince entered while the princess was speaking. He kissed his wife's hand and began, at great length, to tell her exactly where and how he had spent the afternoon. After a while, however, as one or two other friends dropped in, Sansevero talked aside with Tornik.

"You were not at Savini's last night, were you?" he asked.

Tornik looked interested. "No," he said, "but I hear they had a very high game."

"Yes. Young Allegro was practically cleaned out."

"Who won?"

"Who, indeed, but Scorpa! He has the luck, that man!"

"Were you there? I thought you never played any more; have you taken it up again?"

Sansevero, glancing apprehensively at his wife, answered quickly, "I never play." Fortunately, just then the dangerous conversation was ended by the arrival of the Contessa Potensi. She smiled graciously upon the prince as he pressed her hand to his lips, and bestowed the left-over remnant of the same smile, upon Tornik. She also kissed the air on either side of the princess with much affection, and shook hands cordially with two other ladies who were present, but she directed toward Nina the barest glance.

She and Nina, by the way, furnished at the moment a typical illustration of the difference in appearance between European and American women.

The contessa was wearing an untrimmed, black tailor-made costume with a very long train, a little fur toque to match a small neck piece, and a little sausage-shaped muff. Her diamond earrings were enormous, but not very good stones. Nina's dress was of raspberry cloth, cut in the latest exaggeration of fashion—her skirt was short and skimp as her hat was huge. Her muff of sables as big and soft as a pillow—she could easily have buried her arms in it to the shoulder. The elaborateness of Nina's clothes filled the contessa with satisfaction, for she thought them barbarously inappropriate, and she knew that Giovanni was a martinet so far as "fitness" went.

Presently, in spite of her more than rude greeting, she coolly sat down beside Nina. "Will you make me a cup of tea? I like it without sugar and with very little cream." She did not smile, and she did not say "please." Her bearing was a fair example of the cold, impersonal insolence of which Italian women of fashion are capable when antagonistic.

After a time she leaned over and scrutinized Nina's watch, as though it were in a show case. "Do many young girls in America wear jewels?"

Nina found herself congealing; instead of answering, she

handed the contessa her tea, and expressed a hope that she had not put in too much cream.

Taking no notice of Nina's evasion, the contessa, talking indiscriminately about people, arrived finally at the subject of Giovanni. In her opinion, the Marchese di Valdo ought to marry money! Unfortunately, however, she feared he had loved too many women to be capable now of caring for one alone. From this she went to generalities. A man had but one grand passion in a lifetime, didn't Nina think so?

Nina's thoughts were very hazy, indeed, about grand passions, which were associated dimly in her mind with the seven deadly sins—in the category of things one didn't speak of. So she answered vaguely, feeling like a stupid child being cross-examined by the school commissioner.

"Still, he is very attractive, don't you find? Of course, he says the same things to all of us—but then no one understands how to make love as well as he, so what does it matter whether he means it or not? It takes a woman of great experience," insinuated the contessa, "to parry Giovanni's fencing with the foils of love."

Nina was goaded into answering. "You seem to know a great deal about his love-making," she said at last, with the breathy calm of controlled temper.

Half shutting her eyes, the contessa replied: "It is common hearsay. One has only to follow the list of his conquests to know that he must be a past master in the art of making women care for him. That he is fickle is evident; he is constantly changing his attentions from one woman to another, and leaving with a crisis of the heart her whom he has lately adored. I am sorry for the woman he marries—still, perhaps she would not know the difference! He might even be devoted, from force of habit."

Nina, furious, told herself that she did not believe one word that this spiteful woman was saying, but it made an impression all the same, which was, of course, exactly what the contessa wanted.

"Tornik, too, needs a fortune badly," Maria Potensi went on piercing neatly. "It is hard, over here with us, that men acquire fortunes only by marriage. In America, it must be better, for there they can earn their money, and marry for love."

Nina felt her cheeks burn as she listened, but there was nothing she could say. She knew only too well how hard it would be to believe herself loved.

But not all of the women were like the Contessa Potensi, and by the time Nina had been a month in Rome, she had, with the responsiveness of youth, formed several friendships that were rapidly drifting into intimacies, though she chose as her associates, for the most part, young married women rather than girls. Her particular friend was Zoya Olisco, really six months younger than herself, but of a precocious worldly experience that gave her at least ten years' advantage.

The young girls were to Nina quite incomprehensible. Their curiously negative behavior in public, their self-conscious diffidence, seemed to her stupid; but their education filled her with envy and shame. Nearly all spoke several languages, not in her own fashion of broken French, broken German, and baby-talk Italian, but with perfect facility and correctness of grammar. Nearly all were thoroughly grounded in mathematics, history, literature, and science. And yet their whole attitude toward life seemed out of balance; they were like pedagogues never out of the schoolroom—one moment discoursing learnedly, the next prattling like little children. The end and aim of life to them was marriage. Each talked of her dot and of what it might buy her in the way of a husband, very much as girls in America might plan the spending of their Christmas money.

In spite of the unusual liberty allowed Nina, as an American, it seemed to her that she was very restricted. She had, for instance, suggested that they ask Carpazzi to dine with them alone and go to the opera. But the princess had said, "Impossible. Carpazzi, finding no one but the family, would naturally suppose we wish to arrange a marriage between you."

Marry Carpazzi! It was ridiculous; she never had heard of such customs! "Well, then, why not ask Tornik?" she suggested. "He is not an Italian." The princess demurred. It might be possible to ask Tornik—still it was better not. Unless Nina wanted to marry Tornik? Apparently there was little use in pursuing this subject further, so she laughed and gave it up.

They were in the princess's room, at the time, and Nina, dressed for the street, was pulling on new gloves of fawn-colored *suède*. Her brown velvet and fox furs, her big hat with a fox band fastened with an osprey, were all that the modeste's art could achieve.

The princess fastened a little yellow mink collar around her throat over her black cloth dress, selected the better of two pairs of cleaned white kid gloves, picked up her hard, round, little yellow muff, and then went over and sat on the sofa beside Nina. "By the way, darling, I have something to say to you. The Marchese Valdeste has approached your uncle in regard to a marriage between his son Carlo and you. Not being an Italian, I suppose you want to give your answer yourself. What do you say?"

"What do I say!" Nina's eyes and mouth opened together. "Why, I have never seen the man!"

The princess smiled. "The offer is made in the same way in which it would be if you were an Italian. Your parents not being here, I ask you in their stead—or as I might ask you if you were a widow. To begin, then,—no, I am perfectly in earnest—I am authorized to offer you a young man of unquestionable birth. He has in his own right three castles. Two will need a great deal of repair, but one is in excellent condition and contains three hundred rooms, more than half of which are furnished. He has an annual income of twenty thousand *lire* and no—debts! That he is fairly good-looking, medium-sized, has black hair and brown eyes, and is said to have a very amiable disposition, are details."

As the princess concluded, Nina added: "And he has also a most charming mother. My answer is—my regret that I cannot marry her instead."

"You are sure you do not care to consider this offer?"

Nina looked steadily into her aunt's eyes. "I am sure you married Uncle Sandro through no such courtship as this!"

"I did not think you would accept, my dear child; yet such marriages often turn out for the best—at least it was my duty to ask for your answer. You have given it—and now let us go out. The carriage has been waiting some time."

Shortly afterward they were in the Pincio—for the custom still prevails among Roman ladies and gentlemen of slowly driving up and down or standing for a chat with friends. The dome of St. Peter's looked like a globe of gold set in the center of the celebrated frame of the Pincio trees, but as the sun went down it grew chilly, and the Sansevero landau rolled briskly up the Corso. At Nina's suggestion they stopped at a tea shop.

No sooner were they seated at a little table when they were joined by the Duchess Astarte. The duchess had most graceful manners, but she talked to the princess across Nina, and about her, as though she were an article of furniture, or at least a small child who could not understand what was said. She spoke frankly of Nina's suitors. Scorpa's was an excellent title, but Scorpa was a widower and no longer young. Then she begged the princess to consider her nephew, the young Prince Allegro.

It would be a brilliant match, for he was one of the mediatized princes and ranked with royalty. But his properties took such an immense amount of money to keep up that an added fortune would be a great relief to the whole family. Her consummate naturalness did away with much of the bluntness of her speech; but even so, this was too much for Nina's calmness.

"But, Duchessa," she broke in, "have the Prince Allegro and I nothing to do with the arranging of our own future?"

The duchess observed her in as much astonishment as though a baby of six months had broken into the conversation. A moment or two elapsed before she said smoothly: "Oh, the Prince is enchanted at the idea. He danced with you at Court and finds you *molto simpatica*. It is a great name, my dear, that he has to offer you—" and then with a condescension, yet a courteousness that prevented offense: "We shall all be willing, nay, delighted, to receive you with open arms. Your position will be in every way as though you had been born into the nobility."

"Thank you," said Nina quietly, "but I don't think I am quite used to the European marriage of arrangement."

"Ah, but it need not be a marriage of arrangement. If you will permit Allegro to pay his addresses to you, he will consider himself the most fortunate of men. May I tell him?"

"Please not!" said Nina. Quite at bay, she longed wildly for some means of escape. To her relief, two Americans whom she knew, young Mrs. Davis and her sister, entered the shop. Nina rose abruptly, apologizing to the duchess, and ran to them. How long had they been in Rome? Where were they stopping? What was the news from New York? They told her all they could think of. The Tony Stuarts had a son—they thought it the only baby that had ever been born; and as for old Mr. Stuart, he was nearly insane with joy. Billy Rivers had lost every cent of his money; and then—but, of course, Nina had heard about John Derby.

In her fear that some accident had happened to him, Nina's heart seemed to miss two beats. But Mrs. Davis merely meant his success in mining. By the way, she had seen him in New York, as she was driving to the steamer. He was striding up Fifth Avenue, and was "too good-looking for words."

The princess was leaving the shop and, as Nina followed her into the carriage, her mind was full of Derby. It was very strange— she had had a letter the day before from Arizona, in which John had said nothing about going to New York. Then she remembered that her father had hinted at a possibility that John might be sent to Italy later in the winter. Her pulse quickened at the thought, but with no consciousness of sentiment deepened or changed by absence.

Arrived at the palace, she found a note from Zoya Olisco, who was coming to spend the next day with her. Nina handed the note to the princess. "I thought we could go out in the car and lunch somewhere. Or is it not allowed?" Her eyes twinkled as she questioned.

"That depends," the princess answered in the same spirit, "upon whether you are counting upon including me. I am a very disagreeable tyrant when it comes to being left out of a party."

The automobile in question was Nina's. She had wanted one, and with her "to want" meant "to get." Nearly every one thought it belonged to the princess, as it would not have occurred to many in Rome to suppose it was owned by a young girl.

That night another extravagance of Nina's came to light. In the morning they had been at an exhibition of furs brought to Rome by a Russian dealer. Among them was a set of superb sables, and Nina, throwing the collar around her aunt's shoulders, had exclaimed at their becomingness.

The princess unconsciously stroked the furs as she put them down. "I have never seen anything more lovely," she said wistfully, and with no idea that she had sighed. A sable collar and muff had been one of the desired things of her life, but it was utterly impossible now to think of so much as one skin, and in the piece and muff in question there were more than thirty.

That evening, upon their return, the princess found the furs in her room when she went to dress. At first she felt that they were too much to accept, but when Nina's hazel eyes implored, and her lips begged her aunt to take "just one present to remember her by," the princess for once gave free reign to her emotions and was as wildly delighted as a child.

The very next afternoon, however, Scorpa saw the sables, and on a slip of paper made the following note:

| Sables | 80,000 lire |
| 60 H. P. motor car | 30.000 lire |

With a smile that would have done no discredit to his Satanic Majesty, he put the paper in his pocket.

CHAPTER XIV

APPLES OF SODOM

"It amounts to this: do you take a fitting interest in the name you bear, or do you not?" Sansevero was the speaker, and beneath his usual volubility there was an unwonted eagerness. The two brothers were in Giovanni's apartment on the second floor, which in Roman palaces usually belongs to the eldest son, and Giovanni sat astride a chair, his arms crossed over the back.

"I don't think you can ask such a question," he retorted hotly. "I am as much a Sansevero as you! But I really see no reason why—just because you have got a notion in your head that a pile of gold dollars would look well in our strong box—I should tie myself up for life. I am well enough as I am. My income is not regal, but it suffices."

Sansevero, like many talkative persons, was too busy thinking of what he was going to say next himself, to listen attentively to his brother's responses. He was merely aware that Giovanni's manner proclaimed opposition, so, when the sound of his voice ceased, Sansevero continued: "Nina is all the most fastidious could ask. *Noblesse oblige*—are you going to keep our name among the greatest in Rome, or are you going to let it fall like that of the Carpazzi? Shall they say of us in the near future, as they say of them today: 'Ah, yes, the Sanseveros were a great family once, but they are all dead or beggared now'?"

"*Per Dio!* What an orator we are becoming!" mocked Giovanni, looking out of half-shut eyes like a cat. But after a moment, also like a cat, he opened them wide and stared coolly at his brother. "Out of the mouth of babes—" he said impertinently. "My child, thou hast spoken much wisdom! It is, after all, a proposition that has, possibly, sense in it. *La Nina* is a woman such as any man might be glad to make his wife, and yet—this very fact that she is not an insignificant personality, is what I object to! I doubt her developing into either a blinded saint or a coquette with amiable complacence for others. We should lead a peppery life, I fear. But don't you think, my brother, that we are a bit hysterical over our family's extermination? After all, I am only twenty-eight; and in my opinion thirty-five is a suitable age for a man to marry. How old are you, Sandro—thirty-seven, is it not? And Leonora is nearly three years less. Of a truth, you are young!"

He rested his cheek in the hollow of his hand, looking up sideways. "It would be a great amusement if I should marry because I am the heir to the estates, and then you should have a large family—so—" He made steps with his unoccupied hand to indicate a succession of children. Then he laughed, without seeming to consider the difference that the birth of an heir to his brother would make to himself. He arose, lit a cigarette, and, smoking, threw himself into an easy chair on the other side of the room. The great Dane, which had been lying beside him as usual, now slowly got up, crossed the room, and dropped down again at his master's feet.

Meanwhile the prince, hands in pockets, had unaccountably become as silent as he had before been talkative, and Giovanni, upon observing his brother's sulky expression, leaned forward.

"Well?" he questioned, with a new ring in his voice, for Sansevero's moodiness was never a good omen. "What are you thinking of? Come, say it!"

Sansevero paced the length of the room and back; then he burst out: "Very well, it is this—everything is as bad as can be—so bad that if you don't marry money, and at once, the Sansevero burial will take place before you and I are dead. *Nome di Dio!* how are we to live with no money?"

"Since you ask my opinion, I have long wondered why you do not live better than you do," Giovanni answered. "Your income, added to Leonora's money, must make a very handsome sum. But one of the faults of the American women is that they are seldom good managers. Leonora is either no exception to the rule—or else she is getting very miserly. Why, an Italian on Leonora's income would live like a queen!"

"Be silent!" Sansevero, flushing darkly, flamed into speech. "Before you dare to criticise the woman who adorns our house! Here is the truth for you: I haven't one cent of private fortune—I gambled it all away long ago! More than half of Leonora's money is lost—I lost it. Some of it she paid out for my debts; the greater portion I put into the 'Little Devil' mine. I might much better have shoveled it into the Tiber. Do you know what she has done—the woman whom you criticise as a bad manager and stigmatize as mean—I would not care what you said, if you had not thought Leonora mean! *Dio mio*, mean! Know, then, that the very jewels she wears are false; that the real ones have been sold—to pay the debts of the man standing before you—the gambling debts of the head of one of the noblest houses in Italy!"

Giovanni was deeply moved, for this was a wound in his one vulnerable point, his pride of birth. The cigarette dropped to the floor unheeded. He moistened his lips as Alessandro continued:

"They were Leonora's own jewels that were sold, mark you. The Sansevero heirlooms will go to your son's wife intact, as they came to mine! But that is not all: I have given my oath to Leonora never again to go into a game of chance, and really I want to keep it! Yet you know—no, you don't; no one can who hasn't the fever in his veins—if I see a game, it is as though an unseen force had me in its grip, drawing me against my will; I can't resist! At Savini's I was dining, and I did not know they were going to play—I won a very little; enough to pay the interest on what I owe Meyer. But it makes me cold all over to think—*if* I had lost! An enviable inheritance you will get, when it is known what a mess of things the present holder of the title has made!" He dropped into a chair opposite his brother, and buried his face in his hands; between his slim fingers his forehead looked dark, and his temple veins swollen. For a long time Giovanni sat immovable, staring fixedly, but when at last he broke the silence, he spoke almost lightly:

"It is not a very charming history that you have given me— even though it increases my admiration for the woman who has, it seems, been more worthy of the name she bears than has the man who conferred his titles upon her. I wish you had told me before." Then, with a queerly whimsical smile, he said musingly: "To marry the girl with the golden hair—and purse? Not such a terrible fate to look forward to, after all! She would demand a great deal, and I should have to keep the brakes on. Still—that would do me no harm! You look as though you had been down a sulphur mine. Come, cheer up—all may yet be well." Suddenly he laughed out loud. "Funny thing," he observed further—"you know, I am not so sure that I am not rather in love."

He leaned to St. Anthony, and, putting his hand through the dog's collar beneath the throat, lifted the head on the back of his wrist. "Tell me, *padre*, am I in love? Do you advise the marriage?" The dog put his paw up, fanned the air once in missing, and let it rest on his master's knee.

Giovanni laughed aloud "*Ecco!* Sandro, he consents!"

CHAPTER XV

AN OPPOSITION BOOTH IS
SET UP IN THE MARKET PLACE

While Sansevero and Giovanni were in their imaginations refurbishing their escutcheon, two other men, with the opposite intent, stood on the front steps of the agency of "Thomas Cook and Sons." One was proclaimed by the regulation "Cook's" badge on his cap to be a guide; the other, by his military cloak, might have been recognized as an official of the Italian government. Both had shown covert interest in the Princess Sansevero, who, looking particularly lovely in her magnificent set of sables, had crossed the sidewalk with the light, buoyant carriage characteristic of her.

"There, you may see for yourself if it is I who speak the truth." This was said by the guide.

The official looked at him askance as he drew his bushy brows together and pulled at his beard. "I confess it looks serious—and strongly favors your supposition."

"But what else? It is as plain as the nose on your face, I should say! At Torre Sansevero they have been living on next to nothing—my cousin is cook, and I know that every *soldo* is counted. They come to Rome and spend their savings. You will say they have done that for years; but tell me this, should their savings in this year treble the savings of other years?"

Triumphantly he looked at his companion and, throwing back his head, put his hands on his hips. Then, with a return to his confidential manner, he laid his finger against his nose. "I know it for a fact," he continued—"Luigi heard it at the key-hole—that their excellencies contemplated staying at Torre Sansevero all this winter! Her excellency had the look—Maria, the maid, told the servants that much—that her excellency always has when *signore*, the prince, has cut the strings and left the purse empty."

"Furthermore?" The official twirled his mustache with an air of incredulity.

"Furthermore, the great Raphael disappears! Her excellency's renovation story was a little weak for my digestion, and, unless my eyes played me false, she was well frightened. I'll take my oath she was at a loss what to answer."

"You say you taxed her with it?"

"As I told you. She answered that the picture was being renovated. An answer for an idiot—the picture is one of the best canvases extant; in perfect repair."

"Did you tell her that?"

"Partially. I am sure she saw my suspicion."

"I should doubt her carrying out the sale after that. There is where your story fails."

"Ah, but it had already gone! It was perhaps by then in the house of a foreign millionaire. No, no, my story hangs together: The great picture disappears! A month later—time exactly for its arrival in America and the payment for it to be sent over here—her excellency of no money comes out in such a motor-car as that! And sables! I have an eye for furs. My father was in the business. The value of those she has on runs easily into the seventy or eighty thousand *lire*. Here she comes now, out of the banker's where American money is most often paid! Do you want better evidence?"

He had been punctuating all he said with his fingers, and now, with a final snap of arms and a shrug of shoulders, he looked up in keen triumph at his companion.

The other—slower and less excited than the narrator (probably because he was not the discoverer of the plot)—nevertheless showed lively interest. "It is very grave," he admitted at last. "But the Sansevero family is illustrious. We may not proceed against them without due consideration. I shall report the case to the chief of our secret service, and the prince must be—"

A tall, athletic young man who had been changing some foreign gold into Italian, came into the open doorway of the office. A carriage, passing at that moment close to the curb, had prevented the two men from hearing the stranger's footfall, and as the latter stood on the top step, searching in his pocket for matches, he happened to catch the name "Sansevero." At once his attention was arrested, but as the conversation was carried on in an undertone, he caught only vague, detached words. Still, he was sure that he had heard "Raphael" after the name, "Sansevero," "disappearance," and then something like "secret service." But his presence evidently had become known, for as he passed on out into the street the two in blue coats were talking loudly about the excursion to Tivoli and the scenery *en route*.

Walking out into the middle of the square where the cabs stand, he jumped into the first one, but he looked cautiously back toward the men in front of Cook's, before telling the driver to take him to the Palazzo Sansevero.

Here the *portiere* in his morning clothes, very different from

the gorgeous apparel of afternoon, was sweeping out the courtyard. Holding his broom handle with exactly the same dignity
with which, later in the day, he would hold his mace, he informed
the stranger that his excellency the prince was not at home—neither was her excellency the princess. Upon being asked whether
Miss Randolph were perhaps at home, he altogether forgot his
imperturbability. That a *signore* should send in his card to a *signorina* was so far outside the range of his experience that the man
stood with his mouth open, unable even to think what answer to
give. As though he were a somnambulist, the man took the card
and slowly read the name on its face; then he looked the stranger
over from head to foot, read the name a second time, and finally
entered the palace.

The young man watched his retreating figure, and then,
throwing back his head, laughed long and heartily. After which he
fell to studying the details of the courtyard. He noted with keen
interest the deep ruts worn in the solid stone paving under the
massive arches of the gateways, and glanced up at the bas-reliefs
between the windows. At the sound of footsteps he turned and
encountered Nina's maid, Celeste.

Mademoiselle had sent her to bid him mount to the *salon*.
Through the green baize doors—it was the shorter way—and
then, if monsieur would go straight on to the very last of the
rooms— His striding pace made Celeste fairly trot along at his
heels. He went through room after room. Was there no end to
them? At last Nina's slight, girlish figure was seen silhouetted
against a broad window at the end—the light at her back hazing
the gold of her hair, like a nimbus, about her face.

She ran toward him, both hands out. "Jack! Dear Jack! Is it
you, really, or am I dreaming? When did you come? Oh, I *am* so
glad to see you; but what a surprise! Why did you not send word?"

For a moment a light leaped into Derby's eyes. It seemed as
though Nina was looking at him exactly as he, in his day dreams,
had seen her. But his prudence steadied his first impulse, and he
put down her gladness as merely the joy of a person who, far from
home, sees suddenly a familiar face in the midst of strangers; and
they sat on the sofa just as they had sat on the railing of the
veranda in the country, ever since they were children.

In Derby's account of himself, Nina could easily read the confidence that had led her father to send him to Italy. But their talk
had gone little further than the barest outline of his mission when
the prince and princess returned. At the sight of Nina sitting alone
with a man, the princess came forward quickly with the question,

"My child, what does this mean?" as plainly asked in her eyes as it could have been by spoken words. But at Nina's "John Derby, Aunt Eleanor!" the princess put out her hand with all the grace in the world, and as she returned the straight, frank look of his blue eyes, her whole expression became youthful, as if reflecting some pleasant memory of her girlhood.

"I knew your uncle very, very well!" She smiled entrancingly. It was a smile that irresistibly attracted to her all who ever saw it. "You are like him." Then she added softly, dreamingly, as though half speaking to herself, "You remind me of so many things—at home!"

The next minute she had turned to present Derby to her husband, and the conversation became general. But, finally, in a pause, Nina said, "Jack, tell Uncle Sandro what father sent you over to do. Or is it a secret?"

Derby looked toward Sansevero as though measuring the man. "It is no great secret—but I would rather it was not spoken of yet."

"My ears are deaf, and my tongue is dumb." Sansevero put his hand over his ear, his mouth, and finally his heart.

"I have come over to buy, or to lease—at all events, to work—sulphur mines."

As though an electric current had been turned on, Sansevero sat up straight, and his levity vanished. "To work sulphur mines! Will you tell me more? I have a particular reason for wanting to know."

Derby answered willingly. "I can give you a general idea. I was forced into inventing a new method of mining on account of the quicksands, which are found all through our mines at home. Taking a suggestion from the oil wells, I bored just such a well down into the sulphur beds. Ordinarily the sulphur is brought up in powder or rock form, and refined in vats on the surface, so that not only do the miners have to go down into the sulphurous heat, but the caldrons in which the sulphur is refined give out gases that are unendurable to human throats and lungs. In our mines, the sulphur is now refined sixty or a hundred feet below the surface of the ground, and pours out in an already purified state, at the top of the well."

Sansevero looked incredulous. "But sulphur is almost impossible to liquefy. Unlike metals, it congeals again when it has been heated beyond the proper temperature. Also it corrodes any metal it touches, so that a pipe would be eaten away immediately."

"To get over those difficulties is exactly what I am trying to do by my new process," Derby answered. "The sulphur is melted by hot water sent down the pipes, followed by sand, and then sawdust—the sand to carry the heat to the cooler edges, and the wet sawdust to check the heat at the center."

Even the princess drew nearer and laid her hand on her husband's arm as Derby made his explanation. Sansevero trembled with excitement. "But according to that," he cried, turning to his wife; "our mine would be practicable!" Then to Derby: "I ought to explain to you that we have a sulphur mine in Sicily, near Vencata. So far as I know, the sulphur does, as you say, lie in a bed some twenty meters down. Above it are rock and alluvial soil. The volcanic neighborhood makes the temperature below ground higher than can be borne, yet we know that the sulphur deposit is immense."

"Give me more details. From what you say, it sounds as though this mine of yours might be exactly what we are looking for. Does Mr. Randolph know of it, or that you are the owner?"

"No; no one knows it excepting one small group of sulphur owners. I unwisely went into it on the advice of—some one who is very good at all these things; yet the best are liable to mistake. Other mines in the neighborhood, owned by friends of mine, have brought in a fortune. Ours has, so far, been a failure."

The talk lasted until luncheon was served. Giovanni put in an appearance, and Derby was pressed to stay. As di Valdo and the American met, there was a barely perceptible coldness under the Italian's good manners, while Derby's greeting showed a momentary curiosity. Two more sharply contrasted beings could hardly have been brought together. But gradually Giovanni also became interested in the mining plans, and, as the reason for the American's coming to Europe very evidently was business and not the pursuit of the heiress, Giovanni's affability became genuine.

The end of the matter was that Derby agreed to take up the Sansevero mine, commonly known as the "Little Devil"; to be worked on a "royalty" basis. Derby, representing his company, was to pay all expenses, take all responsibility, and to return to Sansevero a percentage of the market price on every ton of sulphur taken out of it.

Furthermore, Sansevero insisted upon giving him a letter to the Archbishop of Vencata, who lived about eight hours on muleback from the mining settlement. The Sicilians, he declared, were a dangerous people for strangers who tried to interfere in their established order of things.

"So then I am likely to have adventures! It sounds exciting!" The American laughed light-heartedly at the sport of it. However, he accepted the letter to the archbishop.

CHAPTER XVI

A MENACE

Derby did not realize until afterward that the entire conversation at the Palazzo Sansevero had been about his projects, and that, aside from a few generalities, he really knew nothing of Nina's winter or of her Italian experiences. He returned to his hotel at about five o'clock, and was striding directly toward the smoking-room without glancing to right or left among the attractive groups that characterize the tea hour at the Excelsior, when he was arrested by some one's calling, "Why, John Derby!"

In the crowd of persons and tables he looked blankly for a familiar face, but, as his name was repeated, he recognized Mrs. Bobby Davis and her sister, Mildred Hoyt. As soon as Derby reached their table, Mrs. Davis glibly rattled off the names of the four or five men who comprised their party. They were all Europeans, who, in regular afternoon attire—frock coats, and flower in buttonhole—were sipping tea and eating cake. Derby was in tweeds, and afternoon tea was by no means part of his daily program.

However, he made the best of it, and also of the remarks that followed, for he was sooner seated than Mrs. Davis turned all her powers of sprightly conversation upon the subject of Nina. Half of the nobility of Italy, she averred, were sighing—or busily doing sums—at the feet of the American heiress. There was a particularly fascinating Sansevero—he was not called Sansevero, but di Valdo (curious custom of having half a dozen names for one person!), who, it was rumored, was simply mad about Nina! People said she was going to marry him—either him or Duke something. And there were crowds of others. That was one of her suitors now—she pointed out Tornik, who was taking tea with a group from the Austrian Embassy. He was most attractive, didn't John think so? In Nina's place, she would have her head turned!

This idea seemed to be a new one to Derby. "Should you?" The question was asked so reflectively that Mrs. Davis almost stopped to think; but the habit of prattling carried her on.

"To have men like that sighing for one—I should call it thrilling, to say the least."

Derby's look questioned. "I wonder why the Europeans make such a hit with you women," he said. "Why, for instance, do you find that man over there attractive? What do you like about him?"

"Seriously?" Mrs. Davis patted her hair up the back with a little smoothing movement of satisfaction. "I don't know how to put it—it is very indefinable; but a man like that has a quality—a polish, I suppose it is, really—that is quite irresistible."

Derby looked rather disgusted. "And you think that is why Nina likes them?"

"Oh, there are other reasons—lots of them. In the first place, Nina has a bad case of '*allure de noblesse.*' In her case I don't wonder! You can't imagine anything so heavenly as her aunt's palace; it is every bit as fine as any of the galleries or museums."

As though this remark added a new link to a chain of old impressions, Derby found himself asking: "By the way—they have a famous picture gallery out in the country somewhere, haven't they?"

Mrs. Davis turned for information to Prince Minotti, sitting next to her; who, as he was not especially welcomed by the Romans, much affected the society of Americans, since to them, as a rule, a prince is a prince, and the name that follows of comparative unimportance.

"Torre Sansevero," he said pompously, "is one of the finest estates we have in Italy. In fact, the gardens are hardly less celebrated than those of the Villa d'Este, and there are a few excellent paintings. Do you ask for any special reason?"

"No," replied Derby casually. "I heard they had a Raphael that was especially beautiful; I should like to see it—that is all."

"Do you, by chance, know the Princess Sansevero's niece, from America, who is captivating Rome this winter?"

"Miss Randolph? Yes."

"Ah, then it will be easy for you to get permission to see the painting. The gallery is not open to the public, though Cook's, I believe, send a party out once a week, to see the gardens."

To Derby the suspicion at once became a certainty that, in overhearing the talk between the Cook's guide and the official, he had by accident stumbled upon something of serious importance to the Sanseveros. He was puzzling over it when, in the smoking-room, a few moments later, he encountered Eliot Porter, an American writer who was making a study of Roman life. At sight of Derby he called out heartily, "Hello, Jack, when did you come over?"

Derby drew up a chair beside him, and briefly sketched the object of his visit.

"Negotiating with Scorpa, I suppose?" asked Porter.

"The Sulphur King?" Derby shook his head. "No, I don't

think I shall need him. I have my hands on a property that promises to be what I am looking for. The duke wants to work his mines himself and in his own way. I am merely trying a scheme; if it turns out well, good! If not, I shall have tested it."

"When do you begin operations? I suppose you realize, my friend, that it is no joke to interfere with the Sicilians? They are as suspicious of a new face as a tribe of savages. Savages is just about what they are, too! And there is another element that you should not lose sight of: If you are going to upset Scorpa's methods, it is not the Sicilians alone that you will have to deal with, but also the duke himself."

"I am not going to try his property."

"No, but he controls the sulphur output. If you come into his market—well, I'd not give a *soldo* for your skin. Besides, that would be the second grudge he'd have against you!"

"Second? I don't understand—"

"He wants to marry your best girl! Oh, hold on—no offense meant. She is having a splendid time of it, if a string of satellites as long as the Ponte San Angelo constitutes a woman's joy. All the same, my boy; put this in your pipe and smoke it: 'Ware Scorpa, don't turn your back to any one who might be in his employ, and bolt your door at night. Will you have my Winchester?"

Derby smoked on, unperturbed. "It sounds as though it might be interesting. I had expected a mere proposition of machinery; the human element always adds. Wasn't it you who told me that?"

"In a book, decidedly!" and then with a sudden impulse, "By Jove, Jack, I believe it would be a good thing for me to go along with you! I might get new copy."

Derby laughed incredulously. "Well, if you mean it, come along! I wish you would." Porter meant it enough to be interested in the project, at any rate, for later the two men dined together, and they discussed arrangements and expedients all the evening.

Derby went to the Palazzo Sansevero the next day, but again he had much to talk over with the prince, and saw little of Nina. In some unaccountable way she seemed changed; nothing definite happened to mark the difference that he vaguely felt, but Mrs. Davis's remark came back to him—"The Europeans are so finished," and he wondered whether Nina found him unfinished; he even wondered whether he was or not—which was a good deal of wondering for him.

At first, Sansevero's investment in the "Little Devil" had seemed to Derby merely the unfortunate venture the prince thought it, but when, in the course of their talk, it came out that

Scorpa was the "friend" who had sold him the mine, Derby was sure that the duke had deliberately saddled him with a property which he knew to be useless. And yet every word that Scorpa had urged as a reason for the mine's value, was—taken literally—true. The mine was in close proximity to his own; the surveys, furthermore, showed the "Little Devil" to be the richest in sulphur deposit of any in the region. But if the mine was as valuable as Scorpa declared, it was scarcely compatible with all that was known of his character that out of purely disinterested friendship, he should put such a prize in Sansevero's hands, while he bought up for himself less valuable mines at higher prices. Derby kept his opinions to himself; but his blood boiled with indignation and, mentally, he resolved to beat Scorpa if it was humanly possible.

As Derby was leaving, Nina deliberately went from the room with him. "I want to speak with John a few minutes," she said to her aunt. "We are both Americans, you know," she added, laughing. In the adjoining room she motioned him to sit beside her, but he stood instead, leaning against the window frame. She looked up with something like apology. "Am I keeping you?" she asked quickly. "Are you in a hurry?"

Almost with the manner of Mr. Randolph, he pulled out his watch. "Not especially. I have an appointment with the Duke Scorpa—but not for half an hour." She had not noticed before the nervously hurried manner of her countrymen. There were many things she wanted to talk to John about—but she might as well have tried to carry on a restful conversation at a railroad station, when the train was coming in.

"With Scorpa?" She tried to hold his attention. "What are you going to see *him* about?"

Derby seemed preoccupied.

"I don't think I'm very sure myself—further than that he wants to buy my patents, which I have no intention of selling, and I want to rent his mines, which he has no intention of renting. Rather asinine, going to see him! Still, as he insists—" There was an eagerness in Derby's face inconsistent with the shrugging of his shoulders.

But Nina's thoughts were not on the processes of mining just then, though they were on Scorpa. She looked at Derby appealingly.

"Jack!"

"Yes, Nina?"

"Do you know what I think?—Aunt Eleanor won't say a word; she hides it all she can, but she must have lost almost her entire fortune. Jack, do you think that Duke Scorpa could be at the bottom of it?"

Derby gave her a glance of keen interest, but he expressed no surprise and asked her no questions. As a matter of fact, the gossip of the Cook's guide had partly prepared him for Nina's revelation about her aunt's fortune, and he had his own theories about Scorpa. "Quite likely," he answered dryly, "but it is also quite likely that we shall get the better of him—" Then, with a sudden change in his manner he looked at her steadily. "But perhaps you don't want us to get the better of him?"

"Do you mean—?"

"I hear he is very devoted—and he has not only the handle to his name that you women seem to be keen about, but he is too rich to be after your money." Derby had no sooner said the words than he regretted them. But seeing Nina color, he misinterpreted her feelings, and spoke under a sudden flash of jealousy. "And I suppose the title of duchess is irresistible."

Nina was deeply hurt. "That is pretty blunt," she said, the pupils of her eyes contracted as though the sun blinded them. "Have you ever seen the man you speak of? No? Well, you would not say such a thing if you had. I *hate* him!"

Derby seemed fated to blunder. Again he made the wrong remark. "Hate, they say, is next to love."

His lack of insight, so palpable in contrast with Giovanni's keenness of perception, was too much for Nina's new sensitiveness. She suddenly congealed, and stood up, very straight, with the little upward tilt of the chin that indicated fast approaching temper.

Derby knew this symptom well enough, but he had not the slightest idea that his own obtuseness was the cause. Without analyzing, he accepted her starting up as a signal to leave, and promptly said good-by. "Good-by, then!" Nina said frigidly; and, turning on her heel, she abruptly left him.

Under the spur of her anger against him, the words framed themselves in her mind—"How unfinished he is!" But down in her heart there was an ache, deeper than could have been caused by mere irritation, or even disappointment. Never before in her life had there been a breach between John and her. She felt it was all the fault of his own density—or was it lack of feeling?

She went to her room to put on her riding habit, for she was going to the meet. Then, as she dressed, the thought came to her that John, a foreigner, and the most venturesome person in the world, was going off to Sicily, into the very center of one of the wildest districts. And gradually fear for him made her forget her resentment.

Just as she was leaving her room a big cornucopia of roses was brought in, to which was appended the following note:

"If we weren't such old friends and you didn't know what a blundering fool I am, I wouldn't dare to apologize for this morning. Judge me by intent, though, won't you—and forgive me?

"Jack."

Nina broke off a rose and fastened it to the lapel of her habit; but the note she tucked in between the buttonholes. Suddenly humming a gay little song, she ran through the rooms and corridors to join her aunt and uncle, who were waiting for her to motor out to the hunt, the horses having been sent ahead with the grooms. As they drove out of the courtyard she noticed that the sun was brilliantly shining.

At the meet the scene was really animated, for the day was perfect, and the Via Appia was a bright moving picture of carriages, large and small, big motors and little runabouts, the road dotted here and there with the brilliant scarlet coats of those who were to hunt and the bright colors of women's dresses in the various conveyances.

There was apparently much lack of system: the huntsmen chatted aimlessly with persons in the carriages; while the hounds scurried around according to their own inclinations, paying little attention to the snap of the whip. The Contessa Potensi, who had appeared in a pink hunting coat, was the cynosure of all eyes. The innovation created quite a stir and no little admiration. She bowed to Nina with unusual civility, and made a formal acknowledgment of the pleasure of riding with her. Yet shortly after, when she joined a group of friends a distance farther on, she was laughing and glancing back as she spoke, in a way that left little doubt that she was making disparaging remarks.

Sansevero and Giovanni had mounted their hunters, and now joined Nina, but that gave her little pleasure, for the contessa immediately returned. Nina was glad when Donna Francesca Dobini and the young Prince Allegro cantered up. Donna Francesca was soon talking with Sansevero, leaving Nina to Allegro— an attractive youth, but light as a bit of fluff.

As for Giovanni, she felt that he was as unstable as the dead leaves which the wind at that moment was blowing around and around. They were graceful, too, those leaves, and Giovanni was fascinating, agile, charming—but in case one counted upon him seriously, where would he be? Smiling sweetly, no doubt, at some other woman, and telling her that her eyes were twin lakes of heaven's blue, or forest pools in which his heart was lost forever.

The contrasting image of John Derby came sharply to mind. John was going to Sicily to do a man's work in a man's way. A little later she noticed Tornik, who was cantering ahead of her: his figure was not unlike John's—he was strong and masculine. She wondered aimlessly if they might be in any other way alike. Supposing, in some unaccountable situation she were to be thrown upon his chivalry for protection, what would he do? Shrug his shoulders and look bored? Or detail a company from his regiment to stand guard over her? The idea made her laugh.

"You are gay this morning," observed Giovanni, light-heartedly joining in her laughter.

With a quizzical little expression Nina looked at him—"I wonder if you would be amused if you knew why I laughed."

"If it gives you pleasure—it is delicious, whatever it is!"

All the softness went out of the girl's brown eyes; they glittered curiously. "Yes," she said, "that is just what I thought." After which ambiguous remark she returned to her former gayety— "Come," she said, "let's go fast; we shall be the last!" Urging her horse, she galloped across the fields.

She would have been at a loss to understand her own vacillations of mood that day: she seemed to feel an unaccountable revulsion against every one. The gesticulations of the men around her, their airs and blandishments, annoyed her. Not an hour earlier she had found John dull and flat by comparison with Europeans. Now suddenly they were effeminate dandies, and John alone was a real man.

But the exhilaration of jumping brought her to a more equable frame of mind, and at the first check she and the Prince Allegro were in the lead. Her cheeks were pink and her eyes bright from the long gallop.

They had stopped on a knoll out on the Campagna, and Nina remained apart from the other hunters, walking her horse slowly, while Allegro went over to the carriage to get a handkerchief for her from the Princess Sansevero. She drew in deep breaths of the fresh air, as she gazed out over the rolling hills to the snowclad tops of the Albanian mountains glistening in the sunshine.

Then suddenly a deep, oily voice jarred through her wandering thoughts. "You are very pensive!" exclaimed the Duke Scorpa, appearing beside her.

Nina started violently, for, besides his unexpected appearance, there was something in this man's personality that always sent a shudder through her.

"The Marchese di Valdo has been telling me that I am very gay," she answered, not so much to give the duke the information as to contradict him.

"Then I am doubly sad, since you are gay with others, and absent-minded when I come." A lurking familiarity in his smile made Nina wince. He ranged his horse so close that his boots brushed against hers, and she pulled aside quickly; he did not move close again, but he checked her attempt to pass him, keeping between her and the other riders.

"Why are you so cruel?" he murmured. "Diana never had so many votaries as Venus."

"I am not interested in mythology," said Nina, her heart fluttering with fright. "Please allow me to pass—I want to join my uncle."

"Sweet, pale little Diana,"—he leaned over in his saddle and purred the words at her—"where mythology failed was in not marrying Diana to Mars. Exactly as—you are going to marry me!"

"I will not! I told you before I would not! Let me pass!" She pulled the reins so taut that her horse reared as she urged him forward, but again the duke ranged his horse close beside her, heading off her attempt to get past.

"A woman's 'won't' as often means she will," he answered deliberately. "It is when she says she is not certain that her irrevocable decision is made."

"I hate you, I utterly hate you!" cried Nina, her anger getting the better of her fear.

The duke laughed maliciously. "I had scarcely hoped to make so deep a mark on your emotions! If you hate me, then truly you will marry me!—against your will, if need be," he added, reining back his horse at last. "I will wait to make you love me afterward."

At this point Allegro returned with the handkerchief, and the duke let Nina pass. Tornik, also, now joined her, the master of the hounds gave the signal, and again the riders were off. Nina, between Tornik and Allegro, was protected from the duke's approach, but she kept apprehensively glancing back. She looked about for her uncle, but could not see him.

As a matter of fact, Sansevero's horse had strained itself slightly in one of the jumps, and he had thought it best to drop out of the hunt. He had gone only a short distance on his way toward Rome when he was joined by Scorpa, who said that he did not care to ride farther but would go back with Sansevero. The prince was glad of his company until Scorpa began:

"You have not yet given me a favorable answer to my proposal for Miss Randolph's hand."

The abruptness with which the subject was introduced irritated Sansevero, and he answered sulkily: "I told you, when you first spoke to me, that it was a matter Miss Randolph would have to decide for herself. An American girl never allows other people to arrange her marriage for her, and I found my niece not at all disposed to reconsider her answer."

An ugly light shone in the duke's eyes. "I do not want to seem importunate," he said, "but—I would do very much for the man who furthered my marriage with Miss Randolph, and you would find the alliance of our families of great advantage. I am a hot-blooded fellow, but I'm not such a bad lot. I cannot help being wounded, though, by your niece's indifference, and in jealousy of a rival I might do things that otherwise would not enter my head. This is—eh—not a threat—but it is a family trait—the Scorpas stop at nothing once their hearts are aflame! Think it over, my friend, before you decide not to help me."

He sighed deeply and then, as though turning his attention to the first trivial thought that came to mind, he said casually: "By the way, I have been reading lately an extremely interesting book on celebrated criminal cases, and I was particularly impressed by the way in which circumstantial evidence can be built up out of harmless trifles. Since reading it I have been rather amusing myself by constructing hypothetical cases. For instance"—Scorpa pursed his lips and lowered his eyes, as though trying to invent a fanciful story—"take a transaction such as your letting me have that picture. One could build a very stirring case upon that!"

"Yes?" encouraged the prince. "How do you mean?"

"Well, to begin, we would send word to the government that your Raphael Madonna had been sold out of the country."

"I don't think that a good beginning, because it is easy enough to prove it is in your palace."

"Ah, of course. But for the amusement of the argument we will say that I *want* to do you an injury and so smuggle it out of the country! Then when I am questioned, I deny all knowledge of it. Yes, I would have you there! It would be quite feasible, because no one saw the picture change hands, and your notes to me—the only proof of the transfer—could easily be destroyed. You see? This really grows interesting! Then comes all the cumulative evidence of the type I was speaking about; for instance: After the supposed sale of the picture, you indulge in unwonted expenditures—of course, it is easy to say that they are those of the American heiress stopping with you"—he paused, in apparent thoughtfulness—"but when, in addition, an enemy buys in Paris a pair of earrings, matchless emeralds, that are recognized as having been worn—"

"*Dio mio!* My wife's emeralds!" Sansevero was startled into exclaiming. Then suddenly he blazed out: "What do you mean by your story? If you have anything to say, say it so I can follow you."

From the gross lips of the duke his apology fell like drops of thickest oil: "I regret you take my pleasantry so ill, and I ask your pardon as many times as you require, my friend! It happened by chance that I saw a pair of emeralds in Paris that were duplicates of the magnificent gems I have often admired when the princess wore them, and the jeweler told me that they had been sold at a sacrifice by a noble lady in urgent need of money. The curious coincidence came to my mind in illustration of the problems I was talking of. Further than that I meant nothing—except that I was serious in what I said about repaying the man who should bring about my marriage."

They had long since passed through the Porta San Giovanni and had arrived at the Coliseum. Scorpa gave Sansevero little chance to answer, but with a friendly good-by, he turned toward the Monte Quirinal. Sansevero pursued his way along the foot of the Palatine. He was disturbed; but he could not bring himself to read into the duke's words a covert threat. His first impulse was to repeat the conversation to Eleanor, but he knew how the mere suspicion that Scorpa had detected her false stones had worried her. Curiously enough, in Sansevero's mind the larger issue of the picture was quite overlooked in the more immediate consideration of the jewels. By the time he reached home he had decided to wait until further events should show Scorpa's intentions. And until then he would say nothing to any one—least of all to Eleanor.

In the meantime Nina was galloping across the Campagna. For a while the fear of Scorpa remained, but when she realized that he was no longer with the hunt, she breathed more freely, and again began to enjoy the day. It was almost as though she were riding through the country at home. She might have been hunting in Westchester, or on Long Island, for any actual difference that there was, and the finish, as at home, was merely anise seed, and the hounds were fed raw meat.

CHAPTER XVII

NINA DUSTS BEHIND THE COUNTER

Kate Titherington, daughter of Alonzo K. Titherington, the Pittsburg iron magnate, had some six years before married the Count Masco. After a short experience of living in his ancestral palace, they had moved into an apartment out in the new part of the city; very handsome, very luxurious and modern in every way. "Deliver me from these musty old dungeons!" she had exclaimed to her husband. "I will give a free deed of gift to the rats, who are really, my dear, the only beings I can think of to whom this tumbledown barracks of yours would be comfortable." Her husband was a meek and inoffensive appendage, who had been well brought up by an overbearing mother and turned over, perfectly trained, to the strenuous requirements of the bonny Kate.

The vivid Countess Masco, *née* Titherington, was looked upon with disfavor by the more conservative Romans, and her position was rather, one might say, on the outer edge of the inner circle. There were those who liked her, and who found her amusing and lively; indeed, that was the trouble—it was her liveliness that had banished her to the outer edge, instead of making a place for her in the inmost circle, where Eleanor Sansevero, for instance, was so securely established.

Nina had known Kate Titherington one summer at Bar Harbor, but her first encounter with this flamboyant personality in Italy was at the Grand Hotel a few days before the hunt. Nina was serving at one of the tables of a charity tea, when she saw a very highly-colored, plump figure, with draperies in full sail, bearing down upon her from the top of the wide steps, at the back of the big red hall. The red of the hall paled beside the cerise costume of the approaching lady. In a voice loud and high-keyed, yet not unmusical, she cried:

"Well, I declare if it isn't little Nina Randolph!" And then with exuberant good humor she called to her husband, who followed lamb-like in her wake, "You see, Gio, it *is* the little Randolph—I told you so!

"This is my husband." She presented him as though he were some inanimate personal possession. "We have been in Paris and Monte Carlo all winter. Got back yesterday. Nice old place, Rome, don't you think? I dote on it, but of course it gets provincial if you stay too long!" At the same moment she caught sight of Zoya

Olisco, and waved to her. To Nina's surprise, the young Russian came forward with both hands outstretched. "Ah, you are back? What was the news in Monte Carlo?"

"Nothing much. They still talk of the *coup* that Tornik—" But before Nina could hear the end of the sentence, the old Princess Malio handed her a five-*lire* note for tea, and Nina had to get change. Then the whole family of the Rosenbaums, eight in number, demanded her services for many cups of tea and as many plates of sandwiches and cakes, and when their change was counted, the Countess Kate and her attendant husband were leaving. The countess, however, called back over her shoulder, "You are dining with me on Friday; the princess said yes for you!"

And so it was that on the evening of the hunt Nina, alone with her uncle—her aunt having stayed at home on account of a headache—found herself entering a big new apartment house, and going up in an elevator, quite as though she were at home in one of the most modern, instead of one of the most ancient, cities in the world.

The Masco apartment was all brand-new—so new that there was still about it an odor of fresh paint and plaster, and the pungency of raw textiles. The Countess Kate, not to be outdone by her decorator, was as new as her surroundings—in the latest style of sheath dress, of a brilliant blue, which she wore triumphantly, regardless of the strain with which it stretched across the amplitude of her bosom.

The company consisted of the Oliscos, Count Tornik, Prince Minotti, Count Rosso, Prince Allegro, Eliot Porter, and John Derby. It gave Nina a sudden feeling of satisfaction to see how attractive John was by comparison with the others. He had a quiet reserve and a forcefulness that Nina thought very effective in this foreign surrounding, and she was ashamed of herself for having judged him by the shallow standard of mere social grace.

The Countess Masco's parties were renowned for their gayety. She was one of those hostesses whose vivacity never relaxes, and whose ready answers pass for sparkling wit. According to her own standard, a party was a success or a failure as it was noisy or quiet. Consequently she talked and laughed continuously. Startling colors were her particular weakness, and by the scent of extract of tuberose she could be traced for days.

Nina sat between Eliot Porter and the young Prince Allegro; but her attention wandered across the table to John Derby so constantly that the Prince Allegro remarked, "You seem to be entranced by that American!"

"Mr. Derby happens to be my oldest and my best friend!" Nina answered. Then, realizing that she had made the statement sententiously, she smiled brightly. "You Europeans so often say that American men are unattractive," she said. "Over there you may behold one of 'our best!'"

Without rancor or jealousy, the young prince seemed entirely to agree with her opinion. "Why is it we so seldom meet those Americans you call 'best'?" he asked, between spoonfuls of *purée d'écrevisse*.

"Because they are those who have to stay at home and work." And then she added, "They are saints—don't you think?"

"They are very stupid, I should say."

Nina let her spoon rest on the rim of her plate. "That's not polite of you."

"Why? Since it is true. Of course they are stupid! They let their women, who are adorable, come over to us. Would I, do you think, if you were my wife, allow you so much as to go out for an afternoon's drive without me? Never! To prove further that your men are stupid—in no country are there so many divorces as in America!"

"It is not because our men are stupid, at all events!"

"Then why is it?"

"Chiefly because our men have too little time to give us." And then she spoke under sudden stress of feeling, without perhaps knowing the full wisdom of what she said: "Do you suppose that if our men at home had time for us, we *would* come over here, to you?"

"Then all the more are the Americans fools!" He raised his champagne glass. "Signorina," he said, "may you find the American who *has* the time."

Involuntarily her glance went toward John. Allegro saw it and laughed. "Ah, ha! So that is why we have no chance? Still," he added on second thought, "your choice does you credit."

"He is not my choice, he is my friend. You don't understand! At home a girl has men friends exactly as she has girl friends. I wonder how I can make it clear to you—we are all like a big family. They might as well be my brothers, many of the men I know; there is not a bit of sentiment in our liking for each other."

"There is no sentiment between you and the man over there?" Allegro twisted the blond down on his upper lip, laughing at her out of the corners of his eyes. "I may be little more than a boy, signorina, but there is one thing that I know quite well when I see it, and that is a person who is in love. Human nature is the same all over the world. Your American men can, after all, have only the same emotions that we have over here. It is as plain as the dome on St. Peter's—you may see it from every direction. That man over there is in love with you! *Ecco!*"

"He is nothing of the sort! You Italians are mad on the subject. I told you you could not understand. You are different, that is all."

Allegro shrugged his shoulders. "As you please! I tell you he is! And what is more, you are in love with him. After all"—he put up his hand to ward off interruption—"I had much rather think you declined my own suit because your affections were already given before I was so unhappy as to see you, than that, while your heart was still free, you would not consider me."

Nina was so surprised that for a few minutes she was unable to answer. Allegro had never said a word to her about the proposal which had been made by his family. Up to that moment she had thought he did not himself know of it.

"Heart?" she said, bewildered. "Did you put any heart into the offer that was made? None has ever been shown to me."

"Is there a chance of your considering my suit?" He asked it very seriously.

Nina shook her head, and Allegro sighed as though dejected; then, having paid her this compliment, he became cheerful again and his candor was as delicious as it was astonishing.

"Shall I tell you? Yes, I will! If you had said 'yes,' I should have found it very easy to love you. As you won't accept my name, however—"

"You don't love me, is that it?" Nina burst out laughing, and Allegro joined light-heartedly, as he nodded his agreement. Their gayety attracted the attention of their neighbors, and for a while the conversation became general. It was suggestive of the Tower of Babel. Nina had turned to Porter with a remark in English, but Allegro added to it in Italian. Tornik, whose Italian was only slightly more villainous than his English, chimed in across the corner of the table in French, but he soon forgot himself and broke into German. Nina found herself mixing her sentences like Neapolitan ice cream into four languages, until finally she put her hands over her ears and exclaimed, "*Attendez, aspetarre, warten sie nur,* oh, do let us decide on one tongue at a time!" They all laughed, and then, as is usual among a group of various nationalities, the conversation went on in French.

Finally, Tornik and Allegro got into a discussion about the Austrian influence in Italy, and Nina was left *tête-à-tête* with Eliot Porter.

She had not met him before coming to Rome. He was a Californian. A Westerner, she put it, but he answered her, "Not at all! I am from the Pacific coast!" He was an agreeable man, much liked in Rome, and he was writing a book on Roman society, a fact that greatly amused the Italians. There was some mild and good-naturedly satirical speculation about what he was going to put in it, but beyond the fact that he acknowledged his subject, nothing was known of either his plot or his characters.

"*Do* tell me what you are going to put in your book. Is it of today, or long ago?"

"The story is to be laid in Rome, the theme society, the time the present."

"How fascinating! Ah, please tell me from whom you have drawn your heroine," Nina continued. "Is she rich or poor? Italian, I suppose, and of course young and beautiful! Is the hero a noble duke or an American on the Prisoner of Zenda or Graustark model?"

"Supposing I should tell you that they were yourself, for the one, and our friend Jack over the way, for the other!"

The coupling of her name with Derby's for the second time in less than half an hour struck Nina, and she became absent-minded; then she said vaguely, "But we are not Italians, either of us."

"Neither are my characters! I will tell you," he said, admitting her to his confidence, "I am going to write of the Expatriates—the people who, to those at home, are always said to be 'abroad.' The story from this side of the water is interesting to me. And the Excelsior is an ideal field for observing them."

"I see!" Then ingenuously, "Are you really going to put Jack in your book?"

Porter smiled, amused. "He hardly corresponds to my aimless nomad wandering hither and yon, with neither ambition nor destination! By the way," he added abruptly, "what do you *think* of Jack? I am not asking this, mind you, just to make conversation, but because I am interested in him as a national type. I confess I was beginning to think that no woman could care for the men at home as any woman might for the Europeans, until he came along the other day." There was no doubting Porter's enthusiasm as he added, "He gave me back my ideals of my own country! He is *real*, I tell you. But this trip he is going to take into Sicily—"

"There is no danger in this day, surely!" she interrupted.

"I am not so sure of it, they are pesky devils!" Then, appreciating her uneasiness, he tried to reassure her. "Jack will be all right, he will be well protected. In fact, to show you how little I really fear from the adventure, I am thinking of going with him. My work is getting stale, and a week or two of change of scene would set me up."

"I don't see that your going proves there is no danger. I should never imagine you the type of a coward."

Porter laughed. "Thank you for your good opinion of my type. But I am not at all certain about it myself. If I thought I was going to run any risk of being stabbed in the ribs, or riddled with bullets, I assure you I would preserve my skin very carefully by staying right here. But to go back to John: Did you ever study physiognomy?" He glanced across at Derby as he spoke.

Nina's lips broke into a smile, as she answered, "No. Did you?"

"Yes. I studied that, and palmistry, and graphology, too. Look at John—he has a remarkably interesting head and hand. You are quite wrong," he answered an interjection of Nina's, "his hands are far from ugly! Spatulate fingers show invention and energy. Just look at his thumb! Did you ever see such cool-headed logic or a better balanced will? Why, all in all, I consider him the best-looking man I know! There are plenty with better features, no doubt, but if I'd had my choice as to looks, I should have been his twin."

Nina laughed joyously. "Do you mean it?" It sounded incredible to her, yet she felt strangely pleased—she looked at John from a new point of view. "I think he has a great many good points; there is something strong and admirable about him, but good-looking—never! His features are too uneven, too big-boned."

"Just like a woman!" exclaimed Porter testily. "I suppose you think that apology on your other side a beau ideal!"

Nina glanced critically toward the small features and blond curls of Allegro. "No," she said, "he is much too effeminate."

"Then who is your Adonis?"

"The best-looking man I have ever seen? Well—I think I'd choose the Marchese di Valdo." The pink mounted over her cheeks into her hair, for she thought Porter was going to deride. To her surprise he agreed with her.

"Of his type, yes, he certainly is good; but I prefer John's. I can see how di Valdo would appeal to a girl, though personally I should ask more masculinity, more bone and sinew."

Nina remembered how Giovanni had nearly choked the Great Dane, and she shuddered slightly. "Oh, but he is strong," she exclaimed; "he is strong as a panther! He always makes me think of Bagheera in the Jungle Book."

"Bagheera was warm-blooded; there was truth and affection in him—for Mowgli, at all events. Your friend di Valdo is as cold a proposition as you could find."

Nina thought this last characterization absurd, and said so.

"All right!" Porter answered. "You mark my word. He is a man swayed by the emotions of the moment. He has feeling, yes—but no heart; he has certain inborn principles, but they are racial rather than ethical. His is the code of *Noblesse oblige*, not of the Golden Rule. In a point of honor he is irreproachable, but it is he, himself, who defines the boundaries of his code."

He paused a moment and continued in a more personal tone: "I don't know you very well, Miss Randolph, but you are a girl from home. And—excuse my frankness—you are one of our great heiresses. I am a stranger to you, and that is why I am going to say something—perhaps all the more forcefully because I have only a racial and not a personal interest: but between marrying Giovanni Sansevero—or that Austrian over yonder—or the golden-headed ornament on your right, and such a man as John Derby, no woman with an ounce of sense could for one minute hesitate. The first, by the gift of kings, are noblemen, but John over there, by the grace of God, is a *man!*"

Nina was so deeply stirred by his words that she sat for a little while quite motionless, looking down at her hands, which were clasped in her lap. Then, before she either looked up or answered, the women left the table.

In the drawing-room, as the other women lighted their cigarettes, Nina stood leaning her cheek on her hand as it rested against the mantel—and for some time she gazed down into the fire, while Porter's words echoed and reëchoed through her mind. When she turned away from the fire her attention was caught by an Englishwoman who had thrown herself full length on the sofa. Her person was a curious mixture of cleanliness and untidiness, her face was even polished by soap and scrubbing, but her frock, although probably quite clean, looked anything but fresh, and lying down among the cushions had not improved her hair, which had been frowzily frizzed anyway. Nina would have thought Lady Dorothy an impossible person were it not for the "Lady" which, as Carpazzi put it, "was pushed before the name."

In the meanwhile Lady Dorothy went off into a long disquisition upon the advisability of having couches at formal banquets as in the old Roman days. The illustration which she was at the moment affording was scarcely, to Nina's mind, encouraging to her proposition. She smoked rapidly and let the cigarette ashes spill all down the side of her neck.

"Isn't it funny what a little place the world is?" babbled the late Miss Titherington, cutting short Lady Dorothy's discourse. "Here we are, you and I and John—just the same as though we were back in Bar Harbor! What a lamb of a child you used to be! Only do you remember the day you nearly drowned me? And he had to rescue us both!"

"Just fancy that!" said the Lady Dorothy from her corner of the sofa. "However did it happen?"

"The water in Maine is so cold one dare hardly go in. Nina was a little girl, she got a cramp, and clutched me around the neck."

"The water cold! How very odd! I had a friend in St. Augustine, who said the water was positively hot. I am sure it must have been, as my friend has rheumatism and could never have ventured into a cold bath."

Lady Dorothy lighted a fresh cigarette and waved the old one helplessly around in her fingers. Nina, afraid that she would let it fall upon the trail of ashes down the front of her dress, went to take it from her.

"Oh, thanks." She threw herself even further back into the cushions and now addressed her remarks to the Countess Kate. She was glad to get away from home. She declared London was overrun this season with enormously, disgustingly, rich Americans. No offense to her hostess was meant, but it was really quite shameful whom one got down to associating with, and yet they were so overloaded with dollars that one might as well, she supposed, gather in some of the surplus! Then she coolly asked Nina's name, which she had not caught. Its announcement had the effect of an electric battery. She raised herself on her elbows.

"The Earl of Eagon is looking for a wife," she announced, and then as though the idea of Nina's wealth were still more felt, she continued almost with enthusiasm, "And there is the Duke of Norchester—his estates need a fortune to keep up, but there are none finer in England."

Nina's expression had a curious little note in it that made the Countess Zoya cross the room and sit on the arm of her chair. Her slim fingers ran lightly over Nina's hair, "You poor child!" she said. "Ah, I am glad I was never so rich. If I were so rich I should be dreadful! I would never believe in any one's caring for me. I should doubt even my Carlo! I could not help it!"

"Don't," Nina said, as though in pain. Zoya impulsively put

her arms about her and quickly changed the subject.

"I want to tell you," she said, "I like your friend the engineer—is that what he is? He is very clever, is he not? I am told he is going to relieve the sufferings of the poor Sicilian miners—is he?"

"Suffering?" Nina repeated, wondering. "I don't know. But it is only a business venture, his mining—not a philanthropic one. At least I have not heard about any poor people who are to be relieved."

Zoya put her hands over her eyes and then her ears as though to shut out both sight and sound. "Oh, it is horrible—horrible in the sulphur mines! You have no idea! Nowhere in all the world is life so dreadful." She shuddered, "But I feel sure, somehow, that your friend the American will be able to do something."

They went on talking until their *tête-à-tête* was interrupted by the men coming in from the dining-room. The servants brought in a big card table.

"Are you going to play bridge?" Nina asked, feeling that the answer was obvious.

But the Contessa Masco, taking her cognac at a swallow, glanced at Tornik with a laugh. "Oh, lord, no! Nothing so dull, I hope, in this house!"

Derby joined Nina, and she looked up at him with pride. "I am glad you are here tonight; I seem to be especially glad—" She broke off, but her intonation conveyed unspoken thoughts.

Derby's eyes kindled. "Why especially? Have you a particular reason, really?" His heart beat so hard, because of the sweetness in her expression, that it seemed to him she must hear it pounding, that she must look through the mask he wore, and read his love for her.

But his mask was impenetrable, and Nina answered lightly: "I wonder which reason you would like me to give? I wonder if it would make any real difference to you whether I said just *glad*—or glad because of something?"

He forced himself to speak with a stolidity that walled in securely his threatening emotions. "I am not a bit good at guessing the meaning of sentences that have no direct statement in them. You see, they are not the kind my grammar book taught me!"

Nina smiled. "You like a regular, straight-out, simple sentence with one subject and one predicate, don't you?"

"That's it! And as few qualifying clauses as possible."

"And as your speech is, so are your actions. No time for trivialities. Big, serious things!" To her surprise she felt a sharp pain in her throat.

"What an old bear I must seem to you—" His sentence broke off as the Countess Masco interrupted them.

"Come along, John—you'll play, won't you? We are waiting!" Count Rosso had already deserted Zoya for the green table.

"Do you need me?" Derby asked.

"Of course we do! The more the jollier; it is dreadfully dull without a lot."

Nina and the Countess Zoya sat apart talking together until nearly midnight. Finally, with a yawn, Zoya suggested that they try to break up the party. For a little while they looked on. Not understanding the game of baccarat, Nina watched the faces of the players.

Suddenly she felt uneasy about her uncle, who had taken a place at the table. Knowing no reason why he should not play, she had thought nothing of that. But now he was flushed, and seemed very excited. Unconsciously taking a leaf out of her aunt's book, she laid her hand on his shoulder. Her touch was, in fact, so like that of his wife that the prince started violently, and a short while later relinquished his place.

After the prince dropped out of the game Nina still stood watching. The Countess Kate played as placidly as though she were dealing cards for "old maid," while her husband reminded Nina of a squirrel sitting up and nibbling at a nut. Carlo Olisco was excited but not unnatural. Porter looked gloomy and taciturn. Minotti and Allegro were both tense and keen, the former arrogant, the latter flushed and excited. John Derby, like the Countess Kate, played exactly as he used to play Jack Straws or *besique*, on rainy days in the country.

From where she had been standing Nina could see only the top of Tornik's head and, obeying an idle impulse of curiosity, she crossed to the opposite side of the table. But no sooner had she caught sight of his face than she started as though some one had dashed cold water over her. Tornik! It was unbelievable! His eyes glowed like coals; his lips, half opened, looked dry and burnt, as with that drawing-in motion of the confirmed gambler he stretched out his trembling fingers to grasp the last of the evening's winnings.

Nina was not in love with him—she had never even for a moment fancied that she was. But nevertheless the revelation of his greed struck at her pride, and she seemed to see herself, or rather her own fortune, being grasped with precisely that avidity by those same long, eager fingers. "He, too!" were the words that framed themselves in her thoughts. Tornik, at least, had seemed disinterested, but it was only her gold that he was after—like all the rest.

She turned away abruptly. The Count Olisco left the table and, as her uncle was already waiting, Zoya and she said good-night to the Mascos and left.

On the way home, Sansevero was decidedly nervous. Something was wrong, that was certain—he was as transparent as crystal; a child could not have shown trouble more plainly. They drove the Oliscos home, but after they had left them, Nina put her hand on her uncle's coat sleeve.

"Can't you—tell me?" she asked him.

Sansevero started, then shook his head. "It is nothing!" he said. But he changed his mind almost immediately, took his breath as though to speak, and stopped again. Nina's manner had been very sweet, very sympathetic. The thought of confiding in the girl beside him had not entered his head; but he might as well have tried to dam up a spring, as to keep his confidence from overflowing at the first words of kindness. He seized her hand, and his fingers during a moment of nervous indecision beat a tattoo upon her glove—then he let her hand drop again.

"I am in the most difficult situation."

"Yes—?" Nina encouraged. "Can't I help?—Oh, I wish I *could!*"

"No!" He threw himself into the farthest possible corner of the carriage. "No, no! I could not let you do that!"

Quickly a suspicion of the difficulty crossed her mind. "Uncle Sandro, I want you to tell me! You know that I love Aunt Eleanor better than almost any one in the world. If to help you is to help her—and it is in my power—I really think you ought to tell me."

He weakened, hesitated. "Give me your promise you will not tell Leonora—?"

"You have it!" She put her hand back into his.

"It is this, then: I am the weakest man imaginable. Tonight I had no idea of playing; I held out for some time, but the temptation was too strong at the end. Also what I lost was very little, but the money was a sum we had put aside to pay household expenses. If I do not pay them, Leonora must know of it."

Between the lines Nina divined a good deal of the whole story. Other vague suspicions that had come to her here and there helped somewhat to the conclusion.

Already they had driven into the courtyard and the footman was holding open the door. Nina jumped out quickly and entered the palace. In the antechamber she stopped for her uncle to catch up with her. "Just wait a moment," she said; "we can finish our conversation quickly." She spoke rapidly and in English.

"How much is it?"

"Five hundred *lire.*"

She caught her breath. "Do you mean to say that *you*—the Prince Sansevero, the owner of this palace, are in need of a hundred dollars, and don't know where to get it? You shall have it tomorrow, the first thing."

Then suddenly she added: "Uncle Sandro—I want you to tell me something! Will you swear on your honor to answer the truth? If you deceive me, I will never forgive you to my dying day!"

He looked at her, puzzled. There was no doubt as to the gravity of her tone. "I will answer if I can." He said it not without alarm.

"Does your brother gamble? Is he also like Tornik and you?" She had no thought for the stigma of her words, and Sansevero was not so small that he resented them.

"No. I can answer that easily enough. Giovanni has not one drop of the gambling blood. That I can swear to you by the name of my mother!" He made the sign of the cross.

Nina sighed with relief. "I'll send Celeste to you with the money in the morning, and you can trust me—I will never let Aunt Eleanor know!" She said it sympathetically and kindly enough, but her tone was a little constrained. "Good-night!"

And then quickly she left him. She felt sure that her uncle had spoken the truth, and that Giovanni was not a gambler; but as she went down the long corridors she felt a sharp contraction in her throat. "Dear—poor—precious Auntie Princess!" she whispered to herself.

CHAPTER XVIII

FAVORITA DRIVES A BARGAIN

As the winter progressed, Favorita's temper showed so little improvement that those whose duty brought them in contact with her at the theatre were on the verge of resigning their posts. Her dresser had a thoroughly cowed expression; her manager consumed more black cigars than were good for him; the *corps de ballet* had hysterics singly and indignation councils *en masse*. In fact, the call-boy, who seemed to enjoy tormenting her, was the only member of the company who took her rages cheerfully.

Finally even Giovanni became uneasy; a well-bred woman could be counted on in given circumstances to do thus and so, but Favorita was of lowest peasant birth: her people were of the mountain districts, so primitive in thought and habit that her early training had taught her obedience to nothing higher than impulse. Superficially, she submitted to the dictates of civilization, just as a half-wild animal submits to the control of his trainer. And in a very real sense Giovanni occupied, in relation to her, the trainer's position. He was the force that held her in check; but though to the audience of the world he appeared perfectly at ease, a definite apprehensiveness underlay his seeming composure.

Matters at last came to a crisis. Giovanni was about to leave the palace one morning a day or two after the Masco dinner, when a neatly dressed woman passed him on the grand stairway. She was wearing a thick veil, but he had an eye for outline and he knew that there was only one woman in Rome with just that half-floating lightness of movement. At once he blocked her way.

She was forced to halt; but her feet did not stand quite still, and there was an effect of briefly suspended motion in her attitude, as though she sought a chance to dart past him.

"Good-morning, signorina!" Giovanni's urbanity was for the benefit of the footmen. For a few seconds there was a straightening of her figure; poised for flight, she held her head a little to one side as she swiftly scanned his face.

Giovanni dropped his voice. "I was just on my way to see you. Come, *cara mia*," he said persuasively. "I have something I want to talk over with you—it is impossible here with lackeys listening to everything we may say. Come, dear."

She looked at him a moment, wavering, then shrugged her shoulders. "Very well," she said, and descended the stairs at his

side. They crossed the wide hall, and she stopped to gaze about it in wonder and curiosity, even though she did not appreciate the splendor of its proportions. The great *baldachino*, of blue and silver, surmounting the Sansevero arms, held her attention.

"Do the broken silver chains in your coat of arms represent mercy or weakness?" she asked.

"Both, probably," he answered grimly, as he caught the sound of an automobile chugging in the courtyard. Feeling sure that it was Nina's car, he slipped his arm through Favorita's to urge her forward, whereupon she grew suspicious and lagged purposely. She looked deliberately about, as though she were a tourist intent upon finding every object starred in Baedeker. To his inward rage and chagrin, Giovanni realized his mistake in having attempted to hurry her, and now changed his tactics. Although his every nerve was strained to catch the sound of Nina's approaching footfall, he went into a long, prosy dissertation upon the history of the ceiling, dwelling purposely upon the dullest facts he could think of, until his tormentor was glad enough to leave.

Once outside the building, Giovanni breathed more freely, although the sight of the automobile confirmed his apprehension. Hailing a cab, he put Favorita into it and got in after her. They had not gone more than five hundred yards when Nina, alone in the car, passed them. Giovanni had stooped over quickly so that she might not recognize him; but Favorita took no notice of this, or anything else, and they drove on in a silence broken only by occasional and casual remarks. It was not until they were safely within her apartment that he demanded:

"And now, Fava, perhaps you will have the goodness to explain to me what you were doing at the Palazzo Sansevero when I saw you, and how you got past the *portiere?*"

"At least it shows you that what I try to do I accomplish," she retorted with an air of bravado. She leaned her elbows on a little table, looking across at Giovanni, her lips parted, her eyes dancing. "Do you wish to hear? Very well. I have a friend who gives the American heiress lessons in Italian. She says it is easy—one has only to talk Italian and make her talk, and tell her when she makes mistakes. My friend is sick. She sent a letter, which I intercepted, and I went in her place. Why not?" Then suddenly her little teeth locked tightly, and she spoke between them savagely—"I'd be a teacher worth employing. I could talk Italian to her that she would never forget! Nor would she forget *me*, either!"

Giovanni's teeth locked quite as tightly as hers. "Will you hush? You must be insane! I told you from the beginning that I would not advertise myself with you. I told you also that if you made a scene, or if you ever tried to interfere with my family or my private life, at that moment all would end between us." As he spoke, Favorita looked frightened, but in a flash her manner changed completely. Long association with him had not been without its lessons, and she answered as sweetly as though no disagreement had ever come between them; as though there were no incongruity between their suspended discussion and her interrupting sentence. "Giovannino," she cooed, "I have had a great offer, an astounding offer from Vienna."

He saw his opportunity. His manner therefore, changed as rapidly as hers had done, and with every appearance of sympathy and interest he asked for her news. She told him with triumph the details of her offer from the manager of a Viennese theatre for a ten weeks' engagement at a stupendous salary.

"You must accept—by all means!" Not a trace of the relief he felt crept into his expression; he looked sad, but thoroughly resigned. "It is time," he added cleverly, "that you should make a name for yourself that is cosmopolitan and not alone of Italy."

So far they had been sitting on either side of a small table, but now Favorita arose and went around to him. Pushing the table away, she sat on his knee, and, with one arm about his neck, held up his chin with her other hand. Then, deliberately, she looked into his eyes with that level, determined steadiness which makes no compromise. She spoke very quietly, so quietly that he was more than ever uneasy. Her turbulence was annoying, but this calmness was ominous.

"I shall accept the offer on one condition:—you go to Vienna with me!"

Giovanni looked quite as though the gates of Paradise were opening before him. Even Favorita believed his enthusiasm genuine as he exclaimed, "Ah, that would be charming!" Then he seemed to be considering the matter eagerly. "That I *want* to go with you—of that there can be no doubt! I am merely wondering how it can be managed."

Now that she seemed to be getting her own way, and her jealousy was allayed, Favorita was soft, and sweet, and affectionate as a little black cat. "Rosso is going to Hungary," she purred. "You can easily say you are going with him on his trip, whereas you can really be in Vienna!"

"That sounds perfect!" he returned gayly; "at least you can accept the manager's offer!"

"Do you promise to go with me? You must swear it!" He hesitated as he rapidly turned the situation over in his mind. Now that he had determined to marry Nina, the main thing was to keep Favorita away, for, should she have an opportunity to unburden her heart to the heiress, that would be the end of his matrimonial chances. But if he could get the dancer to Vienna, and keep her there, then find an excuse for at least a short absence from her, he could come back to Rome, win Nina, be married at once—and then let come what would! An independent American girl would throw him over, he knew that; but a wife would be different! A wife would have to forgive.

"Will you promise?" repeated Favorita.

"Yes, I promise," he said. "Come, we will fill in the contract!"

CHAPTER XIX

A CHALLENGE, AND AN ANSWER

Nina had intended taking her Italian teacher out with her in the automobile. She did this quite often, as it was as easy to practice Italian conversation in a motor-car as anywhere else. But after half an hour—Favorita was nearly that late—she had given up waiting and telephoned Zoya Olisco suggesting that they two spend the day at Tivoli. Zoya agreed, and Nina was on her way to fetch her when she passed Giovanni and Favorita. But she neither saw the former nor recognized the latter.

It was after six o'clock when Nina returned from Tivoli, and she had to hurry to dress for an early dinner, as it was the Sanseveros' regular Lenten evening at home.

Nina particularly liked these informal receptions, where the company was composed, for the most part, of really interesting, agreeable people. There was always music, generally by amateur performers; occasionally there was some other form of impromptu entertainment, an impersonation or a recitation. Throughout the evening there was the simplest sort of buffet supper: tea, bouillon—a claret cup, perhaps, and possibly chocolate, little cakes, and sandwiches; never more. But the princess was one of those hostesses whose personality thoroughly pervades a house; a type which is becoming rare with every change in our modern civilization, and without which people might as well congregate in a hotel parlor. Each guest at the Palazzo Sansevero carried away the impression that not only had he been welcome himself, but that his presence had added materially to the enjoyment of others.

Early in the evening Nina was standing with Giovanni a little apart. Giovanni was unusually quiet, and both had fallen into reverie, from which Nina was aroused by the sudden announcement of a jarring name. Like the ceaseless beating of the waves upon a beach, she had heard the long rolling titles, "Sua Excellenza la principessa di Malio," "Il Conte e la Contessa Casabella," "Donna Francesca Dobini," "Sua Excellenza il Duca e la Duchessa Astarte," and then—"Messa Smeet!"

Nina felt a swift pity for the beautiful woman who was forced to suffer the ignomiy of being thus announced. She had herself been daily conscious of that same flatness when, after the long announcement of her aunt's and uncle's names, came the blankness of "Messa Randolf."

And in that moment, divining the impression made upon her mind, Giovanni seized his opportunity. His eyes looked ardently into hers, his smile was transporting as, with all the warmth of which his voice was capable, he said, "Donna Nina Sansevero, Marchesa di Valdo!"

Nina's heart fluttered strangely, her will was swayed by the moment's thrill, as she heard him continuing: "It can surely not surprise you to hear in spoken words what has long been in my heart to—" But his sentence was broken off abruptly, for a sudden thinning of the crush revealed the Contessa Potensi close beside them. Heedless of Nina, the contessa demanded that Giovanni take her into the supper room for a cup of tea, and Nina was left with Carpazzi, who had at that moment also joined them. He took no notice of her absent-mindedness and kept the conversation going briskly without much help from her, until gradually she became able to focus her attention upon him.

He talked of many things and finally of Cecelia Potenzi. That he should have spoken the name of the girl he loved was quite foreign to his, or in fact to any, Italian nature. But by now Nina had become thoroughly interested in what he was telling her and her sympathetic eyes had a way of urging confidences, and besides, as Carpazzi knew, she was very fond of Cecelia. He spoke quite frankly therefore of his hopes and plans. He was desperately interested in Derby's mining project because he owned a piece of property within a few miles of Vencata and if the Sansevero sulphur mines turned out well probably all the land in the neighborhood would also be leased by Derby's company, and it might be that he and Cecelia could be married.

Nina had already observed the young girl in question and she and Carpazzi made their way toward her. Gradually other young people joined them until a merry group was formed at that side of the room.

The music at that moment was by a young violinist, a *protégé* of the Princess Sansevero's (a brother, by the way, of the peasant Marcella, whose marriage to Pedro the princess had arranged). The boy had real talent, and the princess had denied herself not a few things in order to help him complete his education.

At the close of his second selection the young violinist came over to her, with that look of devoted allegiance which cannot be imitated, and the princess held out her hand for him to kiss. "I am so pleased with your success," she said to him. "Come, I want to present you to the Duchessa Astarte, who was much delighted with your playing." Smiling, she led him away.

The young man traversed the rooms with perfect ease and unconsciousness—this peasant boy who four years previously had run ragged and barefooted, begging for soldos from the tourists who were driving out to Torre Sansevero! From one of the doorways Sansevero watched them. "*Per Dio*, she is wonderful, my Leonora!" he exclaimed to the Countess Masco, whom he had taken to the supper room. "Look what she has made of that ragamuffin! You Americans are an extraordinary people." The countess, as she watched the prince's open admiration of his wife, showed the finest, the most generous side of her cheerful nature. Her expression was scarcely less admiring than his own.

"I'd like well enough to take all the credit for my country," she returned, with her usual good humor, "but in Eleanor's case it is the woman and not the nationality that is wonderful—" Then she added brusquely, "I'm glad you appreciate her." The next moment she tossed the topic aside and discoursed noisily of the latest Roman gossip.

About this time the Count and Countess Olisco were announced. Seeing Derby, who had arrived just ahead of them, Zoya walked up to him without hesitation or manœuvre. "I should like to talk to you," she said; "will you take me to a seat? There is one over there."

He gave her his arm and led her to a sofa at the far end of the room. "Have you been out to Torre Sansevero?" she asked when they had sat down.

"No. We had planned to motor out next week, but I must go to Sicily tomorrow, so the motor trip is postponed until I come back. You asked as though you had something special in mind. Had you?"

"Yes. I might as well tell you—though maybe you know—there is a rumor that a Sansevero painting—the Raphael Madonna—has been sold out of the country. The way I know is secret; but through somebody connected with the Government I have learned that there are grave suspicions against the prince."

Derby gave her his full attention, but said nothing. "Everybody knows," continued the contessa, "that he has spent all his wife's money in gambling, and that they have sold everything that is not covered by the family entail." Her listener did not know it, but his face betrayed no surprise. "This picture, they say, has been smuggled out of the country to a rich American." Her face grew troubled and she spoke lower and more distinctly. "I do not find it possible to think that Sansevero did such a thing. He is weak, if you like; he would fall into temptation; he might gamble or make love to a pretty woman"—she shrugged her shoulders—"but that he would do anything really against the law, I don't believe. Yet—I have never seen such furs as the princess wears this winter. Can't you find out about the picture? Everybody believes it is in America. Think what it would be if Sansevero were put in prison! But I am sure you will set everything straight."

"Your faith in me is flattering, to say the least," he laughed. "But you seem to think that finding an object in America is as simple as though it were mislaid in a fishing village. Do you realize the vastness of the territory which I am to search in the twinkling of an eye?"

"No, no! You must not laugh. I am very serious. I know that America is a land in which everything may be accomplished, even though I may have a false idea of its size. And in you, as an American, my faith is unbounded. You see, I feel convinced that it all depends on you!" Then, under the impulsion of her enthusiasm she clapped her hands together as she exclaimed: "Oh, I am sure you will clear the prince! And then, like the hero in all good story books, win the reward."

"And the reward?" he queried. "What is it to be? Unfortunately, you are asking me to save a prince—a poor prince at that, with no favors to bestow. In the good story books it is always a beautiful princess. To be sure," he added, "the princess is as beautiful as one could wish, but alas! she is married."

"I do not find you at all amiable," the contessa pouted. "I am serious—very serious, and you make fun."

"Not at all. I am very serious, and you talk of fairy tales. Still, if you are my fairy godmother, there is no knowing what stroke of fortune may await me in Sicily." Then, changing his tone, he said earnestly: "I am really sorry, but I am afraid I shall have to leave the picture question until I come back."

"You are going straight off to Sicily?"

"Yes."

"To be gone how long?"

"I don't know; I have no idea. Weeks, perhaps. Months, very likely; why do you ask?"

"May I say something—something very frank to you?" Zoya leaned forward with a sudden direct impulse.

"Say what you please, by all means!" Derby braced himself for her remark, but even so he colored as she said: "Are you in love with Nina? Please, don't be angry; I don't ask you to answer. But if you are, I can't see why you go away to work mines and such things. I should have married her long ago had I been you."

Derby's eyes blazed. "Do you mean I should try to marry her and live on her money?"

"Why not? Since she has enough for two—enough for twenty! There is no need to be so furious. *Per l'amore di Dio!* You Americans have always the ears up, listening for a sound that you can fly at!" Languorously she leaned back among the cushions of the sofa. "It is all so silly—your idea of life." And then she stopped and looked at him curiously. "What *is* your idea of life?"

"Life? One might put it in three words: One must work!"

Zoya shook her head—she did it charmingly. "No, no," she said softly; "you are altogether wrong—though I also can put it in three words. Life lies in this: One must love. That's all there is!"

The conversation ended there, for the Duke Scorpa and Count Masco came up to speak to the contessa. Derby arose and was about to leave when the duke stopped him. Masco sat down to talk with Zoya, and Scorpa spoke to Derby in an undertone. "I hear you are going to Sicily tomorrow?"

"Yes, I leave early in the morning."

"Take my advice"—his glance was sinister—"and stay away."

Derby smiled frankly. "May I ask why?"

"Because your process will not work."

"That might be taken in two ways," Derby rejoined: "either that you believe my patents useless, or else that some means will be taken to prevent my trying them. I rather wonder—after our conversation on the subject—if you intend a threat?" He spoke without stress of feeling, quite simply, in fact.

The duke's unctuous smile was not wholly pleasant to see. "That is for you to decide. Tomorrow morning you intend to go. That is not far off; but you have until then to reconsider your refusal to sell me your patents. I made you a fair offer, which I should in your place accept. However, if you go to Sicily"—he spread out his hands with a shrug—"I shall have warned you, and whatever comes will be off my conscience."

For answer Derby spoke quietly, but with clear, level distinctness. "I go tomorrow to Vencata, to work a piece of land which is the property of the Prince and Princess Sansevero. As their representative, I am vested with every legal right to apply my invention to the mine known as the 'Little Devil.' And I may add"—he put it casually—"that back of me is the full strength and protection of the United States Government." He looked straight into the small rat-like eyes nearly a foot below his own. Then with a smile he bowed to the Contessa Zoya and went in search of the Princess

Sansevero, to say good-by.

He found her in the adjoining room, absorbed in the music; and luckily there was an empty chair beside her, into which he quietly dropped. She smiled her welcome as he sat down beside her, but she had accepted her young countryman into too good a friendship to make either of them feel the need of rushing into speech. After a little she turned to him; even then her sentence seemed to complete a conversation interrupted rather than a new one begun, "Above all, do not forget to present Sandro's letter to the Archbishop! I know you will be drawn to him. His Eminence is one of those rare persons who have not waited to die to become angels." She smiled. "I am sure you will be safe under his protection."

"I wish you would tell me, Princess, why there is so much talk of protection—it sounds as though I were going to explore the interior of Africa! I shall be, at most, twenty-four hours away from Rome."

"There is no knowing what you are going to explore"—a shade of anxiety had come into her face. "The Mafia is there, the people are ignorant, and the lava wastes are as desolate and wild as any spot in Africa. I hope there will be no danger, but it is well to take precautions before going into such a country. You will promise me won't you?—to follow the directions of his Eminence." Unconsciously she put her hand against her heart.

Derby gave his promise easily, and she held out her hand. He kissed it after the European custom; and as he did so he felt her fingers tighten over his, as she whispered with a little underlying emotional vibration, "God bless you, my dear boy!—and a safe return."

Vaguely, as he went through the rooms in search of Nina, the princess's words echoed through his mind, and through some unknown train of suggestion he remembered that Miller, the butler in New York, had wished Nina a "safe return." The association of the two seemed ridiculous, yet a thought held: Was it at all certain that she was going to return home? Was he, perhaps, not going to return from Sicily? He put himself in the category of idiots and banished the idea. But the echo of the blessing that the princess had given him settled softly upon his sensibilities. "God bless *her!*" he said almost aloud.

Presently he found Nina, unapproachably hemmed in, and too near the music to talk. For a moment she hesitated, on the verge of extricating herself or encouraging him to enter the circle despite the general disturbance it must cause. But the moment passed. His lips framed "Good-by" and hers answered, both smiled brightly—and that was the parting.

Derby was in many ways a fatalist—not one of those who thought that by sitting still the gifts from the horn of fortune would tumble into his lap; but one of those who believe (to use his own expression), in pegging away at the thing in hand; further than that, what was to be, would be.

As Derby descended the stairs he encountered the Countess Masco. "Hello, John!" she exclaimed, and then as she held him by the arm, her voice came down to what for her was a low whisper; at twenty feet any one could have overheard her, but fortunately the hall was deserted, save for a couple of footmen standing at the green baize door that led to the outer stairs of the courtyard. "Have you heard the news? Giovanni Sansevero agreed to go on a cruise to Malta with Rosso, and Rosso won't let him out of it! You may imagine he does not relish leaving Rome just now, especially with you again out of the field!"

Derby was not given an opportunity either to accept or to resent her intrusion into his affairs, for the dashing lady immediately fled, and Derby went on. As he waited for his cab, he felt inclined to go back and try to see Nina. He was letting her drift very, very far away. But while he was hesitating, his cab drove up, and without more ado he jumped into it and drove to his hotel. As soon as he reached his room, he began a letter to Nina; but all the things he had vowed to himself not to say, swarmed to the very tip of his pen. He threw it down, therefore, and tore up the paper that showed, under "Dear Nina," an erased "Darl—" After pacing the floor a while, he again picked up the pen, but this time he wrote to Mr. Randolph. At the end of a letter of details relating to the mines, he added:

> "There are rumors now agitating people over here and likely to become public property, that the Sansevero Madonna has been smuggled out of the country. I have reason to believe that the Raphael you showed me in New York is not the duplicate you were led to suppose, but the Sansevero picture. How it was sold, I have not yet discovered, though I do not believe the prince guilty of violating the laws. But I know the Government has its secret agents at work upon the case because of the seeming luxury of the princess, whose new furs and automobile are known to be far beyond her present income. I more than suspect that these luxuries are the result of Nina's generosity, but if the Sansevero picture *is* the one you have, the affair will end badly for the prince. At all events, I consider it best to

carry the matter direct to you."

While Derby was writing to Mr. Randolph, an animated conversation was taking place in a little room on the ground floor of the gigantic palace of the Scorpas. The doors were bolted, and the two inmates of the apartment talked in whispers.

"You understand your instructions?"

"Yes, Excellency."

"Repeat them."

"I take the boat tomorrow—go to Vencata. Keep watch upon the Americano—the one whose name I have here."

"John Derby, yes. But he is very big—a giant. Make no mistake, find the one who is the *padrone!* And—? Continue!"

"I am to watch if it is true that he begins working the 'Little Devil,' and if so—I know the rest. It is nothing! A pig's skin is thick—a man's thin!" As he said this he glanced at the duke, and there was a sinister gleam in the man's deep-set eyes, and beneath the sharp nose the mouth was hard and straight, like a seam across the face.

The duke nodded as though satisfied. "It may be well for you to remember," he observed impressively, "that the reward will make you and yours easy for life."

The man saluted respectfully, but with a dogged surliness that revealed no loyalty. Yet there was in his look a hint of fanatical intensity. Outside in the passageway he smiled grimly. For once the errand on which the duke had sent him fell in with his own inclinations. He opened a window and looked out through the gratings into the night. In his heart he bore no love for the duke, but he was by race and inheritance a dependent of the house of Scorpa. It had always been so—the dukes had been masters since time immemorial. The present duke had made the lives of Sicilians terrible enough, but he, Luigi Calluci, would have no stranger Americano forcing his people to work that hell-mine of the "Little Devil"!

CHAPTER XX

HIS EMINENCE, THE ARCHBISHOP OF VENCATA

Barely two days after the evening at the Palazzo Sansevero, Derby was driving up the Sicilian hills towards the palace—courtesy gave it the name—of the venerable Archbishop of Vencata. Porter, in company with Tiggs and Jenkins—Derby's American assistants—had been left at the inn in the town, but Derby was anxious to present his letter as soon as possible, in order that there might be no delay in commencing work at the mines.

The carriage in which Derby sat had at first sight seemed liable to tumble apart, like so many separate pieces of mosaic puzzle, and he had taken his place on the old cloth cushion rather dubiously. But the driver gayly, and with every appearance of confidence in himself and his equipage, had cracked his whip and shouted all the names in the calendar to the horses, whose muscles gradually became sufficiently taut to impel them onward. A few dozen yards having been made without mishap, Derby felt that the special protection of Providence must be over them, and he leaned back contentedly, puffing at his pipe and enjoying to the full the witchery of a Sicilian sunset. The rickety conveyance clattered slowly up a winding road that seemed like a white band tied about the mountainside, holding here little terraced vineyards, there a huddling group of houses that else would surely have slipped into the ravine. For a short distance it hung out over the sea, then cut inward, as though the band of white had been laced in and out among the silvery sprays of the olive leaves.

Below it all, and beyond, lay the Mediterranean, its blue waters now deepened to indigo, shading into wide lakes of purple, under the reflection of the setting sun, which, like a great red lantern, seemed sinking into the sea. A sharp turn inward and upward brought the conveyance shambling into a little courtyard. It halted before the doorway of a low, white-washed house smothered in semi-tropical vines, which extended from the eaves over a pergola built along the wall at the terrace edge. Beneath this arbor was a rustic seat, on the cushions of which a big gray cat sat up slowly, and stared at the intruders with insolent, unwinking eyes.

A woman's voice droned a dirgeful song that had a half Oriental, half negro suggestion in its monotonous pitch, while from afar, like an echo over the mountainside, came faintly the wailing cadence of the *caramella* of some shepherd boy, and the tinkle of goat bells, interrupted by the hoot of little owls crying through the dusk.

The bells of the flapping harness settled into silence, the droning sing-song ceased, and from the stone flagging within came the shuffle of wooden shoes. An old woman, in the inevitable dark stuff dress of her class, and the blue apron gay-bordered with red and white, stood in the doorway. Her big hoop earrings fell to her shoulders, but were partly hidden by the kerchief which she held over her head with one hand, as if in fear of a draught, while with the other she still grasped the door latch.

To Derby's inquiry as to whether His Eminence were at home, she responded suspiciously—almost contemptuously, as she looked him over from head to toe. Certainly, His Exaltedness was at home. What should one of his venerability be doing abroad at such an hour!

Derby's bow was apologetic. Would Signora have the kindness to deliver the letter which he tendered her?

She turned the envelope over in her hands, looked again at the stranger, and at last stood aside so that he might enter.

Derby waited in the dim, low-ceilinged passageway, which suggested anything but the antechamber of an archbishop's palace. Presently a door opened, a feeble yellow haze filtered into the corridor, and the old woman reappeared and led Derby into a small, stone-paved apartment illumined by a single flickering lamp of the most primitive design, by the light of which the archbishop had evidently been reading. As soon as Derby entered, the venerable prelate arose. In his long *sottana* of violet he looked strangely diminutive and feminine; his pale skin and mild eyes, and the soft white hair like a fringe beneath his velvet cap—all gave an impression of great gentleness, an impression heightened by contrast with the bare, white-washed walls and rigorously meager furnishing of the cell-like room. With the courteous manner of all southern countries, the archbishop placed the best chair for his guest, and said smilingly:

"Do you speak Italian? Ah—I am glad you understand that language! My French is very failing, and as for Inglese—*non lo conosco*. It is too difficult at my age. If I were younger I should like to learn your tongue." He said this with inimitable grace, and added with a gentle inclination: "You are Americano, are you not? Your land has done much for my people! But tell me, Signore, in what way may I serve you? Sua Eccellenza il Principe Sansevero places you under our protection, but he does not tell us what it is that has brought you to us." The archbishop, leaning back in his chair, might so have sat for his portrait—his white hands folded one over the other, and the great amethyst ring on the third finger of his right hand seeming to reflect the paler shadings in the folds of his gown.

"I have come, your Eminence," said Derby, going to the point at once, "to work the 'Little Devil' mine." Before the archbishop could utter a protest, he continued very quickly and distinctly: "I know just such mines as that which are being operated now without danger or suffering to the miners."

Then, briefly as possible, he went on to outline his system of mining. There was no necessity, he said, for miners to descend below the surface of the earth, and he would need only a dozen men—instead of the many workers, including women and children, that were now employed. To Derby's surprise, the old man seemed troubled.

"I grow old, Signore; one does not easily take in new ideas! By your method—am I right?—you will employ a dozen men in place of a hundred. That troubles me, though your plan seems good. If there are but a small handful needed, it must put the others out of work. The mines are hard. A harder existence cannot well be imagined—but the good God must know it is for the best, since he allows it to continue. To be sure," he interrupted himself sadly, "he calls them to him soon!"

"You mean they die young in the mines? That is what I have been told."

"Yes, Signore, in their twenty-eighth year the people are at the end of life; at the age of twelve they are already stooped and wrinkled old men and women. For the children it is most terrible; it is they who climb up the high ladders out of the pits in the earth—it gives one a foretaste of inferno to see such things. *Cosi Dio, m' ajuti*, it is true! Yet so they live—otherwise they must die. What can we do? Since the Santa Maria does not intervene, the poor must work or starve. They have not the money to go away to the country beyond the sea, to America, the land of plenty! If some of the rich abundance might be brought to my people—" He shook his head, looking, it seemed, beyond the white walls of the room, as though he saw a vision.

Then slowly, carefully, Derby explained. It was to bring some of the customs of the land of plenty that he had come. He would pay the men—the father, the brother, the big son—more money than had been earned hitherto by the whole family. No, His Eminence did not understand—the work was not to be harder, but easier! And for the reason that he had already explained: Machinery would take the place of children's hands; steel pipes, and not human beings, would descend into the stifling fumes. He wanted to get a few intelligent men to go with their families to the deserted village clustered about the "Little Devil."

Still the old man sat, looking straight before him.

"All that you tell me, Signore," he said at last, his voice echoing a sweetness, a cheerful patience that was doubtless the keynote to his nature—"it all sounds very beautiful; but, indeed, it cannot be! The great Duke Scorpa has given the matter much thought. The mine owners cannot pay the people more—there is scarcely any profit as it is. The duke has often told me this himself, so I know it to be true."

Derby thereupon said that the great Duke Scorpa had doubtless done everything possible, and that under the old method there had been no help for the conditions, but—and again he expressed himself as clearly as possible—with the new method and with machinery, one man could do the work of many. So the wages might be trebled and yet the mines be made to pay.

As Derby talked, a faint color mounted in the cheeks of the archbishop—his eyes grew eagerly wistful, and at last he leaned forward in his chair, his voice almost breathless as he asked, "Can such a thing be true—that in your country the father can earn sufficient that the little children need not work? Ah, Signore—who knows?—who knows?—may be at last the cry of the *bambinos* has reached the throne of the Santa Vergine!" He sat again silent, but this time with a smile on his lips. Then the old woman appeared in the doorway and the archbishop arose.

"It is the hour for my supper," he said. "I shall esteem it an honor if you will break bread with me." Derby was about to decline, thinking it better to return later, but the manner of the old man left no doubt as to the genuineness of his invitation, and Derby accepted. In the adjoining room a small table was set with very few utensils. Two plates, two forks, two spoons, a cup, and a wine glass apiece—that was all. After the blessing, they were served a frugal meal of bread and goats' milk, a pudding of macaroni, and a plate of figs; there was also wine, acid and thin, which the good Marianna—for so the housekeeper was called—had doubtless pressed herself.

Her son Teobaldo, who waited at table, was dressed in some semblance of a livery—black broadcloth and a white tie. The archbishop ate sparingly—he drank a little of the milk, and tasted a piece of fruit, but his conversation with his guest seemed to satisfy him far more than food could do.

Full of the hope of relief for his people, he now turned to plans for the Signore Americano's protection. Throughout the mountains, the hard life had made a hard people, he said, and unfriendly to foreigners. What could they expect from the hands of strangers when their own nobility, even their priests, were powerless to help! But the Signore should be put under the guidance of Padre Filippo—and also there should be two *carabinieri* for protection. Besides, Padre Filippo would recommend carpenters and mechanics of Vencata Minore—the village nearest the "Little Devil"—good men and honest, who would help in the work.

The meal ended, they returned to the living room. The old woman fussed at the wick of the lamp and then placed a book close to the light and opened it at the page marked by a bit of paper. The archbishop smiled. "She takes good care of me, my Marianna. Once she lost my place, but she is very careful."

Derby looked at the page beneath the flickering dimness. "Does Your Eminence read by this light?"

"Oh, yes, a little. By day I can see nearly as well as ever, but in the evening I can read only the books that have large print—and only for a little time. But what would you have, Signore? My eyesight may not any longer be like that of a boy." Then he added: "The good sun brings now each day a longer time to read, and perhaps by the time another winter makes the days again grow short, I shall be near the Great Light that knows no setting."

"You might have a good lamp and see very well," suggested Derby.

"A lamp? But in this I burn olive oil. It is very good oil, Signore—no one makes it better than Marianna! The reading at night is only for young eyes." Again he smiled.

With difficulty he wrote a letter of direction to Padre Filippo and affixed his seal. Also he promised that two *carabinieri* should be at the inn at eight o'clock on the following morning, to accompany the expedition to the mines. And they should carry a letter to Donna Marcella—in her house the Americans had better lodge. From there they could with ease go each day on muleback to the "Little Devil."

At last Derby arose to leave. And then, although he was not of the Roman faith, he swiftly bent and kissed the ring on the thin, white hand that had been placed in his own. Into the archbishop's eyes came a look of tenderness that yet seemed tinged by a vague fear, as he laid his free hand on the bent head and gave his blessing, "*Deus te benedicet, meum filium.* May you fulfil your hopes for my people in safety!" Very slightly the old man's voice broke.

Derby stood at his full height, towering by head and shoulders over the archbishop as he again thanked him for his hospitality and his protection. He walked back to the inn, his mind full of many things. At the *ufficio della posta* he glanced up, hesitated, and then, with a smile, went in and wrote out the following telegram:

"Miss Nina Randolph,
"Palazzo Sansevero,
"Rome.
    "Send immediately by express one good Rochester burner lamp and barrel of kerosene to
    "Sua Eminenza,
        "L'Arcivescovo di Vencata,
            "John."

CHAPTER XXI

THE SULPHUR MINES

It was nearly nine o'clock the next morning before Derby's party was ready to start. The pack mules, with a bulging load on either side, looked like great bales on legs. Long steel pieces needed for the drills were strapped lengthwise between two mules. The saddled animals, which were to carry the members of the party were held at a short distance while the men were seeing to the final preparations. Four horses had been procured for Derby, Porter, Tiggs, and Jenkins; the *carabinieri* had their own horses, and Padre Filippo his mule.

As it happened, the priest had come to Vencata the evening before, so that the archbishop had been able to turn over at once to his especial guidance the Americanos who had been sent by the Blessed Virgin to rescue the *bambinos* from the inferno of the mines. Padre Filippo was short, rotund, with a ruddy complexion and a cheerful crop of carrot-colored hair. The two *carabinieri* were splendid specimens of men, but after all, to say *carabinieri* is enough: for the Italian cavalry must stand not only a physical, but also a moral examination that goes back three generations. It is not sufficient for a candidate to be above suspicion himself; his father and his father's father must have been so as well. These two men were both over six feet, lean and dark-skinned, with that trace of the Arab which one sees all through the people of Sicily; and they were silent and serious, in great contrast to another type of Sicilians who smile much. They wore the *carabiniere* uniform for the mountain districts—a double-breasted coat with two rows of silver buttons, coat tails bordered with red, two strips of red down the trouser seams, a visored cap, and high black boots. They were mounted on magnificent black horses, with rifles hung across their saddles.

Finally, as the procession started and the hoofs clattered on the hard road leading up over the mountain, people crowded out on the little iron balconies, heads appeared at the windows— heads that seemed gigantic by comparison with the miniature houses, which were painted brilliant pink and blue, mauve and Naples yellow.

As the road ascended, it turned inward away from the sea, and after a short distance narrowed into a rocky mountain path that looked like the dry bed of a stream, winding through the wilderness. After an hour's ride the character of the landscape changed. The semi-tropical vegetation grew gradually sparse, and after a while in the distance, seemingly in the midst of the path, a great rock loomed gigantic and gaunt, cutting in two the blue dome of the sky. Still farther on, they came upon stretches of straggling wild peach, olive, and lemon trees. Beyond again, tangles of hawthorn were interspersed with patches of dried weeds and grass. But as they neared the mining district the soil was bleak and barren. The mountain rivers were dry, and their beds made yawning gaps as though the earth had violently shuddered at her own desolation.

At last, about noon, they came to the village of Vencata Minore, which stood in a little plain of green. The house of Donna Marcella was set on a slight eminence and, compared with the surrounding habitations, was quite pretentious. It was kalsomined white, had a courtyard of its own, and back of it was a little fruit and flower garden. Donna Marcella was a buxom, thrifty, and dominating woman. Had she been a man she would assuredly have migrated to America and become a captain of industry; however, circumstances having placed her under heavier responsibilities, she came smiling to the door, followed by a troop of brown-skinned and curly-haired babies. She courtesied and beamed and gesticulated her delighted welcome of the strangers and, upon being shown the archbishop's missive, kissed the red seal. A few words were intelligible to her, but the reading of a whole letter was beyond the measure of her accomplishments, and she looked to Padre Filippo to explain. She could write the few nouns and do sums quite well enough, though, to make out the bills for her occasional guests,—if in doubt she added another figure.

Sometimes she had guests—ah, but illustrious! The Gran Signore, Sua Eccellenza il Duca di Scorpa—that name to be whispered, and yet to be dwelt upon—no less a personage than such an exaltedness had come to sleep a night under her humble roof! The distinguished *forestieri* should have the very room His *Eccellentissimo* had occupied! She seemed to choose among the Americans by instinct, assigning to Derby and Porter this apartment in which she took such evident pride.

It was, in fact, airy and good sized, scantily furnished, but scrupulously clean, and with two great beds heaped high with the red and yellow flowered quilts which in Sicilian houses serve the double purpose of warmth and decoration: not alone do they lend supreme elegance to the bedrooms, but suspended from the windows, they most gayly embellish the house front on days of *festa*.

As soon as his belongings were unpacked, Porter, with an eye for beauty as well as a view to making himself popular, began to draw a pencil sketch of the little Marcella, a witch of five and beautiful as a doll. Tiggs and Jenkins saw to the unloading of the mules. But Derby and the *carabinieri*, with Padre Filippo, after a hasty luncheon of bread, figs, and goats' milk, pushed on to the mines. Beyond the outskirts of the little village the land soon grew dead again—not a bird fluttered, not a living thing was heard. A few patches of green had sprouted here and there in the lava blackness of the soil, but otherwise the country seemed under a curse.

A new bend in the road brought them close to a small abandoned settlement whose windowless houses gaped, staring like lidless eyes, at the pits which had been dug and left like caverns of the dead—as, in truth, they were. Yet nature had softened the graveyard with straggling spots of new green. A vapor rose from one of the pits as though a monster lay in wait below to destroy his victims with the poison of his breath. This was "Little Devil," the priest told Derby. Through the jaws of that yawning hole many had entered the gates of paradise! His lips muttered a fragment of the prayer for the dead; he crossed himself, and Derby noticed that the *carabinieri* did the same.

During the day Derby had been slowly unfolding to Padre Filippo his plans, and now the priest looked anxiously into the American's face—could he still be hopeful of such a cemetery as this? Derby rode slowly, making a cursory survey of the conditions. It was much as he had expected to find it, he told the priest; he was not disheartened.

They did not stop, as Derby was anxious to go to the Scorpa mines, where he expected to secure his men. He had heard enough to know what lay before him; and even in anticipation he felt oppressed. Another sudden turn in the road gave them a near view of the settlement. Over the arid earth spread a dense haze of smoke and yellow vapor, and down in it—in this vapor whose metallic fumes gripped lungs and throat and burned like fire—crawled human beings! Close to the earth they crept, so that the rising smoke might spend its worst above them.

Derby had thought himself prepared, but with the horrors actually before him, he shuddered uncontrollably; unconsciously, he gripped the pommel of the saddle so tensely that his knuckles whitened. The mine of "Golden Plenty!" From the horrible mockery of the name, the devil might well have taken notes in planning hell! Copper Rock was paradise indeed, compared to this inferno.

Little forms passed by him with faces wizened and wrinkled—were they gnomes?—or what? Surely not children! Small, narrow, stooped shoulders, backs bent under loads buckled to tottering legs. Ragged the creatures were to the point of nakedness, and on their arms and legs were scars fresh and scarlet from the torches of the overseers. Women and men crawled near the caldrons, and down the ladders into the hell pits went the children—up with the heavy loads past the torch and lash of the devil servers, whose duty it was to see that no panting being loitered. Day in, day out, these miserable wretches stumbled under the stinging pain of burning flesh—and once in a while a child's faltering feet slipped from the ladder rungs, his weak hands lost hold—a cry, a fall, and the "Golden Plenty" had swallowed one more victim.

As Derby's party drew near, a straggling group gathered around the strangers. They stared dully and without intelligence, and yet like animals in whom savagery is ever ready to burst restraints. The stronger men among them glowered at the intruders, turning against a strange face with the snarl they dared not show to one grown familiar. Beyond the mines, ranged at different heights on the barren mountain slope, were huts much like the abandoned ones at "Little Devil"—black caverns, smoke-stained and gaping, where stooping human beings moved in and out, maimed and broken like insects whose wings some brutal boy has pulled.

And yet the priest affirmed that to get half a dozen families to leave this place and go to the new settlement would be no easy task. They were too dull to grasp the promise of betterment, and the very mention of "Little Devil" filled them with alarm. It would need many days and much patient handling to convince them that the *forestieri* meant them good instead of harm.

Padre Filippo was the one who most persuaded them—he and a Sicilian workman, a native of Vencata who had lately returned from America. Between these two the miners' fears were partly allayed, and in less than a week's time Derby received a small company of men, women, and children into his new settlement. They came like prisoners, under the guard of the *carabinieri*, and so feeble and debilitated were the wretched creatures that, for a few weeks after their arrival, Derby turned his settlement into a hospital.

Yet suspicion surrounded him on every side. It was one of the *carabinieri*—the taller one—who ventured his opinions one day: "Signore does not know these people! Signore is letting them grow strong that they may the better use their fangs. They cannot believe that Signore is not the devil in paying such wages—in pretending to give them a life of ease. The great Duke Scorpa is their friend—he has been able to do nothing. The good and honorable His Eminence the Archbishop, not even he may help—none in this world; not even the Holy Virgin on her throne in heaven. If any one comes to interfere it must be the devil—since none but the devil comes to such a land."

"That's all right, my friend," Derby answered. "Just you wait and see. Animals never resent kindness, and that's all these poor creatures are—just animals."

In the meantime he and the engineers and the carpenters from Vencata Minore had worked day and night getting up the scaffolding for the first well. The first boiler was set up in a shanty, and pens were hammered together to hold the molten sulphur.

From the moment of Derby's arrival in the Vencata mines, the *carabinieri* kept him under the closest guard and accompanied him wherever he went. But in spite of this there were a few mild outbreaks. One day a stone was hurled at him. Another time some half-crazed wretch tried to stab him; and once a pit was dug across the road, in which his horse broke a leg, so that it had to be shot. This last nearly brought Derby to the point of meting out punishment to the offenders. Yet when he realized again the sufferings of these people, his anger gradually subsided.

However, these disturbances had all taken place within the week after his arrival in Sicily, and at the end of the second week he strongly objected to being guarded. Each day he knew he gained in the confidence of the people, and each day he knew also that they must be improving. He felt sure that as their bodies were put in something like human condition, their intellects must follow. The *carabinieri* protested that he would be making a needless target of himself should he attempt to ride alone in the early dawn from the village of Vencata Minore to the mines. The road led between rocks and underbrush where a man might hide with perfect safety. But the apprehension of the *carabinieri* did not trouble Derby in the least. "Nonsense," he said. "Why, the miners are all beginning to like me—I can see it in their faces."

What he said was true, and under the new treatment the people were beginning to look and act like human beings. Even two weeks were enough to show a settlement beyond Padre Filippo's highest hopes. No child was employed in the mines, neither were the women allowed to work outside their huts and plots of ground. They might dig and plant the soil, but they were barred out of the mines. With the elimination of the refining vats and the reduction of the scorching heat, and with the presence of moisture from the steam and water required in the new mining, conditions became favorable for luxuriant vegetation.

Besides, Derby had received by cable approval of certain quixotic measures: Each family was given a milk goat. The houses were furnished with cook stoves, beds, chairs, and tables. And although it would be some time before "Little Devil" would seem inappropriate as a name, less than three weeks had passed when Derby, sitting in the tent which served as his office, felt a real thrill as he footed up assets and liabilities. One well had been sunk, and the boilers and engines needed to operate it were going full blast. The scaffoldings for two more were nearly up.

In the doorway near him Porter lounged, drawing a picture of Padre Filippo, who, in turn, was writing on his knees, his fine penmanship covering page after page—all about the miracles of the Americano, and addressed to the archbishop.

But his Eminence needed no letters from Padre Filippo to announce miracles, since a miracle had happened in his own house—a marvel that had made Marianna cross her hands in speechless wonder. The new lamp burned on the table, the green reading shade reflected almost as much light on the page as the sun itself, and His Eminence might now read any book he pleased. The archbishop thoughtfully stroked the cat that lay curled on his lap.

"It is not in this world," he mused, "that we shall journey, thou and I, to the land of the Americanos, the miracle workers; but assuredly the Santa Vergine sent the young Signore Americano to bless our people with his miracles—even as he has sent this one to thee and me."

But beyond the bright radius of the good archbishop's lamp a figure waited and watched in the darkness—the figure of a man with a sinister face and across it a mouth that looked like a seam.

CHAPTER XXII

BEFORE DAYLIGHT

In the purple dawn of a morning two or three days later, Derby emerged from the house of Donna Marcella, saddled his horse and for the first time without his attendant *carabinieri*, started for the mines. The faint light showed him only a blurred and indistinct landscape; and in the crisp stillness the leather of his saddle creaked a monotonous accompaniment to the horse's hoofs, which struck the road with clean-cut staccato sharpness.

Meanwhile, in the big best room on the ground floor of Donna Marcella's house, Porter slept. A man's step outside and the fingering of a shutter-latch disturbed him not at all; even when there came a nervous tap on the window frame, Porter slept on. A moment of silence followed, and then a voice breathed stridently, "*Signore!*" Porter stirred in his sleep. A man's head and shoulders appeared over the sill of the open window. "*Signore! Signore l'Americano!*" The tone was louder and very urgent. Porter awoke with a start and seized his revolver. "*Pax, pax!*" came the voice as the man dropped out of sight.

"*Signore, Signore.* It is a friend who would speak to the *Signore l'Americano!*" The syllables were whispered with ringing distinctness. Porter jumped out of bed, revolver in hand. Close to the window, he demanded who was there.

"It is a matter of life and death! May I show myself?"

"Certainly!" said Porter. "For heaven's sake, stand up and let me have a look at you! And give an account of why you are getting a Christian out of his bed at this unearthly hour!" In the glimmering dawn he could see the outline of the man's figure, but he could not recognize him.

"*Signore*, I would speak with the big *Americano*, the one who sent the daylight miracle to the palace of the archbishop. I am sent by His Eminence the Archbishop. I am Teobaldo his servant. See, I carry the archbishop's holy ring to show I speak the truth."

Porter saw the ring distinctly, held between the man's fingers—"Yes! I believe you. Be quick!"

"I have ridden through the night, but I arrive late because I lost my path in the blackness. Last night by chance it became known to the archbishop that there is a plot to assassinate the Americano. I am come secretly to warn him. The assassin is waiting along the road to the mine; it is to be there, and the hour is now!"

Porter sprang back into the room. "Jack, Jack! For God's sake, are you there?" He tore back the covers of Derby's bed, but it was empty. He remembered with horror that the *carabinieri* were not to accompany Derby that morning. He had insisted that they were no longer necessary. Scrambling into his clothes any fashion—his trousers over his pajamas, his shoes over stocking less feet—he strapped on his revolvers, and took the window ledge at a bound.

He jumped astride his horse without stopping for a saddle, and beat and kicked the poor beast along the road as though the very fiends were after him. The horse rocked on his legs and breathed hard, but Porter had no consideration for that. The pale dawn revealed an empty road, along which he sped at breakneck pace, while beads of perspiration gathered on his forehead in his impatience at the seeming slowness of his progress. At last the road cut through a tangled bit of forest with a sharp bend at the end. Just as he reached the turn two shots rang out in quick succession. With his heart almost frozen, he dashed around the corner in time to see Derby plunging into the underbrush. Like a wild man Porter shouted, "I'm coming, Jack, I'm coming!"—impelling his already spent horse to the spot where Derby had disappeared into the thicket.

Derby, like all men who live much in the woods, had almost an animal's instinct for danger, and his ears, supersensitive to wood sounds, had caught a moving in the bushes. To get his revolver in hand and drop forward behind his horse's shoulders had been the act of a second, and the bullet whistled over his head. But the immediate effect of the attack had been to enrage him out of all prudence. Firing point-blank at the smudge of smoke, he jumped from his horse and rushed in pursuit of his assailant.

A second shot Derby thought had grazed his coat; he emptied two barrels of his revolver in the direction from which it came. Another bullet whistled close to his ear, then two shots went entirely wide of him, and the next moment he reached a man lying prone—with blood gushing from his head. Derby knocked the rifle out of his hands, but there was no further danger of its being fired, for the man had fainted.

In a second Porter dashed up, in a frenzy of terror. When he found Derby safe, his fright turned to rage, and he was impatient to put the prisoner into the hands of the *carabinieri*. "Our friend Basso will make short work of him, I'm thinking!" he said grimly.

But Derby had no intention of making such a disposition of his prisoner. "Not at all," he said deliberately; "we will hand him over to Padre Filippo. Priests are better for such creatures than police. Come, help me tie up his head—my shirt will do!" Suiting the action to his words, he pulled off his coat. His shirt was scarlet!

"Great Heavens, man, why didn't you say you were hit?" Porter gasped.

Derby looked down at his shirt and then quizzically at Porter. "Funny," he remarked indifferently; "I thought the bullet had only grazed my coat. It can't be much, as I didn't even feel it; however, you might tie me up, too." He pulled off his shirt. Porter tore it up and bound Derby's shoulder. Then together they made a bandage for the bandit's head.

"He's got an ugly mug!" said Porter, as he wiped the man's face. "By Jove—it's the brigand I noticed coming down on the boat! I told you he looked like a cutthroat."

"Your natural intuition for character?" Derby smiled, but the next minute added soberly enough: "If he came from the mainland we must be up against a good deal more than the poor devils here! Who the deuce can he be? He's no miner, that's certain!"

They had dragged their prisoner out to the side of the road and laid him down. And as Derby insisted, Porter rode off for the priest. Derby sat near his charge, who showed no signs of returning consciousness. His own shoulder ached now, and he gradually became aware of slight weakness. He felt in his pockets for a flask, but found he had forgotten to carry one, so he lit his pipe instead, and fell to scrutinizing the man before him. He was of small stature, but there was great endurance in the long, pointed nose, the strong, lantern jaw; and the face, sinister though it was, retained, even in unconsciousness, an expression of grim fortitude. The more Derby studied the man, the more certain he became that he was no mere skulking coward.

At last Porter and the *padre* appeared over the hill. No sooner had the priest caught sight of the prisoner than he exclaimed, "*Per l'amor di Dio!* It is Luigi Calluci!" There was added horror in his tone as he whispered, "Signore, Signore, he is the body servant of the Duca di Scorpa!"

At this even Derby started, but he said quite calmly, "Poor devil! The question is, what will you do with him?"

"He must be put under the arrest—"

"Well, naturally," chimed in Porter.

But Derby interposed: "He shall be put under nothing of the kind until he can give an account of himself. There is no knowing what fancied grievance he may have against me. Wait until he has been heard. The question of punishment can be considered then.

But in the meantime he must be nursed!"

"You have his brother in the settlement—Salvatore Calluci, the man to whom you have given special duty in the night shaft." The priest's red head wagged mournfully: "It was to the wife of Salvatore you gave an extra goat because of her children!" But then he added, brightening a little at the thought, "I am sure—of a truth I am sure, Signore, that the brother had no hand in this!"

"Very well, then; we will take him to the house of Salvatore. We will say merely that an accident has happened—do you hear? I do not want the story of an attempted assassination to get about." Derby's voice had grown quite weak as he spoke, and the priest and Porter were both too concerned for him to think of opposing any wish he might express in regard to the prisoner. So they laid the man across the saddle of Padre Filippo's horse, and Porter and the *padre* walked on either side of him into camp. Derby rode his own horse, but by the time he reached the mine, he had lost so much blood that he was pretty fit for the doctor himself. Tiggs, a lean, wiry Yankee, sandy-haired and resourceful, was a tolerable surgeon, and he plastered Derby up, pronouncing the injury nothing more serious than a flesh wound.

Luigi Calluci meanwhile was carried into the hut of his brother and put to bed. If Salvatore and his wife had any idea of the cause of his "accident," they said nothing. They were among the most intelligent of the miners, and their gratitude to Derby for the change in their condition, was proportionate.

But it was not alone the Callucis who had made fast strides. The whole settlement had undergone a change that was nothing short of transformation. One reason for the rapid improvement was doubtless the influence exerted by the Sicilian carpenter who had been to America and who had returned a "great man" and rich. Through him as interpreter, all things the American did were good; and the "land of plenty" lost nothing in the telling. The people began to look upon the new mining process as a miracle, and the American as sent by the Blessed Virgin. The wages were stupendous—as much as sixty cents a day! But best of all, they were wages for work that a human being could do. Around the miners' houses were the beginnings of gardens, and several families had, in addition to the goat, a few chickens.

Every day Derby went to the hut of the Calluci. Gradually consciousness came back to Luigi. Slowly, as reason returned, the events of the past weeks formed themselves in distinct sequence. He knew where he was now—at the "Little Devil." Had he not himself descended its ladders into the mine's burning pits? Was not that why he was undersized and weak of lungs? He bore scars that had seared even deeper than through the flesh. He knew the huts, too: caves in which men lived like beasts. It was all clear except the surroundings in which he found himself. The haggard faces of his brother and his sister-in-law were familiar, yet not as he remembered them. The withered bodies of the children seemed not nearly so pathetic! Then, full of bewilderment, he heard his sister-in-law singing. Singing! Could it be possible that a voice could sing in the "Little Devil" settlement! Distinctly he heard another sound, the voices of children at play.

Thinking all this must be merely the creation of his brain, he raised himself on his elbow and made a careful survey of the room. There was no doubt that he was in a good bed, covered by a thick new quilt, and the walls were cleanly white-washed. The air held none of the foul and strangling odors which never had been, and never could be, forgotten. That his brother had moved and had become a well-to-do peasant of the mountain slopes and vineyards was the only explanation possible. He tried to get out of bed, but fell back dizzy, and his mind wandered off again to the semi-conscious vagaries of illness.

In this state of mind, he had become used to a new presence—a very big, very kind personality that hauntingly resembled the Americano—it was, of course, one of those phantoms that appear before fevered imaginations. He realized that, and now he made an effort to detach the dream from the reality.

But even as he was trying to put his thoughts in order, the door opened—and he vividly saw the figure of his vision followed by his sister-in-law. Thinking that his mind was wandering, he lay quite still. Then he heard a kindly voice saying, "I have brought soup for him with me—in this jar. You have only to heat it."

Luigi felt a strong hand clasp his wrist and feel for his pulse. Then came the full belief that this was no dream, but reality, and that it was the Tyrant, the Americano himself, who laid hands on him. With a frantic effort he sprang up and tried to close his fingers around his enemy's throat! But firm, powerful hands gripped his shoulders and forced him quietly down in his bed. Then he lost consciousness.

When he came to, he thought he had dreamed the whole occurrence. His brother and Padre Filippo were sitting beside him, and they would not let him talk. But gradually, as his strength returned, he took in the story. From his brother, from the neighbors, from the priest most of all, he heard, bit by bit, of the work that the Americano had accomplished—the Americano whom he,

Luigi, had nearly slain. Slowly, slowly, he understood that the "Little Devil" mine had been re-christened "The Paradise"—not by the nobles who owned it, but by the people who worked in it. And then little by little the resentment, the bitterness, the grievances of his long, hard life turned him against the Duke Scorpa just as his realization of what Derby was doing won him over to the American.

That Scorpa should have sent a man to stab him was, curiously enough, a fact that did not seem to trouble Derby in the least. It was, after all, no more than he might have expected. Before he had left Rome, Scorpa had warned him. He rather admired him for that.

Derby was heart and soul interested in his settlement. In the short space of time since he had arrived in Sicily, the incredible had already come to pass—and to Derby, as he looked forward, there was every reason to feel assured that the settlement would develop as he had planned. The output of the mines promised to be up to the most sanguine expectation. The whole scheme was organized and started—there was nothing to do now but to keep it going.

In the meantime he received a cable which, when deciphered, ran:

> "Telegraph *Celtic* at Gibraltar, giving Hobson instructions where to find you. Put package he carries in safe keeping. In case of serious development use own judgment."

Hobson was one of J. B. Randolph's secretaries. Derby at once wired to Hobson to await him in Naples. Then, leaving Tiggs and Jenkins in charge, he and Porter embarked.

As they leaned over the deck rail watching the blue shallows where the waters of the Mediterranean curled away from the ship's prow, Porter said:

"It must be good to be going back to Rome with the feeling that you have carried out what you started to do. It's a big feather in your cap, and now there is only one thing needed to make the whole episode a romance from start to finish!"

Derby interrogated good-humoredly, "And that is—?"

"You will probably go up in the air if I tell you."

Derby looked up from the water. "Go ahead—say what you like—"

"You ought to marry Miss Randolph!" Porter declared abruptly, and before Derby could protest he hurried on: "Yes, I know what you would say—she is too rich and she is scheduled to marry a title. But I don't think she is the sort of girl that really puts as much stock in titles as it would seem; and as for money, by the time you have two or three mines like the 'Little Devil' going, you will be pretty rich yourself. Even with your present prospects, no one could accuse you of marrying her for her fortune."

"Prospects are very different from actual money, and compared to her I'm a pauper," Derby answered. "I don't care what people accuse me of, but to marry a girl like Nina Randolph— even assuming the unlikelihood that she'd have me—would be a fatal mistake, unless I had a fortune to match her own. Every changing hour of the day would bring fresh doubt; she would never believe in a poor man's love. How could she!"

Derby stood up straight, thrust his hands into the pockets of his ulster, and as Porter tried to protest, he withdrew from the discussion by declaring that there was nothing to discuss. For himself—he was but a human machine that God had set upon the earth to bore holes in it, and to set swarms of human ants working.

CHAPTER XXIII

THE SPIDER'S WEB

In Rome, after Easter, society blossomed out afresh. Giovanni Sansevero had returned, and to Nina the commencement of the spring season promised a repetition of the winter.

Nina's antipathy to the Duke Scorpa remained unchanged, and to her annoyance it had happened frequently, when dining out, that he had taken her in to dinner. Each time his unctuous, "It is my pleasure, Signorina, to conduct you," gave her so strong a feeling of resentment that she had to exert a real effort to put her finger tips on his coat sleeve. She always kept the distance between them as wide as possible by the angle at which her arm was bent.

On looking back, however, she had to acknowledge that his manner had undergone a radical change. He no longer alarmed her by aggressive pursuit, nor sought to lead the conversation to those personal topics which she had found so repellent. Furthermore, he never alluded to the threat he had made to her that day at the hunt, nor even mentioned his rejected suit. And yet she felt apprehensively that he had not given up his original determination.

In the meantime he was untiring in his efforts to interest her, and evinced an ability to keep the conversation going with great skill—even more skill than Giovanni, whose natural attractiveness could afford to do without the effort that Scorpa found necessary. He flattered her by his assumption that she was a woman of the world, and he disguised the exaggeration of his expressions in such a way that she thought he was speaking but the barest truth. For instance, he dilated upon the particular qualities for which Nina herself adored the princess, until it became apparent to her that, after all, Scorpa must be a man of sensitive perceptions.

Nevertheless, the underlying feeling of terror with which he filled her at the first moment of each encounter was far worse than mere dislike. Intuitively, she regarded him as a menace, and, through his unvarying politeness, she found herself trying to fathom his real intentions. What object could he have had in ranging himself with the suitors for her hand? He was very rich himself. Aside from his own fortune, "poor Jane"—as every one called his first wife—had left a handsome amount, which, according to European custom, was entirely in his control. Perhaps he wanted still more money, and thought that he could find in her another source of supply to be exhausted and practically thrust aside. Many tales that Nina had heard, many things that she had observed were not good for the girl's all too ready cynicism—and the hard little lines around her mouth that the princess so disliked to see, were growing deeper.

The question of international marriage was one on which Nina found herself becoming quite skeptical. She admitted that there were happy examples. Her aunt, for instance. Surely no wife was ever more loved and appreciated than the princess, even though her husband had one serious failing. But then, did not some American husbands also gamble?

In the Masco household too, the bonny Kate was certainly in no need of sympathy. That her position was not as good as her husband's name should have given her was her own fault. She was not one of those gifted with the chameleon faculty of harmonizing with her background. Among the mellow pigments of the Roman canvas she was a glaring splotch of primary color. But she was far from unhappy.

Indeed, so far as Nina's observation could penetrate, the general impression of the average Americo-Italian marriage was of sympathetic comradeship between husband and wife; in nearly every household she had found the indescribably charming atmosphere of a harmonious home.

Yet proposals for the hand of the American heiress were so common that, in spite of the delightful households of her country-women, Nina had long since begun to think—first in fun and then more seriously—of the palaces of Italy as so many spider webs waiting for the American gilded fly. It was at the Palazzo Scorpa that her theory became actuality.

The princess had, very much against Nina's will, taken her to see the duchess on the day after their own dance. But a serious indisposition had prevented the duchess from receiving—not only on that particular day, but for the rest of the winter. Toward the end of March, however, in response to a note, Nina was finally obliged to enter the Palazzo Scorpa.

It was a rugged gray stone fortress of a place, "like a monster," Nina said, "of the dragon age, that sulkily remained asleep and hidden among the narrow, twisted streets that had crept around it."

Through the yawning gateway they entered a sunless courtyard. Even the porter at the door, notwithstanding his gold lace and crimson livery, was austere and forbidding. Within, the palace had been refurnished in the most lavish Florentine period, but the effect of the high-vaulted rooms was that of a prison.

One room, however, through which they passed to reach the reception apartments of the duchess, gave Nina a little thrill in spite of her antipathy. The Scorpas had belonged to the "Blacks," that is to the ecclesiasticals, and this room was not repaired in modern fashion, but hung in tattered purple silk. On one side stood a solitary piece of furniture—a great gilt throne upholstered in red velvet, and above it hung a portrait of Pope Alexander VI, the whole surmounted by a canopy of red velvet.

"Was he a relation of the duke?" Nina whispered, aghast at the resemblance.

"Who, child?" asked the princess.

"Rodrigo Borgia."

"No one knows. Hush!"

"But why the throne? Were the Scorpas kings—or what?"

"Before the secular unification of Italy," the princess answered, "the Holy Fathers used to visit the Scorpa cardinals. There has always been a Scorpa among the cardinals. The one now is Monsignore Gamba del Sati. Del Sati is one of the numerous names of the Scorpa family."

Nina cast another glance at the portrait of Alexander VI. The sinister face was so like the present duke's that it made her shudder, and her imagination at once pictured slaves and prisoners being dragged along these same stone floors. At the end of ten or twelve rooms, each gloomy, yet over-rich with architectural adornments and modern elaboration, two lackeys lifted the hangings covering the last doorway, and announced:

"Sua Eccellenza la Principessa Sansevero!"

"Messa Randolph."

The Duchess Scorpa was very gracious to the American heiress. But, unaccountably, Nina had a strangled feeling, as though she were a bird and had been enticed into a cage. It was a ridiculous notion, for, even following out the simile, the door was open, she knew; and, for that matter, the bars were too far apart to hold her, as soon as she should choose to slip through. But the feeling of the cage was oppressively vivid, and she clung as closely to her aunt's side as she could. Friends of the princess rather monopolized her, however, while the duchess neglected her other guests to talk to Nina. To add to the girl's distress, the duke, stroking his heavy chin with his fat hand, stood beside her chair with what seemed a proprietary air, and a smile that was intolerable. "Well, my guests," his manner seemed to say, "how do you like my choice? She is not all that I might ask for, but she will do—quite nicely."

Nina glanced appealingly at her aunt, but Eleanor's back was turned. Involuntarily she looked toward the doorway—Giovanni was to meet them there, and she longed to see his slender figure appear between the *portières*, to hear the announcement of the well-known name which was no less great than that of the odious man who was trying to compromise her by his air of proprietorship.

Nina could stand it no longer, and sprang to her feet, in the very midst of a long-winded story about—she had no idea what the duchess was saying to her, but she realized that she had done an inexcusably *gauche* thing, not only interrupting, but in starting to go before her chaperon made the move. And her discomfiture was increased by a quick sense of the Potensi's derisive criticism. Recovering herself, she exclaimed rapidly: "I am so much interested in sculpture; may I look at that statue?"

The duchess, far from showing resentment at the interruption, was apparently delighted with the opportunity of impressing upon her guest the greatness of the palace and the family of the Scorpas. "Certainly," she cooed, as nearly as a snapping turtle can imitate a turtledove; "that is a genuine Niccola Pisano. The original document is still intact in which he agreed with the cardinal of our house to execute it himself. The portrait of our ancestor who ordered the statue is in the gallery."

Before Nina could resist, she found herself being conducted between mother and son through the numerous rooms which terminated finally in the gallery. Unlike most of the collections of Italy, this included many modern canvases.

Before the portrait of a thin, heavy-boned, frightened-looking English girl, the duke assumed a deeply sentimental air, sighing as though out of breath. "That is the portrait of my beloved Jane," he said. "It was painted by Sargent while we were on our honeymoon." The artist, with his consummate skill of characterization, had transferred a crushed, fatalistic helplessness to the canvas. Nina found herself, partly in pity, partly in contempt, scrutinizing the face of the woman who had brought herself to marry such a man.

Suddenly an indescribable feeling of oppression seized her. She looked away from the picture, and then, glancing around to speak to the duchess, she saw the edge of her dress disappearing through the hangings of the doorway, while between herself and her retreating hostess stood the stolid figure of the duke, with the most odious smile imaginable upon his horrid face.

With a flush of anger that made her temples throb, Nina realized that a dastardly trap had been sprung upon her. To leave a young girl even for a moment unchaperoned was against the strictest rule of Italian propriety. The duchess had brought her all this distance on purpose to leave her with the villainous duke—in a situation that, should it become known, would so compromise an Italian girl that there would be no place for her in the social system of her world afterward outside of a convent. Her marriage with the duke would be almost inevitable.

Determined to give no evidence of the terror that gripped her, with the most fearless air she could assume she attempted to pass the duke; but he blocked her way so that her manœuvres came down to the indignity of a game of blind man's buff. Nina held her head very high and looked straight at her tormentor. "Please allow me to pass." She tried hard to speak quietly and to keep the tremulousness out of her voice.

For answer Scorpa quickly closed the intervening distance between them, and the next thing she knew the grasp of his thick, hot hands burned through the sleeve of her coat, and his face was thrust near to her own. In a frenzy of fury she wrenched herself free, and without thought or even consciousness of what she was doing, she struck him full in the face.

Instead of recoiling, he caught and pinned her arms in a grip like a vice. "Ah, ha, so that is the mettle you are made of, is it, you little fiend! Don't think that I mind your fury—you will be a wife after my own heart when I have tamed you! I am a man of my word—I said I would marry you, and I will! Not many men would want to marry a woman of your temper, but you suit me!"

In her horror Nina felt her throat grow dry. She stared at the thick, red, cruel, animal lips of the man with a loathing that almost paralyzed her power to move; while his hands pressed numbingly into the flesh of her arms.

"Let me go! Do you hear"—her voice shook with fright and rage—"let me go! At once! You coward! You beast!"

And like a beast he snarled his answer: "Scream all you please! You could not be heard if you had a throat of brass!" Then mockingly he sneered, "Come, won't you dance with me, as you did with the pretty Giovanni? You had his arms around you lovingly enough! But, by Bacchus! the way to win a woman is to seize her, after the good old customs of our ancestors!" And with that he drew her close to him—so close that, though she screamed and struggled like a fury, his lips drew nearer—nearer—

Then a jar struck through her blinding rage; in a daze she felt herself released, and realized that Giovanni had appeared; that he had gripped Scorpa around the throat until his eyes started out of their sockets; and then sent him sprawling to the floor.

With the relief and reaction, everything seemed to recede from Nina and grow black. Dimly she felt that Giovanni had put his arm around her to support her. "Come quickly, Mademoiselle, before there is a scene"—she heard his voice as though it were far off. But she was perfectly conscious. She knew that Scorpa still lay on the floor as Giovanni hurried her through another set of rooms and led her down a staircase that brought them to a second entrance door—one by which, as it happened, Giovanni had come in. The footman on duty looked as though he were going to bar their egress, but Giovanni ordered him to open the door quickly. "The lady is fainting," he said, and a glance at Nina's face too well confirmed it. Besides, the man would hardly have dared disobey a Sansevero. Once in the open air, they lost no time in going around to the main entrance. The Sansevero carriage was waiting, and Giovanni put Nina in. "Wait here a moment—I will go up and tell Eleanor."

Nina was shaking from head to foot. "No—no—don't leave me; take me away!"

"It is not seemly to drive with you, Mademoiselle; I will return in a moment."

But by this time Nina was hysterical. "No—no—please take me home," she begged. "The carriage can come back." And she began to sob.

Giovanni hesitated, then jumped in quickly, telling the coachman to drive home as fast as possible.

"It must have been a frightful experience," he said, as they started. "Thank God I came even when I did."

A shudder ran through Nina. Instinctively she drew away from Giovanni, merely because he was a foreigner, and of the same race as Scorpa. She could still see those thick, loathsome lips approaching her own, and the recollection gave her a nauseating sense of pollution. Holding her hands over her face, she sobbed and sobbed.

Giovanni let her cry it out. It was not a moment to play on her feelings—they were too strained to stand any other emotion. Yet had he considered nothing but his own advantage, he could not better have used his opportunity than by doing exactly what he did.

"Listen, Mademoiselle"—his voice was soothing—as kind and unimpassioned as though he were talking to a troubled little child. "Promise me that you will try not to think about this afternoon. It will do no good. Try to forget it, if you can. That man shall never again in any way enter your life. At least I can promise you that! Here we are! Now," he added in English, as the footman opened the door, "go upstairs and lie down. I will go back immediately and tell Eleanor that you felt suddenly ill and that the carriage took you home. It is not likely that Scorpa has given any version of the affair."

But a new fear assailed Nina. "You cannot go back! The duke will kill you! He would do anything, that man!"

There was pride in Giovanni's easy answer. "He is not very agile," he laughed; "to stab he would have first to reach me!" Then seriously and very gently he added, "You are overstrung and nervous, Mademoiselle. On my honor I promise you need never fear him again."

"What do you mean by that?" Startled, she put the question.

"Nothing," he rejoined lightly, "only that a man never repeats a performance like that of the duke. The Italian custom prevents!" he added, with a curious expression of whimsicality over which Nina puzzled as she mounted the stairs to her room. Even in her shaken state, she marveled at the contrast between Giovanni's finely chiseled features and the elastic strength that must have been necessary to overpower the bull force of the duke. She thought gratefully of the sympathy in his gentle voice, as well as in his whole manner during the ten minutes which were all that had elapsed since the duchess left her. She realized with what perfect tact and perception he had treated her on the way home. And suddenly her heart went out to him. She felt now, as she went through the long stone corridors and galleries toward her room, that instead of drawing away from him, were he at that moment beside her, she might easily sob her emotions all peacefully out in his arms.

In the meantime Giovanni returned to the Palazzo Scorpa and, ascending the main stairway, entered the antechamber of the reception room. The old duchess was hovering anxiously at the entrance of the rooms leading to the picture gallery, the closed *portières* screening her from the guests to whom she had not dared to return without Nina. The rugs laid upon the marble floors dulled all sound of Giovanni's footfalls, so that he appeared without warning, and with his own hand hastily lifted the *portière*, disclosing her to her waiting guests. She had no choice but to precede him, doubtless framing an excuse for Nina's absence. If so, she need not have troubled, for Giovanni spoke in her stead, and with such distinct enunciation that the whole roomful heard:

"Miss Randolph felt suddenly ill and asked to go home. I came just as the carriage was disappearing, and found the duchess much disturbed over it, though I assured her it was quite usual for young girls to go about alone in America."

His look at the duchess demanded that she corroborate his account.

"It was too bad," she said, glibly enough. "I should have accompanied her as I was, without hat or mantle even, but Miss Randolph was gone before I really had time to think. It is, after all, but a step to the Palazzo Sansevero."

Eleanor Sansevero arose. Through a perfect control and sweetness of manner the most careless observer might have read displeasure. "Of course," she said, enunciating each word with smoothly modulated distinctness, "in America there could be no impropriety in a young girl's driving alone, but I am sorry you did not send for me. Your son left the room at the same time—he has not returned."

The American princess towered in slim height above the stolid dumpiness of the duchess. From appearance one would never have guessed rightly which of the two women could trace her lineage for over a thousand years.

The mouth of the duchess went down hard in the corners, and her dull, turtle eyes contracted, then her lips snapped open to answer, but Giovanni again saved her the trouble. "I met Scorpa on the street about ten minutes ago. He was going toward the Circolo d'Acacia."

"Ah yes, Todo was filled with regret, as he wanted to show Miss Randolph the portraits," haltingly echoed the duchess, but she glanced uneasily at the door. "I was glad he did not see her indisposition—he has a heart as tender as a woman's, and it would have distressed him greatly! I do hope, princess, that you will find her quite recovered on your return. I think it must be the effect of sirocco."

The other guests supported her in chorus. "The sirocco is very treacherous," ventured one. "She was perhaps not acclimatized to Rome," said a second. "I thought she looked pale," chimed a third.

The princess made her adieus at once and, followed by Giovanni, left the palace. For a few minutes the various groups, disposed about the Scorpa drawing-room, conversed in low whispers, but by the time the Sanseveros were well out of earshot the duchess had turned to the whispering groups with a hauteur of expression conveying quite plainly that it was not to be endured that a Sansevero, born American, should imply a criticism of a Duchess Scorpa, born Orsonna.

"A headstrong young barbarian from the United States is quite beyond my control," she shrugged. "How can I help it if she chooses to run from the palace, like Cinderella when the clock strikes twelve!"

One or two of those present who were friends of the Princess Sansevero may have resented the implied slight to her democratic birth. But though there was a vague appreciation of something beneath the surface in this American girl's sudden departure, there was nothing to which any one could take exception.

The Contessa Potensi, however, had long waited for just such an opportunity, and seized it. "I felt sorry for Eleanor Sansevero," she said sweetly. "It puts her in an unendurable position to have to defend such a person. Naturally she *has* to defend her, since she is her niece. I am sure she did not want her for the winter—but her parents would not keep her. It is no wonder they would be willing to give her a big dot!"

There was general excitement. "What do you know?" the company cried in chorus. "Tell us about it!"

But the Potensi at once became very discreet. For nothing would she take away a young girl's character. Besides, Eleanor Sansevero was one of her best friends—it would not be loyal to say anything further. More definite information she would not disclose, but her manner left little to the imagination.

"Surely you can tell us something of what is said," insinuated the old Princess Malio, adjusting her false teeth securely in the roof of her mouth as if the better to enjoy the delectable morsel of scandal that she felt was about to be served. But the contessa, with a "could-if-she-would" expression, refused to say anything more, and the old princess turned instead to the duchess with, "Tell us the *truth* about Miss Randolph's sudden illness!"

The truth, of course, was out of the question. Public sympathy must have gone against her and her son, and she hedged to gain time, "It is not all worth the thought needed to frame words."

The old Princess Malio made a swallowing motion, still waiting. "Yes?" she encouraged eagerly.

"Any one could see what happened," said the duchess reluctantly, as though she were loath to speak scandal. "The American girl, through lack of training—it is, after all, not her fault, poor thing—knows no better than to try to arrange matters for herself!

She wanted, of course, to have an opportunity of talking to my Todo alone. Her plan to go into the picture gallery here, however, necessitated my chaperoning her, and then—contrary to her expectations—Todo, who did not fall in with her scheme, said he had an engagement and at once left. She could not, of course, declare the picture gallery of no interest, so I took her, but in her disappointment she quite lost her temper, so much so that it made her ill. And then she took the matter in her own hands and went home—I was never so astonished in my life! She ran off with Giovanni Sansevero so fast I could not catch up with them. I *suppose* he put her in the carriage, but for all I know he took her somewhere else. I followed to the front door and waited, not knowing what to do. Just as I returned to inform Princess Sansevero, for whom I have always had the highest regard, Giovanni commenced with his own account. What could I do except agree to his statement?"

She looked inquiringly from one to the other. "That is the whole story! But I have made up my mind to one thing"—she spread her fat fingers out—"not even her millions would induce me to countenance Todo's marriage with such a self-willed girl as that!"

The old Princess Malio looked like a bird of prey whose prize morsel had been stolen from it. "There is more in this than appears," she whispered to a timid little countess sitting next to her.

The latter's half-hearted, "Do you think so, really?" voiced the attitude of nearly all present. The Scorpas were, to use the old Roman proverb, "sleeping dogs best let alone," and the Sanseveros, though not as rich, were none the less too great a family to side against.

While the voice of the duchess was still echoing in the drawing-room of the Palazzo Scorpa, Nina had thrown herself into the corner of the sofa in her own room. She had a perfectly normal constitution, but she had been not only infuriated and horrified, but really frightened, and her nerves were unstrung.

As she grew calmer, she thought more clearly; and she found that the afternoon's experience, horrible as it was, held some leaven—Giovanni's behavior stirred her deeply. She had realized the power of his muscles under his slight build before—when he had held the Great Dane's throat in his grip—and she had seen his flexibility, in turning instantaneously from fury to suavity. Yet his masterful attack upon her assailant, followed by his sympathy and comprehension on the way home, thrilled her as with a revelation of unguessed capacities. John Derby could not have come to her rescue better, nor could she have felt more protected and calmed with her childhood's friend at her side in the carriage, than with this alien of a foreign race.

She went into her dressing-room and bathed her eyes and cheeks in cold water. Then, thinking the princess must surely have returned by this time, she decided to go into the drawing-room. On her way she met her aunt coming toward her, followed closely by Giovanni, who put his finger on his lips, just as the princess exclaimed, "Nina, my child, what happened to you? You did very wrong to run off home alone. I can't understand your having done such a thing. It was not only ill-mannered, but it put you in a very questionable light."

Over the princess's shoulder Giovanni was making an unmistakable demand for silence. "I'm very sorry," Nina faltered— Giovanni was looking at her intensely, pleadingly, his finger on his lips—"but I—never felt like that before. I got terribly—nervous, and I felt that if I did not get away from that house I should go mad." Even the recollection made Nina look so distraught that her aunt's indignation turned to anxiety, and she put her arm around the girl and led her into the drawing-room.

"It is not like you, dear, to lose control of yourself," she said tenderly, and then, as she scrutinized Nina's face in the better light, she added: "You do look white, darling. You had better lie down here on the sofa. I think I will prepare you some tea of camomile," and then, with a final touch of gentle admonition, she added, "We must not have any more such scenes!" Nina hoped for a chance to ask Giovanni why she might not tell the princess what had happened, but the latter did not leave the room. Having sent for the camomile flowers, she made Nina a cup of tea, and the subject of the afternoon's occurrence was dropped.

CHAPTER XXIV

WEIGHED IN THE BALANCE

All that evening Nina was tense and nervous, not only because of her experience at the Palazzo Scorpa, but because of something portentous in Giovanni's unexplained demand for silence. He was not at the same dinner party with her, but she went on to a dance at the Marchese Valdeste's, feeling sure that she would have a chance to speak with him there. He always danced with her several times during a ball, and, as he was not very much taller than she, she could easily talk to him without danger of any one's overhearing.

Her partners undoubtedly found her *distraite*; her attention vacillated from one side of the ballroom to the other, as she searched for a well-known, graceful figure and a small, sleek black head. All the time, too, she was fearful of seeing a square-jawed face that kept recurring to her memory as she had last seen it that afternoon—distorted, with mouth open, and eyes protruding from their sockets. Vivid pictures of the terrible incident flashed before her as she tried to listen to her partners; now she was swept with horror and revulsion, and again she felt a strange thrill at thought of the steely strength of Giovanni's arms, as he had half carried her down the stairway. But she looked in vain for her protector—neither he nor the duke appeared.

"What is it, Signorina?" Prince Allegro's voice broke jarringly upon her recollections. "I am afraid I dance too fast!"

Nina recovered herself with a start. "Oh, no! But I feel—a little tired; I wish we might sit down."

"Let me conduct you into the next room—or shall I take you to the princess? Perhaps it would be better for you to go home."

Nina smiled. "No," she said, "I am all right. The room is very warm, I think."

The Contessa Potensi, walking for once with her husband, passed through the adjoining room just as Nina had finally succeeded in focusing her attention upon Allegro's sprightly chatter. As they passed, the contessa stopped a moment to say to Nina, "I am so glad to see that you have recovered from your sudden indisposition of this afternoon." But her tone was neither solicitous nor sincere, and she hid her hands in such a way that she might have been making with her fingers the little horns that are supposed to be a protection against the evil eye.

"I am much better, thank you," Nina answered simply.

"Don't let me keep you standing. I merely wanted to be assured that you are recovered. I would not interrupt a *tête-à-tête!*"

The contessa's manner suggested to Nina that it was perhaps questionable taste for a young girl to sit out part of a dance. Instead, therefore, of resuming her place on the sofa, she asked Allegro to take her to the princess.

During the rest of the evening she had an uncomfortable conviction that the Contessa Potensi was talking about her. She always had this impression in some degree whenever the contessa was present, but tonight it was strong and unmistakable. And after a while she became aware that other people's eyes were upon her with a new expression, that was not idle conjecture nor unmeaning curiosity. The old ladies against the wall whispered together and glanced openly in her direction, as their gray heads bobbed above their fans.

At the end of the evening, as she was descending the staircase with her aunt and uncle, she was joined by Zoya Olisco, who whispered excitedly, "Tell me, *cara mia*—what happened this afternoon?"

Nina started. "What have you heard?" She tried to look unconcerned, but her face was troubled, and she drew Zoya out of her aunt's hearing.

"It is rumored that you lost your temper—oh, but entirely! and walked yourself out of the Palazzo Scorpa without so much as saying good-by or waiting for your chaperon."

Nina hesitated, then said in an undertone, "Yes, I am afraid it is true. Was it a dreadful thing to do?"

The contessa laughed softly. "I told you that you were a girl after my own heart. In your place I should have walked myself out of that house as quickly as I had entered, but all the same—that would not be my advice. However, this is not the serious part of the story." Even Zoya's buoyancy became restrained as she concluded: "All Rome is asking what you have done with the duke. He followed you out of the room and has not been seen since. Giovanni is said to have spoken of seeing him at the club—and that is known to be untrue. Carlo was at the Circolo d'Acacia all the afternoon; so was that Ugo Potensi, as well as a dozen others—and neither Scorpa nor Giovanni was there! So where is the duke? Come, tell me!"

A look of terror came into Nina's eyes, and the young contessa darted her a swift returning glance of comprehension. "Listen, *carissima*," she said, "I am your friend, therefore don't look so frightened—you are a regular baby! The situation is not difficult to read. Obviously there was a scene between you, the thick duke, and the agile Giovanni. Just what it was all about, of course, I can only surmise; but I *do* know that Giovanni is deep in it, and, what is more important, I know also that the result is likely to be troublesome for you. For men to quarrel between themselves is one thing; but when a *woman* comes into it, one can never see the end."

"Woman? I know nothing of any woman." Nina shook her head.

"I told you that you were a baby! But we can't talk here. I shall come to see you tomorrow, but not until late in the afternoon. I shall then perhaps be useful, for in the meantime I am going about like the wolf in the sheep's pelt, to see what news I can pick up. Till then—have courage!"

Just then the Sansevero carriage was announced, and Nina was obliged to hasten after her aunt. At the door she glanced back at Zoya with a half-questioning look, which the contessa answered by blowing her a kiss.

That night the little sleep Nina was able to get was fitful and broken by dreams. The duke and his mother appeared to her as cuttlefish in a cave under perpendicular cliffs that ran into the sea. Nina was out in a little boat alone, and the waves dashed the tiny craft nearer and nearer to the cave where the cuttlefish were waiting; finally she came so close that one tentacle seized her. Terrified, she awoke. After hours of half-waking, half-sleeping, formless confusion, she dreamed again. In this dream she and Giovanni were on horseback. She was sitting in a most precarious position on the horse's shoulder, but was held securely by Giovanni's arm around her waist. Behind them she heard the pounding of many horses in pursuit. The whole dream had the underlying terror of a nightmare, and just as the distance diminished, and they were nearly caught, the ground gave way and they pitched over a precipice. As they were falling and about to be dashed on the rocks at the bottom of the ravine, she heard a woman's laugh, and recognized it as that of the Contessa Maria Potensi.

She awoke, trembling, and lit her lamp. It was nearly four o'clock, and she had slept but half an hour. Near her bed was an American magazine; she read the advertisements, to fill her mind with thoughts commonplace and practical enough to banish dreams. The sun was rising when at last she fell asleep, and she did not awake until nearly noon.

The morning's mail brought her a letter from John Derby—a good letter, simple and frank, like himself, full of enthusiasm and of plans for making the "Little Devil" a model settlement. He would arrive in Rome, he told her, within a week. But even John's letter gave her only a few moments' relief from her distressing memories.

Knowing that she had to pay visits with her aunt again that afternoon, she put on her hat before lunch, in the hope of securing an opportunity to speak with Giovanni while waiting for Eleanor, who always dressed after luncheon. When she was nearly ready to go down, Celeste answered a knock at the door, but, instead of delivering a package or message, disappeared. After at least five minutes she returned, and, with a noticeable air of mystery, locked the door, and then gave Nina a letter. "I was told to give this into Mademoiselle's hands, without letting any one know," she said.

Nina felt an undefined misgiving as she tore open the envelope. Though she had never seen Giovanni's handwriting, she had no doubt that it was his. It looked as though it might not be very legible at best; but on the sheet before her the shaking, uneven letters trailed off into such filiform indistinctness that she had to go through it several times before she could decipher the following, written in French:

> "Mademoiselle, I understand you well enough to be sure that you will ask for the truth at all costs, but in giving it to you, I also depend upon your honor to divulge to no one, not even Eleanor, what I tell you: I fought Scorpa this morning and have sustained a bullet wound in the arm. Unfortunately, it was impossible to hide, as the bone is broken and it had to be put in plaster. Scorpa's condition is, I am told, serious. If it goes badly, I shall have to leave the country, though I doubt if he allows the real cause to be known. I rely upon your discretion as completely as you may rely upon my having avenged an insult offered to the purest and noblest of women.
>
> "I beg you to believe, Mademoiselle, in the respectful devotion of the humblest of your servants.
>
> "Di Valdo."

Nina folded the letter and locked it away in her jewel case, moving as if in a daze. She felt faint and suffocated. Giovanni had risked his life—for her sake! He was hurt—what if the wound should prove serious, what if he should lose his arm! Oh, if only she might go to her aunt and pour out the whole story! But she was in honor bound to say nothing without Giovanni's permission, and she must master herself at once in order to appear as usual at luncheon.

A little later, as she entered the dining-room, she heard the prince saying—"Pretty serious accident." He turned at once to her:

"You have heard?" he said, and as she merely inclined her head, he hastened to explain: "Giovanni, it seems, slipped this morning and broke his arm. But, though the fracture is a very serious one, he is in no danger."

Nina tried to speak, but her tongue seemed glued to the roof of her mouth. Naturally enough, both Eleanor and Sansevero interpreted her pallor and agitation as a sign of interest in Giovanni. "He broke the elbow," the prince continued; "a 'T' break, it is called, which may leave the joint stiff. There was a piece of bone splintered." Nina gripped the under edge of the table—she knew what had splintered the bone! She almost screamed aloud, but she set her lips, held tight to the table, and tried to appear calm; while Sansevero, in spite of his anxiety for his brother's condition, could not help feeling great satisfaction in what looked so encouraging to Giovanni's suit.

"Giovanni went to the surgeon's," he continued. "Imagine— he walked there! He should never have attempted such a thing. He had quite an operation, for the splintered portions of the bone had to be cut away. The arm is now in plaster, and they won't be able to tell for weeks whether he ever can move his elbow again. They brought him home a couple of hours ago. He is now a little feverish, but a sister has come to nurse him, and we have left him to rest." Then Sansevero turned to his wife: "It all sounds very queer to me, Leonora. What was the matter with the boy, anyway? Why did he not send for me? And why did he not go to bed like a sensible human being and stay there?"

Nina was on tenterhooks. She so wanted to ask her aunt and uncle what they really thought! She wondered if they truly had no suspicions. Or were they perhaps dissimulating as she herself was trying with poor success to do? She could not understand how the princess, who was usually quick of perception, could possibly be blind to the real facts of the case. She felt choked—as if she herself had fired the shot that might bring far more horrible consequences than her aunt and uncle knew.

The princess, seeing Nina's face grow whiter and whiter, asked anxiously if she felt ill.

"No—not a bit!" Nina answered, looking as though she were

about to faint. After several unsuccessful attempts to turn the conversation into happier channels, the princess met with some success in the topic of John Derby and the miracles with which rumor credited him. Nina listened with half-pathetic interest, but her hands trembled, and the few mouthfuls she took almost refused to go down her throat. In her heart, at that moment, everything gave way to Giovanni. She reproached herself deeply for lack of belief in him. Always she had acknowledged that he was charming, but the doubt of his sincerity had weighed against her really caring for him. She had accepted John Derby's casual words, "The Europeans do a lot of beautiful talking and picturesque posing, but when it comes to real devotion you will find that one of your Uncle Samuel's nephews will come out ahead."

All that was ended; there was no more question about what the Europeans would do when it came to a test. Giovanni had done far more than say beautiful, graceful things—he had proved to her that her honor was dearer to him than his life, and she was stirred to the very depths of her soul. In the midst of Eleanor's talk of John Derby, she tried to imagine what John would have done in Giovanni's place. He would have thrashed the man within an inch of his life—that she knew. But, manly as that would have been, it could not compare with Giovanni's course in silently waiting fourteen or fifteen hours and then deliberately going out in the dull gray dawn and standing up at forty paces as a target for Scorpa's bullet. She thought how, while she had been merely tossing in her bed, unable to sleep, intent on herself, dwelling on her injured dignity and the horror of that brute's touch, Giovanni had been sitting up through the same long night, putting his affairs in order, and looking death in the face! And she found herself forced to realize that Giovanni—whose instability had been the strongest argument against allowing herself to love him—had paid a price so high that his right to her faith must henceforward be unquestioned.

She had only a vague idea when luncheon ended, or what visits she and her uncle and aunt paid that afternoon. She went through the rest of the day as though dazed. Fortunately, her agitation seemed natural to the prince and princess, and her apparent interest in Giovanni was so near to the truth that she did not mind. Late that afternoon she and Zoya Olisco sat together behind the tea table, for most of the time alone. Zoya had the story pretty straight, but Nina simply looked at her dumbly—answering nothing. She was relieved, however, to hear that, so far, people had evidently not ferreted out the facts.

They were not to find out through the papers. On the morning after the duel, the *Tribunale* had this paragraph:

"Society of Rome will be sorry to learn that the Duke Scorpa is seriously ill at his Palazzo. The doctor's bulletins announce that their illustrious patient is suffering from a malignant case of fever which at the best will mean an illness of many weeks."

But it was not until the next day that there was a paragraph to the effect that the Marchese di Valdo had met with an accident. A passer-by had seen him slip in front of his club, the Circolo d'Acacia. It seems the wind carried his hat off suddenly, and, as he put his hand out to catch it, he fell and broke his arm. Following this came several other social items, and then the second day's bulletin about the Duke Scorpa, saying that the gravity of his condition remained unchanged.

Nina quite refused to be moved to pity by the news of Scorpa's critical state. Her only anxiety in connection with him was, what would they do to Giovanni, in case Scorpa should die? For *how* was Giovanni to be got out of the country, when he was said to be delirious in bed! By day she thought, and by night she dreamed, that they were going to cut off his arm.

As the excitement was dying down, John Derby returned from Sicily. He noticed that Nina looked nervous and ill, but she tried to convince him that it was the result of late hours and dancing. Besides, he had no opportunity of talking to her alone, for in consequence of his success, all who were interested in Sicily or mines flocked to the Palazzo Sansevero as soon as it became known that Derby was there. The fuss made over him pleased him, of course; for, after all, he was quite human and quite young, and there was great exhilaration in being the bearer of good news. He would not promise any definite amount to the holders of the "Little Devil." There would be some money, but that was all he could say. He did not yet know how much. To Nina's delight, he actually got Carpazzi to accept the position of Tiggs, who had to return to America. The plant, once started, no longer needed both engineers. And Carpazzi's tumble-down castle not far from Vencata, enabled him to go without hurt to his European ideas of dignity to "look after his own property."

In spite of her explanations, John was very much worried about Nina. She certainly was not herself. Several times he caught a half-appealing look in her eyes, as though she had something weighing on her mind. Yet she gave him no chance to ask her confidence. Finally he had the good luck to be left with her for a few moments alone, but there was a lack of frankness in her face that he had never seen there before, and she had an apprehensive, frightened manner that alarmed him.

The question he was almost ready to put, in spite of his resolution, remained unasked, and he said instead: "Look here, Nina, I don't think you are well! You're awfully jumpy. I never saw you like this at home. Has anything happened?"

Nina shook her head.

"Honest and straight?"

She looked at him with a distracted expression that reminded him of a child afraid of losing its way.

"Jack"—she hesitated; her voice sounded constrained—"please don't look so—so serious. It is nothing—that I can tell you! Don't notice that I am any different. Really, I am not. You are my best friend, and the first I would go to if I needed help."

Yet, as she said the words, she felt with a sudden, poignant pain that they were no longer true. Her mind was in a turmoil, and at that very moment, had she followed her inclination, she would have screamed aloud. She did not understand why she was so wretched; but one thing was certain—it was Giovanni who filled her thoughts!

Perhaps Derby interpreted the change in her. He put a question suddenly, "Nina, you couldn't really care for an Italian, could you?"

Nina flushed. "I don't know whether I could or not," she said. "I think there may be just as wonderful men over here as at home. I know there are some that are quite as brave."

Derby frowned. "Nina, Nina—"

But Nina did not even hear his interruption. "I wish you knew Don Giovanni, Jack," she said. "You would like Italians better, I think!"

"It is not that I think ill of Italians—quite the contrary; but—I should not like to think of your marrying Don Giovanni."

"And why shouldn't I?" The question came near to summing up the problem of her own meditations, and his opposition—with its carefully maintained impersonal quality—piqued her and made the smoldering consideration of marrying Giovanni suddenly flame into a definite intention.

"Well?" she repeated.

"Because I think American men make the best husbands."

Nina was brutal. "You say that because you are an American yourself!"

He let the injustice of her remark pass unnoticed. "I merely repeat," he said calmly, "that, married to the Marchese di Valdo, you would be a very unhappy woman. That is my straight opinion. If you don't like it, I can't help it."

"Why should I be unhappy?"

"Don't let's discuss it."

"That is just like an American. Do you wonder women care for Europeans? A man over here would sit down sensibly and tell you every sort of reason."

"Yes, and one sort of reason as well as another. For, or against, whichever way the wind might happen to be blowing!"

In spite of herself, Nina was disagreeably conscious of the truth of his judgment. But she shut her mind to it, as she exclaimed, "And you say you don't dislike Italian men!"

"No, I don't! You are altogether wrong. I have been over here often enough to admire them tremendously, in a great many ways. But I don't like to see the girl I—the girl I have known all her life, marry a man that I feel sure will break her heart."

"Aunt Eleanor's heart is not broken!"

Derby walked up and down the floor, then stood still, stuffed his hands into his pockets, and looked down at his shoes as though their varnish were the only thing in life that interested him.

"Well? Is Aunt Eleanor's heart broken?"

"Perhaps not; but, even so, you and she are very different women. From her girlhood she was more or less trained for the life she leads. She went from a convent school to the house of a brother-in-law—in other words, from one dependence to another. She is the type of woman who weathers change and storm by bending to the wind."

"Aunt Eleanor! Hers is the strongest character I know!"

"Of course it is! But it is exactly because she is apparently unresisting and pliant to surrounding conditions that her spirit is unassailable. You, on the contrary, would snap in the first tempest! Or, to change the simile, have you ever seen a young bull calf tied to a tree, and, in a frantic effort to get loose, wind itself up tighter, until its head was pulled close to the tree? That is exactly what you would be over here. No girl has ever had her own way all her life more than you! Believe me, you have no idea what it would mean to be tied to a rope of convention that would tighten like a noose at any struggle on your part. As the wife of a man like di Valdo, you would be bound by endless petty formalities. Another thing— which your aunt has made me realize—as an American, you would have to excel the Italians in dignity in order to be thought to equal them. Things perfectly pardonable for them would finish you. You need only take your aunt and Kate Masco for your examples. Kate's behavior is not any worse than that of plenty of the born countesses, even. But that's just it—she *isn't* a countess born, and her ways won't do! Your aunt, on the other hand, is '*grande dame*' in every fiber of her being. Hardly another woman in Rome has her graciousness and dignity. These qualities were hers, doubtless, from the beginning, but you needn't tell me even she found it as easy to be a princess as it would seem!"

Nina looked up at Derby in open-eyed amazement. "Gracious, John! I never dreamed you were so observing! In a way, I imagine you are right, too. But at least, if a woman has to follow conventions to earn a position over here, that position is real and worth while when she does get it. And a woman like Aunt Eleanor is far more appreciated here than she would be at home."

"Humph!" was Derby's retort. "You needn't think that all the appreciating of women is done in Italy, though the men at home may not put things so gracefully as these over here, who have nothing else to do but learn to turn beautiful phrases. I don't think that I am flattering myself in saying that if I were to give up my life to the one accomplishment of artistic love-making, I might make good, too! However, that is pretty far out of my line. I'm a blunt sort of person, but I—well, I care a lot for you, Nina! I'd rather see you marry—Billy Dalton, any day!"

As Derby brought in Billy Dalton's name, Nina had a sense of flatness that she would have been at a loss to explain.

"Jack!" she cried suddenly, her surface vanity piqued, but before even the sentence which crowded back of her exclamation could frame itself, Giovanni's image flashed before her mind and pushed out every other impression. She seemed to see him racked with suffering, and all for her! She hated her own vacillation. She despised herself for a fickle flirt. What else was she? Here she was imagining all sorts of vague heartaches that were utterly unworthy of her loyalty either to Giovanni's love or to Jack's friendship. Jack was her best friend, almost her brother, and she had no right to feel so limp because—she did not finish the sentence even to herself; yet she was swept into such a turmoil of emotion—friendship, love, pique, doubt—that she could restore nothing to order. She knew Derby thought Giovanni wanted her money—instinctively her mouth hardened as she thought of it—but then—every one wanted it except Jack! And at once, with an unaccountable baffling ache, she was brought face to face with the fact that Jack, as it happened, did not want her at all!

Then, hating herself because she had for a moment thought of Jack as a possible suitor, and more especially because of the detestable and unworthy chagrin that his not being a suitor had caused her, she became hysterically erratic, aloof, and impossible, and began suddenly to talk like a paid guide about the sculptures at the Vatican! At the end of some minutes, during which Derby failed to get anything in the way of a natural remark from her, he arose to go. He left with a strong desire to send a doctor and a trained nurse to take Nina in hand.

Down at the entrance of the palace a very pretty woman was speaking with the porter. She was talking vehemently and with much accompanying gesticulation. As Derby passed out, she looked up into his face. He put his hand to his hat, in a vague remembrance of her features, wondering where he had met her, and what her name might be. As he went through the archway into the street, the recognition came to him. She was the celebrated dancer, La Favorita.

CHAPTER XXV

"THY PEOPLE SHALL BE MY PEOPLE—"

The following morning, for the first time since his injury, Giovanni was brought into the princess's sitting-room, and propped up on a sofa. As occasionally happens in early spring, midsummer seemed to have arrived in one day, and the windows stood wide open to the morning breeze.

Sitting in the full light of the windows, and close by Giovanni's couch, Nina was making a necktie—a very smart one, of dull raspberry silk; but she was knitting rather because the occupation steadied her nerves than for any other reason, and the charmingly tranquil picture that she made was very far from representing her feelings. She had never been less happy or peaceful in her life.

The princess, within easy earshot, was busily writing at her desk. But after a while, in answer to an appealing look from Giovanni, she left the room. Nina felt no surprise either at Giovanni's appeal or at her aunt's response. She knew very well what he would say, and she had long been trying to make up her mind what her answer should be. Yet no sooner had the *portières* closed than an unaccountable dread took possession of her, and she had an overwhelming desire to escape.

She knitted industriously, her head bent, her eyes intent upon her needles. For a while Giovanni lay back against the pillows, idly watching her progress; then he raised himself on his unbandaged elbow and leaned forward. Even this exertion revealed his weakness: an increasing pallor overspread his transparent features, and he spoke as sick people do—with difficulty and as though out of breath: "Mademoiselle, you know—what I have in my heart—to say—"

"Don't, ah—please—" Nina sprang up and put out her hand in protest.

But he paid no heed. "Donna Nina," he implored, "will you do me the honor to be my wife? *Carissima mia—*" she heard his voice as though from afar, as he fell back against the pillow—"I love you! Even a portion of how much I love you would fill a life!" He took her hand as she stood beside him, and pressed it to his lips.

She felt how thin his hand was, and how it trembled. Her conscience smote her—it was all because of her! And for a moment the answer that he sought hung on the very tip of her tongue—hung, faltered—and then raced down her throat again. Her hand drew away from his clasp, and she almost sobbed, "I can't, I can't. Oh, I would if I could—but I can't!"

Then she heard him say gently: "Give me an answer later—I am not such, just now, that I can hold my own—I will wait till I am strong again. Will you give me your answer then?" Half choking, she nodded her head in assent and hurried from the room.

St. Anthony, the great Dane, who, since Giovanni's illness, had attached himself to Nina, stalked after her. She went through the intervening rooms into the picture gallery, and there dropped down upon a low marble seat and took the big dog's head in her arms.

She believed in Giovanni's disinterestedness; he had given her every reason to think he truly loved her. It seemed to her that she had seen his real feeling grow gradually. If she could believe in any one *ever*, she must believe in him. Even the astute little Zoya Olisco had confirmed the impression by saying that all Rome knew that Giovanni cared nothing for money. There had been a very rich girl—all the fortune hunters were after her—and she was so strongly attracted to Giovanni that she made no effort to disguise her preference for him. But he showed no inclination to marry a rich wife.

These and many other things were enough to convince Nina that his love was real, without the final proof when he had risked his life for her. In mere gratitude she would have made the effort to care for him. And yet the more she tried to encourage her sentiments, the more they baffled her. From the first she had felt timid of something unknown in Giovanni. She had thought herself in danger of being attracted too much, but now she felt that, throughout, the fear had been of another sort, a fear which she could not analyze.

"What is the matter with me?" she whispered brokenly to St. Anthony. "We love Giovanni, don't we? We do! We do!" But her words were meaningless sounds that echoed hollowly.

Then slowly she noted the great gallery filled with things flawless—the mellow canvases of the old masters, the marvelous statuary, perfect even in the brilliant light streaming through the eastern windows; and her thoughts turned backwards to that day when the allure of antiquity had most strongly held her—that day when she had first seen Giovanni dance. As the recollection grew in vividness, she was again aware of the same strange sensation that she had felt then. It was as though she were living in a past age, with which she, as Nina Randolph, had nothing to do. Her name might be Tullia or Claudia!

And then once again the memory of Giovanni's high-bred charm, no less than of his great estate, which she was now asked to share, seemed to hold a spell of enchantment. His words, "*Carissima*, I love you," swept through her memory with a thrill that the spoken words themselves had failed to carry. She laid her cheek down on the dog's great head, her mouth close to a pointed ear. "We *do* love him, thou and I," she whispered in Italian, "and we will stay here always—always."

She unclasped her arms from about the dog's neck and sat up straight, determined to hurry back through the rooms, before the queer fear should seize her anew. She would not wait to analyze her feelings again; she would go straight to the sofa and say to Giovanni's ardent, appealing eyes—his beautiful Italian eyes— "Yes."

But even as the resolve was shaped, there followed swift upon it an overwhelming wave of doubt that made her clasp her hands to still the turmoil within her breast. It was as if an inner voice repeated, clearly and insistently, "You don't love him! You don't love him!"

The dog lifted one huge paw and put it on her knee, his head went up, he pushed his cold nose against her cheek, and as she lifted her chin, to escape his over-affectionate caress, her glance fell by chance on a picture of Ruth and Naomi. On the day when she had first come into the gallery Giovanni had repeated, in French, the words of Ruth; and now, as she gazed absently at the picture, she found that she was saying to herself, not in French but in English, "Thy people shall be my people—" Gradually an indescribable, comforted, soothed feeling crept over her, as she looked into the true, steadfast eyes of the pictured Ruth—hers were indeed the eyes of one who could follow faithfully to the ends of the earth.

"'Whither thou goest, I will go,'" repeated Nina—yes, that was the test. Giovanni away from his surroundings, and apart from his name—she could not picture him. And should she put her hand in his, whither would he lead her? Where did his path of life end? She could not with any certainty guess. "Thy people shall be my people"—how could they ever be? They were so widely different—so utterly different—she had never realized it before— and then without warning, as a final move in a puzzle snaps into place and makes the whole complete, with a little cry she started up. For she now knew that the more she tried to focus her thoughts upon Giovanni, the more they turned to another quite different personality. Until at last, as in a burst of light, she awoke to the consciousness that the words of Ruth were bringing a great longing for the sight of a certain pair of eyes whose expression was like those in the canvas! "'Whither thou goest, I will go—' Ah!"—exultantly and with no fear of doubt; it was true! To the uttermost parts of the earth! . . .

But she must tell Giovanni—she must tell him at once, decidedly and finally, "No."

Sadly, regretfully, she crossed the room again, her hand slipped through the great Dane's collar as though to gain encouragement from his presence. In the antechamber of the room where Giovanni lay, she stopped and kissed St. Anthony's head—as though the dog in turn might help Giovanni to understand that she was not in truth as heartless as she seemed.

The stone floors were covered with thick rugs, the hangings were heavy, and her light footfall made no sound. Without warning she parted the *portières*, took one step across the threshold, and halted, stunned—the Contessa Potensi was kneeling beside Giovanni's couch, and the sound of Giovanni's voice came distinctly, saying, "For her? But no! But because she is of the household of the Sansevero." And then with an ardor that made the tones which he had used to her sound flat and shallow by comparison, she heard him say, "*Carissima*, I swear I shall never love another as I love you."

The *portières* fell together, and Nina fled. Two or three times she lost her way in the endless turnings of the palace before she finally reached her own room. Once there, she wrote the shortest note imaginable, declining in terse and positive terms Giovanni's offer of marriage. The pen nearly dug through the paper as she signed her name. Besides giving Celeste this missive to deliver, she sent her upon a tour of trivial shopping—anything to be left alone.

When the door was closed, Nina threw herself across the bed, still hardly able to credit her senses. Giovanni had asked her, Nina, to be his wife, not half an hour before—he still had the effrontery to hope for a change in her answer. He had dared to tell her that he loved her, he had dared to call her, too, "*Carissima!*"

With her head buried in the pillows, she did not hear the door open, and the princess reached the bed and took Nina in her arms before the girl knew that she had entered.

Nina poured out the whole story. The one clear idea that she had in mind was to leave Rome at once. She wanted to go away! Above all, she wanted to go away! She was by this time quite hysterical.

The princess's coolness gradually dominated as she said finally: "The thing is incredible—you must have misunderstood. I don't know what the explanation is, myself, but the worst blunder we can make is to judge too hastily. I am sure it will come out differently than it seems, if you will but have patience."

Savagely Nina turned on her. "Are you against me? *You*, auntie! Do you side with him? And that Potensi?"

With an expression more troubled than angry, the princess answered gently, "Of course, my child, I don't side against you—but I can't believe that they were really as you thought they were."

A sudden violent knocking interrupted, and at the same moment Sansevero, who had been looking for his wife everywhere, rushed in, quite beside himself, with the announcement that Scorpa was dead. The Sanseveros had for some days known the cause of his illness, and the doctor who had been at the duel had kept them informed of his condition. Now there was not a minute to lose! The news of the duke's death had not yet been made public, but Giovanni must be got out of the country at once, or there would be trouble! A train would go north in an hour, and the prince and princess hurried off to complete the arrangements for Giovanni's departure.

Left alone in her room and to her own thoughts, Nina's anger gradually lessened. Giovanni's danger, and his having to be taken away so weak and ill, appealed to her humanity and helped to soften her resentment. Whether it had been for love of her or not, it was on her account that he had been placed in his present unfortunate situation. He was going out of her life—it was not likely that she would ever see him again—but it took an hour or two's turning of the subject over in her thoughts before she came to the conclusion that, instead of being resentful, she ought to be thankful for her escape. She had finally reached this frame of mind when there was a knock at the door.

"May I come in, my dear?" Zoya Olisco entered as she spoke. She stood a second on the threshold, then, closing the door after her, crossed the room quickly and, taking Nina's face between her hands, looked at her with a half-quizzical grimace. "You silly little cat," she said softly, "surely you have not been melting into tears over the duke's death—nor yet for Giovanni's departure?"

"How do you know about it? Aunt Eleanor didn't tell you, did she? Is the news of the duke's death out?"

Zoya's raised eyebrows expressed satisfaction, and she exclaimed triumphantly: "I knew I was right! Really, it is extraordinary how things come about! No one has told me a word. Yet the whole story unrolled itself in front of me. Listen"—she interrupted herself long enough to light a cigarette, then sat down tailor fashion on the foot of the lounge—"I was but a moment ago at the station—my sister went back to Russia this morning. As I was leaving, whom did I see but Giovanni being piloted down the trainway! He looked really ill, and it would have struck any one as strange that he should be traveling. Then all at once I thought to myself, 'Hm, Hm! Signore il duca has descended into the next world, and the one who sent him there is being banished into the next country!' Thereupon I thought further, 'That child of a Nina will be hiding her head under the pillows of her bed'—exactly as you have been doing! How do I know? Look at your hair, and look at the pillows—and here I am to scold you!"

Nina looked at her in amazement. "You have put it all together, you wonderful Zoya! Compared to you, I never seem to see anything! Oh, but this whole day has been full of horrible surprises. I never dreamed what sort of man Giovanni is—and yet I can't help feeling sorry to think of his being sent off ill and alone!"

"How *very* pathetic!" exclaimed Zoya sarcastically. "It is the very saddest thing I have ever heard of." Then her tone changed. "I would not waste too much sympathy on him for his loneliness, however," she said briskly, "as he has a very charming companion, who, if accounts are true, is not only diverting but devoted. That spoils your sad picture somewhat, does it not?"

"The Potensi!" escaped Nina's lips before she knew it.

Zoya blew rings of smoke unperturbed. "So you have found *that* out, have you?"

Nina colored with indignation. "Have you known that, too, and never told me? Zoya, you call yourself my friend!"

But Zoya met Nina's glance squarely, as she asked in turn: "What difference does it make? Though, for that matter, I've made it plain all winter; any one but a baby would have understood long ago. But after all, why such an excitement over such a commonplace fact?" Then, with far more interest, she said: "You certainly are funny, you Americans. What in the world do you think men are? And since Giovanni is not even married? However, to finish my story: it was not the Potensi with your hero, but Favorita."

"Favorita—the dancer? Zoya, what do you mean?"

"Exactly what I tell you." Zoya inhaled her cigarette deeply and then shrugged her shoulders. "When I saw Giovanni, I did not believe it possible, that, even on so short notice, he would go off as you said, ill and alone. So I went back along the station and waited. In a moment, I saw Favorita come out on the platform and pass hurriedly down the train, peering into every carriage. When she came to Giovanni's she flew in like a bird. I waited a moment longer, and saw the guards lock the door and the train pull out!"

Though Nina understood only vaguely what it all meant, she was human and feminine enough to find a certain grim satisfaction in the thought that Giovanni was no more to be trusted by the Potensi than by herself.

A short time afterward Zoya got up to go. "I shall see you tomorrow, *cara*, yes? Will you lunch with me? And—I shall like very much if you bring the American."

"Do you mean John?"

Zoya burst out laughing and then mimicked Nina's tone. "Is it indeed possible that I could mean him?" She leaned over and kissed Nina affectionately, then hurried to the door. On the threshold she paused to call back, "One o'clock tomorrow, and be sure of John!" She smiled, blew another kiss, and was gone.

Nina looked after her, her thoughts in strange turbulence. A moment later she ran a comb through her hair, pinned up one or two tumbled locks, washed her face, polished her nails, took out a clean handkerchief; after which, she felt quite made over, and went in search of her aunt.

If she imagined that the day's emotions were ended, she was destined to be mistaken, for just as she went into the princess's room, a messenger came with a note from the prince, saying that he had been arrested. It was a very cheerful note and sounded rather as though he considered the whole situation a joke. He begged his wife not to be alarmed. The police had evidently mistaken him for Giovanni, so he had given no explanation and refused even to tell his name. When Giovanni should have time to reach the frontier, he would prove his identity and return home.

The princess's chief anxiety was therefore directed toward Giovanni, and she dreaded lest Sandro's identity be discovered before his brother should be safe. As for Nina, she cared no longer what might happen to Giovanni. She had had too many shocks and too little time for recovery. All her sympathy was for her poor Uncle Sandro who, in the meantime, was sitting in jail! Yet the thought of his situation in some way struck her as ludicrous—almost like comic opera.

But following this there came a second letter, very different from the first, written by the prince in great agitation, and saying that his arrest was not for the death of the duke, but for the smuggling of a Raphael out of the country.

At the shock of this news, the princess for once lost her self-control and turned to Nina in frightened helplessness.

Nina's first thought was to send for Derby, and to her relief the princess not only made no objection, but grasped eagerly at the suggestion. Fortunately, she got him on the telephone just as he was leaving his hotel, but in her agitation she did not stop to explain further than that her uncle was under arrest somewhere because of something to do with a picture. Derby answered that he would come at once, and the reassurance that she felt from the mere sound of his voice partly communicated itself through her to the princess, as they went into the sitting-room to wait for him. A few minutes later the *portières* were lifted—but instead of Derby, it was the Marchese Valdeste who entered.

Happily he had been at a meeting in the Tribunale Publico when the prince was arrested, and, as an important official and a great personal friend of Sansevero's, had hurried to inform the princess what had happened, and to place himself at her service. The case was very serious not only because of the evidence against the prince, but because of the lofty way in which the latter had replied some weeks previously to an inquiry from the Ministero. Sansevero said his Raphael was in the possession of the Duke Scorpa, but the duke, who had been chiefly instrumental in discovering the sale of the picture, was unable to shield his friend. Sansevero was questioned again, and refused to say anything more. He had answered once, and that, in his opinion, was sufficient for a gentleman.

The government thereupon had sent a representative to the Scorpa palace, where Sansevero averred the picture was. The duke's servants were catechised, but none had ever seen it. To add to the complication, the duke was far too ill to be questioned further, and Sansevero was at present injuring the case by making every moment more and more confused statements about his alleged transaction with Scorpa. First he said he had loaned it—because Torre Sansevero was cold; then that he had sold it for one hundred thousand *lire*; then that no money was received; then that he had let the duke have it as security, and that there was an agreement whereby he was to get his picture back. When he was asked to show a receipt in writing, he went into a rage.

The princess, quick enough to see the treachery of Scorpa and the net of circumstantial evidence that he had thrown about them, felt utterly helpless. "It is true, even I did not actually see the duke take the picture," she said, "and I am the only one who knew anything about it. As Sandro's wife—my word will have no weight at all!"

Valdeste solemnly shook his head. "I fear it is graver than that—for even Miss Randolph's word that she had made certain unusual expenditures would not be believed. The picture might too easily have been sold and paid for through her. Unless it can be produced *here in Italy*, the end may be bad. Somehow we must find a way to do that."

Nina was getting every moment more and more nervous—she could not understand Derby's delay. Why did he not come? Since she telephoned, he could have covered the distance from the Excelsior half a dozen times. Every second of glancing at the door seemed a minute, and the minutes hours. After the disillusionments she had suffered she actually was beginning to think that he, too, would fail her in the crucial moment, when, at last, the *portières* parted, and Derby entered carrying—the celebrated Sansevero Madonna!

The princess and the marchese were so astonished that only Nina seemed to notice Derby himself. With a cry of *"Jack!* How *did* you do it?" she sprang up, staring at him in bewilderment.

The sound of Nina's voice drew the princess's attention to Derby, and she, too, started toward him.

"John! What does it all mean?" she exclaimed, quite unconscious that she had called him by his first name.

"It means a rotten plot—neither more nor less—to ruin Prince Sansevero, concocted by a man whom the prince believed to be his friend! The Duke Scorpa has just died, which ends the affair for him, but I have the whole chain of evidence that clears the prince. The picture was taken in exchange for a promissory note of the prince's, for one hundred thousand *lire.* The duke tore the paper up and threw it into the waste-paper basket. Luigi Callucci, who was his servant, gathered the scraps out of the basket and pasted them together. This same Luigi also wrapped up the picture and carried it to Shayne. That's all, officially. Actually, there is a good deal more. The facts are that the duke sold it with perfect knowledge that it was to be smuggled out of the country. I have all the information necessary."

"It is incredible, incredible—the duke Scorpa!" exclaimed Valdeste. "But that the Prince Sansevero is cleared is the main thing." Then, turning to Derby, he continued, "I hope you will allow me to express to you my admiration and congratulation for the way in which you have brought it about."

Upon this the princess joined the marchese by holding her

hand out to Derby. "I never can thank you enough for what you have done! But for you, we should be in a very bad way. I quite agree with the Archbishop of Vencata that you must be a miracle worker!" Her voice was a little tremulous as she broke off. Then, including the marchese also, she added: "But now, my good, kind friends, go, please, and get Sandro out of his situation. My poor boy must be in a terrible state of nerves. And—thank you both again!"

The marchese and Derby hurried out, Derby carrying the picture. Nina followed them out of the door and stood looking after them until they had disappeared down the vista of rooms. Then she exclaimed: "Really, John is wonderful, isn't he? Wasn't it just like him not to say a word all the time! So many people talk, and do nothing!" Then Nina noticed that the princess was holding her hands over her face. She hurried to her anxiously. "Aunt Eleanor, what is it?"

The princess put her hands down. "I am just thankful—that is all. It threatened to be so dreadful, I can scarcely realize the relief yet. What a chain of circumstances! It is almost impossible to believe that even Scorpa would plan them! But it is true I never trusted him. When there is a race feud over here it seems never to die out." She paused a few moments, and then continued as though half to herself, "Although, in this case, I think it was chiefly on account of Giovanni. If you had married him, and the duke had lived, I believe he would have spent the rest of his life in scheming to injure you and everybody connected with us."

At the suggestion of the marriage which might have taken place, all the experiences of that varied day came rushing back to Nina—Giovanni's proposal, the revelation of his falseness, and the conversation with Zoya which had given her the true key to him who had until then been something of a mystery.

With a strained intensity of tone, she suddenly demanded, "Aunt Eleanor, tell me, supposing I had *wanted* to marry Giovanni, would you have made no protest?"

The princess answered thoughtfully: "I am glad you are not to marry Giovanni—yes, I am glad. Yet even so, he might make a good husband."

Instantly the blood rushed to Nina's head, "Don't you love me more than to let me risk a life of wretchedness?" she exclaimed, but the look in her aunt's face brought from the girl an immediate apology, and presently the princess said:

"I don't think I should want you to marry over here at all. At first I hoped it might be possible—but I am afraid you would be unhappy. There are plenty of girls who might be content, but not you!" The princess took her sewing out of a near-by chest and began hemming a table cloth.

"You mean," said Nina, "that when one reads of the broken hearts and lost illusions of Americans married to Europeans, the accounts *are* true? Why did you not tell me before?"

"I don't know, dear. Probably because such accounts are, to me, purely sensational writing—and yet at the bottom of them lies a certain amount of truth. In the majority of such cases of wretchedness, if you sift out the facts, you will wonder not so much at the outcome, as that such a marriage could ever have taken place. When it happens that a nice, sweet, wholesome girl marries a disreputable nobleman, who is despised from one end of Europe to the other, American parents seem to feel no horror until she has become a mental, moral, and physical wreck. To us over here it was unbelievable that a decent girl could think of marrying him; that her parents could be so dazzled by the mere title of 'Lady' or 'Marquise' or 'Grafin' or 'Principessa' that they were willing to give her into the keeping of an unspeakable cad, brute, or rake. Do you think that it is the fault of Europe if such girls know nothing but wretchedness?"

The princess paused, then continued: "On the other hand, if a girl marries in Europe as good a man, regardless of his title, as the American she would probably have chosen at home; and, above all—for this is most essential—if she is adaptable enough to change herself into a European, rather than to expect Europe to pattern itself upon her, she will have as good a chance of happiness as comes to any one. Marriage is a lottery in any event. Of course, *if* it turns out badly abroad, it is worse for her than it would have been at home—much worse. Everything over here is, in that case, against her: custom, language, law, religion; she is literally thrown upon her husband's indulgence. In a contest against him she would have no chance at all—there is no divorce; there is no redress.

"Yet, so far as my personal observation goes, numberless international marriages have been happy. The American wife of a European finds many compensations—for although her husband does not allow her freedom to follow her own whims, and may not even permit her to spend her own money, he gives her a ceaseless attentiveness that never relaxes into the careless indifference of the husbands across the sea.

"It is after all a question of choice—do you want the little things of life very perfectly polished or do you prefer rough edges and heroic sizes! European men know how to make themselves charming to their wives, because with them to be charming is an aim in itself. They have versatility, ease, and grace of intellect, where the American men are bound up in their one or two absorbing ideas, outside of which they take no interest. The Europeans are brilliant conversationalists, they make an effort to be agreeable and to take an interest in whatever occupies the person they are talking to—even though that person is a member of their family.

"But, of course, as in everything, there is a price one has to pay. One can't have rigidity and flexibility both in the same person. For the pliancy of understanding, the easy sympathy, one has to relinquish a certain moral steadfastness."

Suddenly the princess looked away and spoke very lightly, as though merely brushing over the surface of the thoughts in her mind: "What would you have, dear? Men are men—it is well not to question too far. Even the best of them have to be forgiven sometimes." Under the light tone, there was an unwonted vibration, and though the princess's face was partly averted, Nina caught a shadow of pain in her eyes. But the next moment she smiled. "I can tell you a story," she said, "about a young bride whose husband was very fascinating to women. The young wife, with suspicions of his devotion to another lady, went in tears to her mother-in-law. But the old lady asked her, 'Is not Pietro an admirable husband? And is he not a most devoted and attentive lover as well?' And the bride sobbed, 'Oh, yes, that is the worst of it—it is almost impossible to believe in his faithlessness, he is so adorable.' And her mother-in-law answered: 'Then, my child, be glad that you have in your husband one of the most accomplished lovers in the world, and do not inquire too closely where he gets his practice.'"

"Do you mean to say that a woman can be happy under such circumstances?" Nina demanded. "If that is a typical foreigner, then I am glad American men are different! I'd rather my husband were less accomplished and more entirely mine."

"Yes, dear, I am sure you would," the princess rejoined. "That is one of the reasons why I told you. For you, I think a European marriage would be—not best." She looked up quickly. "You ought to marry some one—I'll describe him—some one quite strong, quite big, quite splendid. And his name is easy to guess—of course it's John."

"John!" echoed Nina dolefully. "John is just the one person above all others who does not want to marry me—or even my money!"

"Your money, no! But *you*, indeed yes."

Nina shook her head. "No—he is not in love with me. In nothing that he has said or even looked, has he indicated it."

"You are a little mole, then," said the princess, smiling. "Every look he gives you, even every expression of his face in speaking about you, tells the story."

Like a whirlwind Nina threw herself at her aunt's knees, pulled her sewing away, and claimed her whole attention. "Tell me everything you know," she demanded hungrily. "Why haven't you told me before? Why do you think so? What has he said to you? Dearest auntie princess, tell me every word he has said. Quick! Every word—"

The princess, between tears and laughter, looked down at Nina. "Every word? Oh, my very dear," she said tenderly, "his love is not of the little sort that spends itself in words."

And then suddenly they heard the sound of two men's voices, and the next moment the *portières* parted, admitting Sansevero and Derby. Both the princess and Nina sprang up; the princess in her joy ran straight to her husband's arms. It was like a meeting after a long separation that had been full of perils.

A little later she put out her hand to Derby. "I don't think I shall ever be able to thank you enough; it was quite worth all the anxiety and distress to have found such a friend." Her smile was entrancing. The charm of her was always not so much in what she said, as in the way she said it—in the way she gave her hand, in the way she looked at one, in the varying inflection of her voice, in her sweetness, her calm, her dignity, and, under all these attributes, always her heart. And never had she shown them all more vividly than now as she put her hand into Derby's.

Then they all four sat down—the princess in a big chair and her husband on the arm of it leaning half back of her. And nothing could stop his talk about his friend the American, and the effect upon the members of the committee when the picture was produced and Derby presented his chain of evidence. They had been more than polite and courteous to the prince, that was true, but they *had* detained him; him, a Sansevero!—and in the telling he again grew indignant. And yet it had been a terrible chain of evidence, and he had not seen how it was to be broken.

Then he branched off from his own affair, and went into an account of all that he had just heard of the experience of Derby himself with Calluci; and the adventure, in spite of Derby's protests, certainly lost nothing in the recital. The princess and Nina had not heard of this, and Nina sat and gazed at the hero in mute rapture. In fact, the only one whose feelings were at all uncertain was Derby. Not but that it was pleasant to hear such praise of himself but it is very hard to be a hero unless one has no sense of humor at all. When the prince had used up half the adjectives of praise and admiration in the Italian language, and was about to begin on the other half, Derby succeeded in interrupting.

"By the way, princess," he said, "I have something I meant to show you this morning, but the other matter put it out of my mind." He drew a paper out of his pocket and handed it to her. She opened it, the prince looking over her shoulder. It was a sheet of foolscap covered with fine writing and many figures in groups and in columns.

"But what does it mean?" she asked.

"It is our first balance sheet at the mines. These are the tons of ore taken out," he answered, pointing to various totals, "this is the present market price paid for the first shipment, and this is the amount we are turning out now per day. At the same rate, the year's payment, at a conservative estimate, will be that amount. At all events I shall send you a check the first of August for fifty thousand *lire*."

"Fifty thousand *lire!* Oh, Sandro!" The instinct of the woman showed, in that her husband was her first thought; and her voice vibrated joyously. "Fifty thousand *lire!*" they both repeated as though unable to comprehend—and then, the full meaning of it dawning upon him, the prince threw his arms about her in wild exuberance.

"Oh, my dear one!"—he punctuated each phrase with kisses—"now you shall have everything . . . everything . . . your heart can wish! Stoves you shall have . . . servants and dresses. . . . Yes, and your emeralds! And your pearls! You shall have . . . emeralds set in a footstool! Every *soldo* is for you, *carissima*, it is all *yours*, yours!"

Gently she stopped him. "Sandro," she smiled, "Sandro *mio*, not the mines of the Indies could supply your plans for spending!" Then her voice broke, but she laughed through her tears and buried her face against his throat.

After a moment the princess recovered herself. She looked up, blushing like a girl—a little self-conscious that any one should have witnessed the scene between herself and her husband. "We are very foolish," she laughed. "But it is good to feel so joyous as that!" She got up and, as she passed Nina, she put her hand caressingly under the girl's chin. "It has not been a bad day, after all, has it?" she said. "And when fortune begins to come, it always comes in waves—the difficulty is to make it begin." Then she looked back at her husband, "Sandro, come with me, will you? These children will not mind, I am sure, if we leave them for a little while, and I want very much to talk to you." She smiled her apology to Nina and Derby, who both stood up. Then she and the prince went out of the door together, his arm about her waist.

When they had gone, Nina said softly: "They are dears, aren't they! Oh, Jack, aren't you proud to think you are the cause of every bit of the gladness they are feeling today?" She glanced up at him, her eyes alight with a brilliant softness and tenderness. But he did not look at her, and so answered merely her words: "I guess it would have worked out all right, anyway." And then he seemed to study the pattern of the carpet, and there was silence.

Nina stood leaning against a heavy table, and Derby stood near her with his hands in his pockets and his attention engrossed on the floor. Both seemed incapable of speaking or moving, as though a hypnotic spell had fallen upon them. Twice, while her aunt and uncle were in the room, Derby had looked at her with an expression that set Nina's heart beating, but now they were alone it had entirely vanished and he kept his head persistently turned away. She wondered how she could ever have failed to find his profile splendid. But he seemed so detached, so bafflingly absorbed, that all the old ache that she had felt that day when he had advised her to marry Billy Dalton—and since—came suffocatingly back. The old doubt suddenly gripped her—could her aunt be mistaken?

Finally, it came to her, intuitively, that her whole future was hanging on this moment, and the impulse was overwhelming to forget that she was the woman. It seemed that she must herself force the issue and end the doubt, at all hazards—this doubt which hammered at the door of her intellect and yet which her heart refused stubbornly to accept.

"Jack"—she tried hard to carry out her resolve not to let the false pride of a moment perhaps spoil her whole life; but the inborn reserve of generations of womanhood rebelled. In her uncertainty and anguish each moment of silence seemed weighted into leaden despair, but she was utterly unable to say what she had intended. At last her lips parted and, like the wail of a lost child, "Jack—" she cried. It was all she could say before her eyes filled and a queer little gulp came into her throat; then, with superhuman effort yet hardly articulate, came the whisper, "H-have you n-nothing to say—to me?"

All at once he turned and looked at her—looked again and caught her by the shoulders. The love and ardor of which the princess had spoken flamed unmistakably in his expression now—she saw him swallow hard, and it seemed to her as though her very soul were wandering lost in the blue spaces of his eyes as they searched hers, and then through it all his voice came huskily.

"Nina!"

For another long, intense moment he gazed at her earnestly, then "Nina! Nina!" he cried again, the wonder breaking through his tone. "Do you understand—do you *mean* what you are looking? Do you love me like—that?"

She tried to answer, but could not, though a little smile quivered in the corner of her mouth, and the dimple in her cheek was softly visible. Then she looked up again through her tears. A radiance indescribable lit the man's face, making his rugged features beautiful—then swiftly he stooped and gathered her to his heart.

THE END